THE
GUARDSMAN

P.J. BEESE AND TODD CAMERON HAMILTON

PAGEANT BOOKS

For my father, the storyteller.
I haven't forgotten.

P. J. B.

and

For Luanne McHenry Hamilton.
You taught me well.

T.C.H.

PAGEANT BOOKS
225 Park Avenue South
New York, New York 10003

Copyright © 1988 by P. J. Beese and
Todd Cameron Hamilton

PAGEANT and colophon are trademarks of the publisher

Cover artwork by Thomas Kidd

Printed in the U.S.A.

First Pageant Books printing: July, 1988

10 9 8 7 6 5 4 3 2 1

GALACTIC
REBELLION

Somewhere in this room a very frightened someone was contemplating trouble.

"We must consolidate the empire," Emperor Ozenscebo said from his throne. "We must find a way to bring the worlds together."

Ki edged closer, turned his head, and sniffed again. A nondescript servant approached the emperor with a goblet—but there was already a goblet in Ozenscebo's hand. There was a blur of motion that was Ki and a sliding, savage sword that moved into an eerie, dreamlike lack of sound, and the servant's head skipped down among the envoys, spraying blood among them as it rolled.

The emperor looked away from the ball-shaped object that had been a head, and directly at Ki. There was only mild surprise on his jaded face. "Amusing. But why?"

"I could not permit him to kill." Ki re-sheathed his blade, blood and all, and stooped over the body. From somewhere inside the assassin's full gown, Ki removed a high-carbon plastic needle—strong, sharp, and totally invisible to metal detectors. "It's been poisoned," he said to the emperor.

■ ■ ■

The Guardsman is a well written adventure filled with artistry and color by a promising and talented writing duo."

—John Varley

"We have a fine new talent here—or should I say two of them. *The Guardsman* is a rich, colorful, full-bodied tale with exciting action and characters one is eager to know."

—Hugh B. Cave

Prologue

———◆———

THE BLADE FLASHED DOWN, swift and hard, severing the umbilical. Captain Ki Lawwnum watched the small spurt of blood, then lifted the blade in salute to the new child. Taking a small square of silk, he wiped the blade carefully, then turned to the empress. Her ladies were attempting to make her comfortable, so he did not approach. She was tired, tried to her limits. Even so, he thought, she was the most regal human woman alive. It had not been an easy birth. Even Ki, Lionman of the Imperial Guard, was tired, the hours having taken their toll, and yet his only job had been to watch and wait. And still Elena Accalia, Empress Imperia of the Grand Imperium Alligantia, after her pain and exertion, retained all her grandeur. A squall from the new infant drew Ki's attention. A nurse held the babe on an open blanket in outstretched arms for the emperor's inspection.

Royal lips pursed in distaste, bringing the emperor's full sensual mouth into a tight circle. His dark brows drew together over muddy brown eyes, giving him the look of a hunting bird of prey.

"Unsatisfactory, Elena. Most unsatisfactory."

The dragons embroidered on his golden robe writhed around each other as he swirled out of the sterile sea-foam green chamber.

Ki's hands—the right one natural, as tawny as the rest of him, strong-nailed and fine-fingered, the left mechanical, gray metallic—automatically straightened his meticulous uniform.

"Your Majesty," he said, the sorrow he felt for the emperor's reaction thickening his deep, rich voice.

Elena Accalia regarded this Lionman carefully. The distaste he felt for the emperor's reaction did not escape her, even now in her extreme weariness. How long had he been with her? Ever since she had been sent from her own planet to Homeworld to be the wife of the emperor. He had been among those sent to escort her. His mane had been totally dark then. It seemed the years spent in this emperor's court took their toll even on the long-lived Lionmen. The gray-white streaks in his mane now were not unattractive, however, and Elena remembered the many kindnesses to her that had probably added to them as she took his metallic hand in hers.

Ki "felt" the pressure of her touch, the softness of her skin, through his sensory receptors, but none of her warmth. That was not one of the hand's capabilities.

"Ki, the child is a girl. Firstborn, and a girl. Her life is in danger from her first breath."

Elena took the square of silk and lifted it into his line of vision. "Her blood and mine are tied to your sword, Ki. Protect her. Love her. Stay with her as long as you can. Teach her the things she needs to know. Ki Lawwnum, I put her in your care." Elena tucked the silk into Ki's hand.

Ki bowed to his empress, acknowledging her wishes, awed by the responsibility and the trust placed in him, and inserted the square of silk carefully into his sash. He felt unworthy in spite of his long association with the empress. He gently withdrew his hand from her grasp, promised again with his eyes to do his best to obey her command, and backed respectfully out of the room to go to the royal nursery to stand guard over his newest charge until utter fatigue forced him to seek rest.

Chapter One

———◆———

THE DOOR SLID aside into its pocket and Aubin stepped back involuntarily, startled, as a rumbling war cry reverberated down the palace corridor. Looming over him, glowing menacingly in the bright yellow light from the hallway, was a wild Nidean dressed in the deep desert robes of his people, untamed golden-brown mane free to the winds and stippled with braided-in beads. The warrior's face, with the ocher-and-scarlet tattoos that denoted his pride, was a hardened mask of determination. The outstretched gently curved hoj, the longer of the two blades Nideans traditionally wore, swept past Aubin's face. He shied as he felt the cold breath of air that followed it, too late, though, to have avoided the stroke had it been intended to be deadly.

Then, from behind the Nidean, Aubin caught a flash of blue-white skin, and he sank heavily against the wall of the wide palace hallway, shaking with warm relief.

"That's a damned puppet!" he exclaimed as his heart rate slowly began to recede to normal. "Ki Lawwnum, how could you do that to me?"

Lawwnum answered with his rumbling Nidean laugh, and dropped the massive puppet's head and built-in harness from its place on his wide, well-muscled shoulder.

"I was a little homesick, and the 'general' here was helping me to practice my pridecraft. Surely you remember 'General' Haarwaa?"

Aubin forced himself away from the wall, and tugged at the royal-blue skinsuit he was sporting on his stocky frame. "I'm afraid I don't," he said, with just a little acidity.

Ki grabbed the puppet's hair and raised the face so that it peered down into Aubin's. "Look again, my friend. He's been hanging on my living room wall ever since I took over these quarters."

Aubin studied the mask. Now that it was not animated, and therefore decidedly less vicious, he recalled. He nodded to Ki, then, drawn by this masterwork of the carver's craft, reached out to touch the heavily defined features with a tentative finger. He leaned in closer, and the distinctive odor of the wallumnar wood from which such puppets were traditionally carved reached him. It was an odor he loved, rich and clean, and it brought a smile to his world-weary face.

Ki gently pulled the puppet back. Aubin followed it, and Ki closed the door.

"You remember who Haarwaa was, don't you?" he asked Aubin.

Slightly embarrassed, the lunar envoy answered, "Sorry. I'm not up on such things."

Ki seated himself on one of the padded wooden benches that served as furniture in his spartan quarters, and began to adjust the buckles that held the puppet's feet to his knees. "It was Haarwaa who united the prides to keep the Imperium from overrunning Nide." Then he stood, and raised the puppet's head so that it fitted with its harness over his left shoulder. He placed his hands into those of the puppet, and suddenly "General" Haarwaa lived again, a vicious, antique Nidean come to life out of dusty history.

"Please, sir," the "general" rumbled in full Nidean intonation. "Take a seat. There's a story to be told."

The hair on Aubin's arms rose, and he felt his skin prickle. The Nidean rumble, raspy and harsh, always did that to him. He collapsed into the offered chair, afraid to speak, wanting very much to see the living history of Nide's oral tradition, something very few outsiders were ever permitted.

The "general" began to move, stalking an invisible quarry, eyes shifting, head turning, shoulders lifting, hands gesturing, all with the fluid grace of water over stone, and Ki no longer existed except as a white nimbus, a shadow, a ghost to match Haarwaa's movements.

Aubin forced himself to look away from the puppet and to his friend of some twenty years. Ki's leonine face with its broad, flat nose was only partially visible behind the cloud of Haarwaa's hair, but its fierce Lawwnum pride tattoo of rose-colored swirls on the cheek and short black downward strokes at the corners of the mouth was still impressive. Ki's mane, worn in the full style similar to that of the Lionmen of the Kabuki theater of old Japan, floated like a blue-white halo behind the puppet's head. Then the "general" began the tale, and Ki once more faded from existence.

"When the Eighth Ozenscebo held the throne," rumbled "Haarwaa," "he began the era of exploration. Many worlds were brought under his sway, and one was not. That one, *vateem*, friend, was Nide.

"When the emperor's ships first filled our skies, we watched. When the soldiers landed, we killed them."

Aubin marveled at the tidal fullness of the motions, the wholeness, the reality of what he was seeing. This was a wild Nidean, untamed by contact with the "civilized" worlds. Of course he knew Ki was still there, but he had diminished into insignificance. Aubin was amazed to realize that at that moment, only the puppet was real.

"When more soldiers landed," the "general" continued, drawing his hoj, "we killed more!" This was accented with a broad arc of the sword.

"But we were a backward people," the "general" said sadly, "at least to those with technology. And the technology was defeating us. It killed us faster than we could kill in return."

Aubin's throat was suddenly constricted. How painful it must have been to those warlike creatures to lose! And how in blazes had that emotion been communicated? What a huge effort it must be to move the monstrous puppet with such grace and ease!

"But I knew we were fierce! I knew we were many! As Didentaar, Aashtraar, Lawwnum,

Streestawwn, Gelshanaam, we could not win. But as Nideans we could not lose!"

Aubin's head bobbed as he nodded assent.

"We joined our people into one, and we began to win, destroying the technology that had destroyed us."

There was a long dramatic pause, and Aubin waited breathlessly for the "general" to continue.

"This Ozenscebo was not a fool. He saw us as fighters, and recognized us as the best in the known worlds. He came to me, the emperor himself, and made this offer. We on Nide should have autonomy in perpetuity if we would swear fealty. But if we did not swear, our world would be destroyed." The "general's" head dropped in weariness. "It was a hard decision, and many preferred to fight on. But at last we swore."

Aubin wanted to cheer! They'd made the right choice.

The "general" turned his head quickly in Aubin's direction, and caught some hint of the envoy's emotion. His puppeteer was extremely attuned to the human audience, refining the motions to ones the human could comprehend, smelling his reactions, listening for the little clues such as indrawn breaths and subvocal sighs.

"But that is not the end of the tale, cub!" he hissed, menace spitting from voice and pointed finger.

Aubin quickly subsided, a slight shiver of fear stealing down his spine.

"This emperor knew he needed fighters such as we, and he was...intrigued by our appearance, like the demons of their legend. And so we became his special soldiers, his Guardsmen, and he called us Lionmen in their honor."

The "general" faced Aubin squarely, and step by step approached in a most menacing fashion. Aubin found himself retreating further and further into the cushions of the chair.

"And we still do not allow your kind on our world, human!"

Then the "general" was gone, his head thrown to one side, Ki's hands slipping from those of his ancestor's. Aubin slumped in his chair, emotionally drained, surprised at his responses. And perhaps a bit embarrassed.

"Ki, that was marvelous!" Aubin said enthusiastically as he stood to pat his friend on his muscle-hard back. "I've never seen anything like it!"

"Nor will you, I hope. That was appallingly bad."

"Bad! It was wonderful. I felt it all! All the emotion! No wonder your people know their history so well!"

Ki shook his head in denial. "No, Aubin. It was not good. At my finest I was barely acceptable. I was never even in line to be puppetmaster. And now I'm grossly out of practice."

Aubin pouted. He did not like having his praise shunted aside. "I thought it was good."

"You are uneducated," Ki responded with typical candor.

Aubin's eyes opened wide in surprise. "Nobody's told me that for a long time. I thought I was rather worldly."

"Ah," Ki replied. "But which world?"

Aubin laughed, a rich and full sound that told anyone listening here was one who enjoyed life. Then he shook his head. "Capitol Center and

Luna, but obviously not Nide." He cocked his head and studied his friend.

Ki was dressed only in fundoshi, a white loincloth that covered the minimum, and Aubin noticed the pattern of the hair on the Nidean's body that covered a broad area across the chest and then ran in a narrow line down the hard, flat stomach to disappear into the cloth had indeed lost its youthful reddish gold. But in spite of the labor of working the heavy and demanding puppet, there was not the smallest sign of exertion, not even a heavy breath. The finely honed, slim, lithe body worked to perfection, every motion as supple as Ki's blue-white skin. His legs were as powerful as ever, and longer than the norm.

Ki's nose twitched, and Aubin noticed, raising an eyebrow in question.

"Nothing. A scent from the garden."

Aubin nodded, and added to his inventory the fact that Ki's extraordinarily fine olfactory sense was as sharp as ever. But as Aubin's green-flecked brown eyes stayed locked with Ki's golden slatted ones, he could not quite keep the humor out of them.

"I may be uneducated in the ways of Nide, but may I point out you are hardly appropriately attired for an imperial banquet at Capitol Center?"

Ki's lip curled back, partially exposing semi-pointed teeth, and a snarl rumbled heavily in his throat. "I have no use for imperial banquets where hangers-on and leeches guzzle the emperor's roed until they're drowning in their own senses!"

Aubin nodded. He had no use for the drug either. He had seen many a fine mind lost to the siren song of the enhanced sensory input and long, long life that roedentritic quopapavaradine provided. Though it was supposedly non-habit-forming, in fact many would suicide rather than do without their daily dose.

"Nonetheless," Aubin said, "you are the commander of the Imperial Lionman Guard, and your presence is required."

Ki sneered, making a wonderfully exaggerated wild face. "I've never needed a human to tell me my duty," he rumbled.

"Perhaps not," Aubin returned as he flipped an item from an end table in Ki's direction, "but maybe you need a nanny to see you properly dressed."

Ki grabbed the missile out of the air with his left hand unerringly, though his eyes never left Aubin's. There was a soft *chink* as the metallic hand closed over it, and any humor that had been in Ki's face fled with the sound.

"If you've damaged it, human..." he rumbled threateningly from deep in his inflated chest.

Aubin winced. "I'm sorry, Ki," he said sincerely. "Check it."

Ki opened his hand. On it rested a beautifully crafted ring, an unusual affair that wrapped completely around the hand and was constructed of tarsh, a flexible silvery metal that, in the presence of body heat, moved as its wearer did. Set in it were two opals, one larger than the other, but each of excellent color and quality. It was intact, and Ki nodded his acceptance of that fact.

Aubin let out a breath he hadn't realized he was holding. He really had no idea how Ki would have reacted to the destruction of the last gift he'd received from his now-dead wife. Relief that he wouldn't need to find out flooded over him.

"Aubin, will you always try my patience?" Ki asked with great exasperation.

With a silly smile that reflected his relief, Aubin answered, "Almost certainly."

"Spoiled. All spoiled." Ozenscebo XVII, the 150-year-old emperor, was muttering to himself as he made his way angrily through the palace to his seraglio. Though ancient, his addiction to roed kept him looking, and largely feeling, as if he were in his upper fifties. In his wake came many of his most ardent followers. Having just left the emperor's expansive banquet, one would have expected the group to be in a better humor. But the emperor was unhappy, and therefore everyone in his company must share his mood.

"How dare she! How dare she preempt me?" he asked, snapping the full skirts of his heavily embroidered court robes. "Discussing affairs of state right beneath my nose! And at my own table! She knew this was to be a pleasant evening with my friends!" He looked angry and pleading at the same time. "How could she do such a thing?" He knit his heavy brows together over his muddy brown eyes.

Mercer Parry, Avoy's envoy, who had no great love for Elena Accalia, was not about to let this opportunity slip by. "You know your empress is a...most difficult lady." *Carefully*, he thought to himself, *carefully. It will not do to go too far. I would like very much to see another dawn*. He looked down his hawklike nose as he decided what to say, twisting his scrawny fingers in his cheap gown. "She has never been the sort to be aware of the ...sensitivities of Your Majesty."

"True. True." The emperor sighed. "She never has understood me. If it weren't for that damned treaty, I would have put her away years ago!"

Parry, as much as he wanted Elena out of the way, did not want it to happen because of something he said. Whatever occurred, his name must not be linked in the emperor's mind with having caused the empress's demise. "Now, Your Majesty, you know she has also given you two fine children, and she does leave you to yourself most of the time. And the rest of the night will be interesting, don't you think?"

The emperor threw back his head and laughed, his ugly turn of mind disappearing as quickly as smoke. "Interesting isn't the word for it, Mercer. Not nearly the word. I have something special to show you tonight." He draped an arm across Parry's shoulders in a confidential fashion. "I have a new toy. That new world ...what's it called again?"

"Delena," Parry interjected helpfully. "Mostly water, I hear." Parry was wildly enthusiastic about the emperor's ability to be diverted. It was Ozenscebo's only asset.

"Yes, yes, that's it. Delena. Delena has sent her new emperor a gift. Something quite special, I'm told. I haven't seen it yet, but the reports are extraordinary." The emperor stopped, and looked behind him at the train of twenty or so that followed him down the long white marble corridor. His toy was too new to share with so many. He did not want that kind of distraction. "Send them away. I don't want it frightened."

Parry shooed the others off quickly.

The emperor was breathing heavily by the time he and Mercer reached the seraglio, followed only by Ozenscebo's personal guard. The walk was a rather long one from the hall the banquet had been in and the emperor was not used to exercise. Sweating, he said a brief thanks that his own rooms were just off his arena of play. He needn't even return to them if the effort seemed too much. He thought tonight the effort might be too much after the strain of the dinner spoiled by that bitch, Elena. As he entered the seraglio reception room, the guards who had followed him dispersed, disappearing into specially built alcoves that hid their presence nicely. It gave Ozenscebo the illusion that he and Parry were totally alone, doing something naughty.

The emperor sank down gratefully on one of the heavily upholstered sofas that banked the walls, and rested his head back to look out the specially constructed sunroof. It was tinted pink because long ago Mama-san had told him that pink was the most becoming light a woman could be seen in. The rich coloring of the polarizing filter gave the stars a look of pink diamonds, rare, and just out of reach. The huge fountain in the center of the room splashed merrily, cooling the air and drowning the usual tiny sounds of occupied dwellings. He rested for a few moments, hoping no one would disturb him —especially not Parry. He knew a weasel when he saw one. But a weasel was more fun than a cow like Elena.

"Your Majesty! I didn't expect to see you this evening! I thought you would be engaged at the banquet." Down the curving central staircase came an older woman. She had probably been a beauty once, and one could still see touches of it when she smiled. Her gown was long and flowing, pink to match the marble and lights and overstuffed chairs of the reception room. Her perfume was heavy and sweet, very, very sweet, and it reached the emperor before she did, for she did not really hurry. When she finally stood before the emperor she bowed slightly. "I'll bet I know why you've come. You couldn't wait to see the new one."

"Ah, Mama-san, you know me so well," Ozenscebo said as he chucked her playfully under the chin. He didn't have to move much to do so, as Mama-san was exceptionally short. "How long have you been here?"

"Longer than any woman likes to remember, Your Majesty." She pulled herself up proudly. "I have had the pleasure of being in Your Majesty's service ever since you took the throne. And I served your father before you, too, for almost two years."

"My father was scum," Ozenscebo said conversationally, "but you have always served me well, Mama-san. Now, where is this new treasure?"

Mama-san looked uncertain for the first time. "As I said before, Your Majesty, we did not expect you tonight. The creature has gone to its mineral bath. It must have them, you know. I will call it immediately. Perhaps you would like one of the others to keep you company until it's prepared?"

"Mmmm. In the bath, you say? Show me the chamber. This is bound to be more enjoyable than that disastrous banquet."

Mama-san led the way through the interconnecting corridors of the seraglio. Though the

hallways intersected, twisted, and turned back
on themselves, their outlets to the rest of the
palace being very few and carefully monitored,
she could have toured them with her eyes
closed. The chamber she sought was one she
thought Ozenscebo might not remember. It had
originally been designed as something of a hot-
house for the plants of one of the ladies who had
been a favorite of the emperor's some time back.
Although Ozenscebo had indulged the lady's
fancy, he never shared her botanical interest
and did not meet her there. The lady, like the
plants, had not survived long. The room, of
course, had been totally redone in order to satisfy the need of the latest occupant. A pool, almost a small lake, really, had been installed.
The surrounding flooring had been ripped up
and replaced with handmade tiles. The walls,
too, were covered with tiles in blues and greens
so subtly shaded that it almost gave one the
feeling of being underwater. Another fixture
from the original that had been retained was the
cut-glass skylight. Sunlight filtering through the
room would fill the chamber with rainbows because a special misting system that had once
watered plants had been adapted to carry min-
eral-rich water into the room's atmosphere, pro-
viding a moist environment. All in all an alien
feeling, even for a place as cosmopolitan as
Homeworld.

Mama-san was praying silently that the emperor would be beset with devils. She had been
working for this moment ever since she knew
the creature was to be sent, some three months
ago, almost the day after the conquest of Delena. She had had the room refurbished, ordered clothing that would complement the

female's exotic aura, had replayed in her mind over and over again exactly how she would present the thing. Done properly, Mama-san felt she could probably have anything she asked for for some time to come. As it was, the emperor's timing was execrable. She had not prepared the new acquisition for the emperor's arrival, nor had she even had the time to make certain the creature understood its duties. It had only arrived this morning, and had spent most of its time soaking. It was a lovely thing, and Mama-san had intended to show it in the best possible manner. As it was, Ozenscebo would be catching it in its bath, totally unprepared. If that creature caused any trouble ...

Mama-san opened the door with a flourish and a prayer that the female would keep its mouth shut and do as it was told, and the emperor stepped through. He stopped short, so short that Parry almost ran into the back of him. Rising slowly, languidly, from the pool was a living gem, skin flashing pinks and greens in the roomlight, hair a mass of shining green crystals. Heavy, mineral-laden water slid off her slowly in large drops and small rivulets, as if it were reluctant to leave its magnificent perch. She moved slowly, almost as if she were tired, every gesture delicate and deliberate, as she rose step by hesitant step from the pool, her long, thin fingers extended gracefully forward as if in warm welcome.

"She's solid opal," Parry breathed. He had known such creatures were reputed to exist, but he was not prepared for the sight of her. More beautiful in the silicon humanoid flesh than any figment of imagination, even the jaded Parry was awed.

"Not solid," Ozenscebo corrected. "Look at that hair." His eye had been caught by the spikes of perfect crystals that showed brilliant parrot green. "Is it emerald?"

"No, Highness," Mama-san put in, glad for the chance to show off the homework she had spent hours on. "It's peridot, grown in the same matrix as opal. If you will be so kind as to notice, Sire, the color is less intense than emerald, softer, and somehow richer." She turned toward her newest charge. "Come here. Quickly. The emperor wishes to look at you."

"What's her name?" Parry found his voice was hardly more than a whisper.

"I've taken to calling her Opal. No one here has managed yet to say her proper name. Apparently one almost has to be gargling in order to even come close." Mama-san looked at Opal and saw no appreciable progress in her approach to the emperor. As she was used to immediate obedience, anger quickly flooded through her system. "I said quickly!" she shouted.

Ozenscebo put a restraining hand on her shoulder and gave her a slight shove back in the direction of the door. Although Mama-san took this as dismissal, bowed, and left, the emperor did not notice. His eyes were only for the gem that was slowly, elegantly, nakedly, making its way toward him. A serving girl approached with a robe. Ozenscebo snatched it from her and hissed, "Out!" The girl fled, and he threw the robe aside impatiently.

Parry was totally absorbed in watching the tiny droplets of water that had been captured in the fine, curly strands of peridot that made up the creature's pubic hair. The drops seemed to glisten and pulse as they hung suspended in fragile purchase, then slid silently down a twist to her skin or fell in graceful arcs to her thighs. He wanted very much to know what that fine pelt felt like, if it was hard and brittle, if it would break instantly like some cave formations he had read about that would shatter if you breathed on them, or if it was as warm and soft and erotic as promised. But he was so bewitched he could not move, and would not even if he could. Parry knew the emperor would not have approved his instinctive reaction to feel.

At last, and much too quickly, Opal's progress toward the emperor reached an end, and she stood before him with bowed head.

"Highnessss," she said. The word was clear, understandable, and yet, especially in the drawn-out sibilation of the last sound, one almost heard the swishing of waves on a shore.

Ozenscebo could contain himself no longer. He touched her. He had expected her skin to be cool and firm. Instead, she was warm, although not as warm as he, and although he felt a certain resistance to pressure, her skin dimpled much as his would have. Curious, he pinched her, hard.

It seemed as if nothing happened. She did not squeal as a human would have. She had not even moved. But then her head slowly came up, until her eyes met Ozenscebo's.

"They told me I would be treated well here, Majesty. Did they lie to me?"

The question was asked softly, and with no hidden anger. It was merely a plea for information. And that plea left the emperor nonplussed. He had expected pain and/or resentment.

"No, dear, no. They did not lie to you. I will

take very good care of you, for you are a rare beauty indeed." He took her slender, well-curved arm in his hand and led her toward a bench that sat in front of a bed of mosaic sea-weed. "I am Ozenscebo, the seventeenth emperor of that name to rule the empire. I am very glad to have your planet, Delena, added to our reign."

She sighed, again with the sound of the waves. "Not all of my people are glad, Highness, but I am here to see that we become friends."

The emperor sat. "Oh, we will be friends. I'm sure of it. In fact, I order it. Sit. Sit here beside me."

He watched as she seemed to float into position over the bench and hover there like an opal cloud before she began to sink to the wood. Apparently this slowness in motion was natural to her, but it was beginning to irritate Ozenscebo.

"Why do you move like that?" he asked.

She raised her hand languidly. "Do you mean at this speed, Majesty? I am used to moving through water, not air. All of my kind move as I do. To me it seems that you humans flit like insects."

The emperor was insulted by such a comparison, and an angry retort came instantly to mind. But he did not wish to frighten this thing away from him, so he merely smiled. "What else do you think about humans?"

"You're not very pretty, are you?" she asked guilelessly. "Where are your colors? How do you tell one another apart?"

"We manage. Stand!" he ordered, as he was far too eager to put his hands on her, and he wanted this meeting and all its good intentions to last a long, long time. "Move there, beneath the light."

She did as she was told. While it pleased Ozenscebo that she did not pretend to modesty, in fact she was being totally modest. Clothing was alien to her. She was used to wearing an elegant gown of sheerest water. As long as the drops on her skin did not dry, she considered herself fully clothed. She did not appreciate how lucky she was that Ozenscebo did not comprehend.

Marveling at the way the light set off flashes of color from within her, the emperor wished to see what occurred when she moved with the light behind her. "Raise your arm!"

She complied, somewhat bored, and brushed at the crystals that crowned her head. To the shock of her audience, they moved, swayed, then settled in a slightly different array than they had had before.

"Impossible!" Parry muttered.

"Hold your hand to the light," the emperor ordered.

Opal moved slightly so her face was more toward the lamp, and held her hand between it and Ozenscebo. He was fascinated. He could see that most of the color, the life, came from the upper layers of what would have been the epidermis on a human. Her skin was essentially clear; beneath it was a more opaque layer, white, with some tones of pink. Then he looked from her hand to her face, which was still near the lamp. Her nose was almost entirely translucent. He could see faintly the outline of her opposite cheek behind it.

"Turn around."

In her achingly slow fashion she pirouetted for his pleasure. But she was beginning to dry.

Even in this room with its controlled moist atmosphere, she was beginning to find herself uncomfortable.

"Your Majesty," she said, "the trip here was a very long one for me, and I traveled under very difficult circumstances. I was not allowed enough space to bathe. I had to keep myself moist by constantly sponging my skin. Although I obviously survived, my moisture level is seriously depleted. I therefore humbly beg your permission to return to the pool."

Return to the pool! Certainly not, Ozenscebo was thinking. She would not deprive him of the sight of her so easily! Then came a wonderful idea.

"Certainly, my dear. By all means, return to the pool. I would not like it if you were uncomfortable. In fact, the pool sounds lovely. I could do with a swim myself to wash away the awful taste of this dreadful day. I think I will join you." He threw over his shoulder as an afterthought, "Parry, you are dismissed."

Chapter Two

———◆———

THE PLACE WAS very busy, and Loni loved it. She stood in the lobby of the bordello section of her entertainment center and drank it all in. The crystal chandeliers, authentic Louis XIV brought by stable hovercraft from Paris, older

than old. The wallpaper, copied by hand from
the Suki Wall at what had been Nikko Park before Fuji blew its top, on fabric as rich as silk.
The water sculpture from Delena that had cost
her a fortune to move and install (not counting
the bribes she'd had to pay to customs officials
to get it onto Homeworld—Delena had not been
part of the empire when she had commissioned
the piece). All of it was hers. Who would have
believed it thirty years ago when she was just
starting out, an overeducated brat from the
lower northern quadrant of Osaka. And now her
place was as busy as could be. She couldn't be
happier. If this kept up until the midwinter holi-
days, she would be able to pay her amusement
taxes, and maybe have a little left over for herself—not to mention that no one was likely to
notice the extra traffic that flowed directly into
a back room. That party of twenty-two from the
sticks, while an annoyance because they hadn't
given her any advance notice, was also a blessing. She had been able to accommodate them,
using some of her less urbane girls, and still feel
she had a full complement ready for the rest of
the evening. And their exuberant entrance had
covered quite nicely the arrival of several
others, a few of them rebel inner circle, who had
headed directly for the door marked Staff Only.
Her only work-related problem now, in fact, was
that some of the boys were becoming downright
lazy. She chuckled. They'd work hard enough
once the countessa arrived for her vacation.
How that lady loved to get into Osaka and off
the dreary little backwater planet her husband
insisted on living on.

"Loni?"

The madam responded quickly to the inquiry

from her desk clerk, swinging her white heavily beaded gown as she crossed the room. "Yes, Jane?" Loni checked the girl over automatically. Her short dark curly hair was neatly in place, and she was dressed quite well in a fitted slacks-and-jacket ensemble that allowed enough to show to tantalize. But Loni, although not tall herself, never could figure out how the tiny girl managed to see over the top of the huge mahogany counter that had once been a bar in what used to be the United States.

"This gentleman is looking for a companion for the entire night, someone to take to dinner, have a good time with. Who would you recommend?"

Sara Korlon, known to the entire empire as Loni, had an excellent memory. On an ordinary evening she would have known off the top of her head exactly who was available. Tonight, however, was far from ordinary, because of the meeting being held in her back room. Fourteen of the most powerful or currently important men in the rebellion were on her premises. She knew each of them—had dealt with them, in fact—and knew she could control them in one way or another on an individual basis. But how she would fare against a group of them had not yet been proven. She was somewhat rattled, and she had to consult the status board kept underneath the counter to know who was free. She looked over the customer, too, without his being aware of it. His clothes indicated a traveling type, slightly tired from a trip, and probably more interested in conversation than gymnastics. Must be new, because she never, ever, forgot a face. That was bad for business.

"Ellen. You definitely want Ellen. Jane, call her. I'm going to take this handsome man over to my table and buy him a drink. Maybe we can get acquainted." She turned to the customer. "What's your name, honey?" she asked as she drew him across to the booth where she frequently held court. Many of the famous of this world and others had been delighted to be asked to join Loni at her table, and this poor fellow was thrilled.

"Stanton. Akihito Stanton," he answered shyly.

"Is this your first trip to Loni's Place?"

"Yeah. I don't get into Capitol Center very often. I spend most of my time hopping from planet to planet. Sometimes I wonder if it's worth it."

"Here, let me pour you some sake." She pulled the antique bottle, black raku ware, from its heater built into the table. She took the matching cups from a small display of things behind her, mostly carved jade and authentic silk scrolls, and poured as elegantly as any geisha of old. "Ellen should be here soon. She'll show you what Loni's Place is all about." She lifted her tiny cup. "Kampai."

"Kampai," he responded, and tossed off the sake she had poured for him. Loni refilled his cup while he looked around. "This is really a nice place you've got here. Promised to bring the wife on our next vacation."

"Thanks. I think she'll like it. Have you been down to the resort section yet?"

"Only when I checked in ..."

"Loni, who's your handsome friend?"

Loni smiled as Stanton's face lit up with a wide grin when he saw Ellen. Ellen was probably not to be considered a classically beautiful girl. Her face was too broad for that. But she had a smile that touched all of her and made her large brown eyes gleam. Her dark blond hair was as natural as all her other charms. Her form was just the way Loni liked her girls, lush without being too full. Ellen also had a way of talking that made the men in her company feel they were the sexiest, most interesting men ever to cross Loni's threshold. This guy was in for the evening of his life, and Loni was glad for him. Poor slob looked like he could use it. She watched with some satisfaction as the two made off for the Paradise Restaurant down on the public fifth floor. There was certainly more spring in Stanton's step now that he escorted Ellen, who wore that short blue dress that wrapped her fanny just so.

But when Loni stood, all traces of a smile fled. She had to get into that back room and find out what was going on. If she left them alone too long, they'd probably find a way to blow up the entire damned planet!

"Jane, I'm going in the back. Don't call me unless God Himself arrives."

The corridor in the back was blissfully quiet until she opened the door to the conference room. Shouts of anger and dissatisfaction caused her to cover her ears after she slammed the door behind her. Fourteen people were arguing volubly in small groups.

"What in the hell is going on in here?" Loni demanded.

Her query was greeted with a chorus of yells as every one of the people present tried to make himself heard at the same time. At last one voice, being stronger than the others because of the violence backing it, was heard clearly.

"The banquet! He was serving at the banquet! The perfect opportunity and he didn't use it!"

"Colwin, shut up!" Loni shouted at the rangy young man. Then she turned to the rest of the group. "All of you! Shut up!"

"But, Loni!" Colwin spit into the infant silence. "This bastard was serving the emperor! Standing right at his elbow! All it would have taken is one thrust with his dagger! Our problem would have been solved!"

"Colwin Dene, you shut your mouth. Did you expect the man to commit suicide? How long do you think he would have lasted in a room full of Lionmen guards? And just how would he have gotten a dagger into that room in the first place?"

Colwin did not like the fact that Loni ordered him around. Any place but this, everyone listened to him. Men followed him into battle, died at his command. Yet, somehow, when he came here, he was treated like the tolerated toddler. Resentful, he pulled a designer chair covered in cream suede from under the walnut-burl table, seated himself firmly on the table by wriggling until he was perfectly comfortable, and planted his heavy boots, none too clean, on the seat of the chair. He followed that action with a look of intense satisfaction at Loni. She may have told him off, but there was always a way to get even. He did, however, remain quiet.

Loni put her hand on the shoulder of the short and stockily built man that had been the object of the dissension. "The rest of you. Out. At least until I can find out what happened."

There were mutters, and the beginnings of

one or two questions, but Loni glared at them all and they subsided. They made their way out in relative quiet.

"Stay where I can find you!" she called to their backs.

"Not you!" she snapped at Dene when he stood to follow the group. She put her hands on her hips and looked intently at him. "Colwin, you're a good man and a good leader. You have charisma. The men like and respect you. But I don't think you understand just how dangerous a thing charisma can be. People will follow you without thinking, without understanding the consequences of what you ask them to do. So you have to learn to do the thinking for them in order to give them a fair chance at surviving. And you'll never make chief around here until you learn to think, for yourself and for them. This isn't the first time you've heard me say this, either. Now, keep your mouth shut and listen!"

She turned to the man still seated quietly in the chair. His dark brown eyes looked tired. "Thomas, what happened at the banquet?"

"Nothing. Yes, I was within striking distance of the emperor"—he shot a killing glance at Dene—"but there was nothing I could have done. That Lionman commander was just a few seats away. I would have been dead as soon as I moved."

"You must have served others. Did you hear anything of note?"

"No. The emperor was surrounded by his usual group of degenerates, and I was serving that end of the table. The only new person was the man sitting next to the empress. I think he was an envoy, but I'm not sure. He was partly sloshed, and bending Elena's ear about moving some people around."

Loni looked disappointed. She had hoped to learn *something* from this banquet. Enough important people had been present. Evidently, they had all been subdued by the emperor's desire for a "good time."

Colwin had subsided once more to the table-top, and Loni, in her disappointment, turned on him.

"Colwin, you know you're my favorite, but that table took all the profits from this place for more than three months. If you've scratched it, I'm going to take the cost of having it repaired out of your hide. Now get your sweet little ass off my table!"

Surprised, Colwin jumped up like a kid caught with his hand in the cookie jar.

Loni turned back to Thomas. "Nothing? Nothing interesting happened?"

"Wellll . . ." Thomas began eagerly, sitting forward on the edge of his chair, some light coming into his eyes. It was obvious to Loni he had given what he was about to say a lot of thought. "It isn't important yet, but it could be. Mercer Parry winked at me."

Colwin exploded into raucous laughter, much to the chagrin of both Thomas and Loni. They glared at him, both sets of eyes flaming.

"Parry winked at you! Oh, gods! And I'll bet you just loved it, too," Dene screamed through his laughter.

Thomas started to rise from his seat, obviously intent on murdering Dene, but, with difficulty, Loni restrained him. *That Dene!* Thomas thought. *Thinks he's the only guy around capable of killing. If it weren't for Loni, I'd tear him apart.*

Colwin saw something of the viciousness in Thomas's glare, and laughed all the harder. He knew, and he saw that Loni knew also, he could have torn Thomas's head off without a whole lot of difficulty, in spite of Thomas outweighing him.

Then Loni said coldly into Colwin's braying, "You're a good man, Colwin, but if you want to be a live one, you'd better learn to think, starting right now."

Something in Loni's tone hit home with Colwin. There were ice-cold rage and deep affection both intertwined in her words, and he stopped laughing to hear her.

"Listen to what Thomas is about to say. If I understand him, and I think I do, you're about to find out what real courage is."

Chapter Three

————◆————

ELENA, A SMALL, delicate woman with blond hair and fragile blue eyes, sat in the throne room feeling slightly bored, and just beginning to be angry. How many times had they gone over this? At least six she could recall clearly, and that did not include the several times she had been waylaid in corridors and the like. Yukio Yuichi was still rambling on. And Elena, though she looked as attentive as ever, was beginning to drift. Yukio's initials. Y. Y. His mother must

have asked "Why?" twice when he was born.
Suddenly Elena shifted, and brought her attention sharply back. It was dangerous as well as
unwise to be mentally elsewhere. Something
important might be said, and she must not miss
it.

Aware now, she listened to Yuichi with half an
ear, but turned the rest of her attention to her
daughter, who sat behind and below her. She
shifted slightly on the throne so that she could
see what Natanha was doing, and smoothed her
skirt so it did not wrinkle. She had been worried
about the children ever since that disaster of a
banquet two weeks ago. The timing of their arrival to say good-night had been the worst—
and best—possible. Ozenscebo preferred to be a
father only when it suited him. That the children should arrive when he was angry was dangerous, both for Elena and for the children. But
their arrival had probably diverted an even
larger disaster by sidetracking her "loving husband" from his intended public chastisement of
her. Still, she had been very grateful that somehow Magnus, a wild seven-year-old, had seen
Ozenscebo's displeasure in time to abort his
leap to the emperor's lap. Although the boy had
always been the emperor's favorite, she was not
sure what the result of his impetuousness would
have been. Natanha, almost a woman at thirteen, had never behaved like Magnus. She had
always been a restrained and serious child.
Even as an infant she had never cried unless
really troubled or uncomfortable. Now Natanha
sat quietly, never fidgeting, head slightly bent,
although Elena could see the child's eyes took in
every movement. The empress was fairly certain
the various advisers and courtiers who were

present had totally forgotten Natanha was among them. But the child had not forgotten them. Elena knew Natanha was storing away every word, every reaction. Pride and love soared in her. This girl would be capable of running the empire one day, and, more importantly, her people would love her mild and thoughtful ways.

It was Elena who fidgeted. The throne was massive, so large there was really no way Elena could sit comfortably in it. If her legs folded neatly over the front, her feet would not reach the floor and her back would not reach the backrest. If she leaned against the arms, they dug into her side just under her ribs. And no amount of cushioning could disguise the fact that the chair was made of constanadium, the native metal of Changwo, the first extra-Solar planet conquered by Ozenscebo's forebears, not after her body had endured the cold, hard surface for more than three hours. Elena had learned long ago to hate the thing, in spite of its beautiful lavender color and the amethysts that ringed the back, in spite of the technical achievement it represented—it had been carved from the largest block of constanadium ever poured. But she would not give up sitting in it when she ran the business of the empire, though she really had no right to it. She felt she was doing the work that should have been her husband's, that she represented the empire, and that she had, in the beginning at least, needed all the trappings of legitimacy.

In truth, she sighed to herself, *I don't suppose it would matter now if I sat on a tatami. The passing of time and necessity have granted me legitimacy.*

Elena decided she hated the throne room, too. It had been finished to Ozenscebo's taste—that is to say, as costly and intricately as possible— and she was nowhere reflected. The ceilings and walls dripped with gold on structural pieces between masterworks of the finest artists. She had seen old holos of the ceiling of a thing called the Sistine Chapel, a tiny place of worship that had been somewhere in backwater Europe. She remembered it distinctly from her lessons on ancient Earth history before she had come here to Osaka. It looked like it had been done by an orangutan, when compared to this hall. But where the Sistine Chapel breathed, this room suffocated, despite its never being warm enough. The columns supporting the enormously high and drafty ceiling were twisted, convoluted shafts of the rarest marble—lavender, naturally, to complement the throne—and wrapped around them were vines and leaves of yet more gold. The floor was an immense map of the empire, crafted by a method in which precious stones were processed until they were molten, poured into cells, much like cloisonné, then polished till they gleamed. While it was beautiful, it was also ornate, ornate, ornate. But, on further reflection, Elena supposed she could live with the floor if some of the other gaudiness was removed. Like the draperies over the floor-to-ceiling window way at the back of the room. Blue, red, and purple, though all considered royal colors, were not her choice of color scheme. And the sconces. They would have to go too. Yellow dragons added nothing to this decor.

Elena shook herself. It was not likely Ozenscebo would give her leave to redecorate his throne room, even if he was rarely there. And Yuichi was still babbling about new taxes.

"Advisor Yuichi, it is too soon to impose new taxes. We implemented a new tax plan less than one Solar year ago. Our people are being very hard-pressed."

Unfortunately, Elena saw, Yuichi took her remonstrance as a personal insult, bowed, and withdrew slightly without further comment. But the respite was short-lived, as Counselor Keisuke Shishi took his place.

"Empress, it is true we cannot tax the people of Earth yet again. As you say, it is too soon. But that does not preclude further taxes on the colonies. You have been very lenient with them in the past."

Shishi's oily, ingratiating voice had always annoyed Elena. Though she wanted to take his robe, every bit as ostentatious as something the emperor would wear, and stuff it down his throat so he couldn't produce those sounds anymore, she asked instead, "How would you propose we collect these new taxes, Counselor?"

"Simple, Your Majesty," he whined. "Send a cadre of those magnificent Lionmen. We pay for their upkeep, after all, and they haven't really been useful since the Avoyan uprising."

Elena sighed again, this time audibly. "Force, I'm afraid, gentlemen, will not bind the empire."

This comment was met with a cacophony of voices raised in various sorts of protest. Some were arguing in favor of the proposed new taxes, some were saying the Lionmen had outlived their usefulness, some that the empire's strength rested in its ability to use force when necessary, some were talking merely to hear themselves.

Elena let it run on, hoping it would sort itself out, but it did not, and there were some signs that tempers were beginning to fray. Finally, one voice was heard above the others. "How are we going to pay for all our programs if we don't raise the taxes?"

Elena responded immediately to keep this meeting from getting totally out of hand. "I suppose I could always retain fewer advisers."

There was an instant silence, born, most probably, of fear. If the emperor had said that, more than likely some of them would not have seen tomorrow's dawn. But this was Elena, and some nervous laughter began to filter into the quiet.

"This is enough for today, gentlemen. I will consider what you've said. Leave us."

Natanha rose from her chair, mounted the few remaining steps to the throne, and sat next to her mother. "Will you really remove them?" she asked in her light and warm voice.

Natanha reminded Elena so much of herself before she had become the bride of the emperor. Her daughter's long blond hair hung in fine wavy tendrils down her back, held in place with only a ribbon. Natanha's eyes were the same crystal blue as her own. Their features were even remarkably similar: strong, high cheekbones, slight hollows in the cheek; well-formed mouths, richly pink, that rarely needed makeup. There was little of the father in this daughter. Elena, of course, had been happy before she came to Osaka. She didn't know if Natanha really understood the word happy, having grown up amid the intrigues and violence of Ozenscebo's court.

"No, child. I won't dismiss them. I much

prefer to keep them where I can see them. Keep your enemies always in your sight."

There was a pause while Natanha considered, then she asked, "Does that include Daddy?"

Elena was no longer shocked by her daughter's perspicacity, but this question saddened her. She hugged Natanha to her as she answered, painfully, truthfully, "Yes, child. I'm afraid so."

Natanha nodded, then pulled away from the hug. "Did Yuichi seem resentful?"

"Oh, his nose was a little out of joint, but he's mostly harmless. Don't ever turn your back on Shishi, though."

"Has there been any further news about the rebels?"

For just a moment Elena froze. There were so many things she needed to explain to her daughter. But now was not the time. She touched Natanha's hair. "Never go near anyone you don't recognize, Natanha, and don't trust even those you know."

Ki's nose was twitching. Something was wrong. All things have their peculiar scent, and a Lionman, born to use his senses to hunt, trained to use his senses for his own protection and the protection of those in his care, was keenly aware of the world about him. He changed his path from the one that led into the palace, and followed instead the one that led off to the practice field. He was supposed to meet the empress, but she would understand if he were delayed. She valued the men who served her.

He sniffed. It was there, among the dust and

the sweat and the body-generated heat. One of the new recruits was bathed in arrogance. The odor of it was so strong it almost wiped away the traces of Nide that still clung to the new arrivals.

Ki walked to the edge of the field, then stopped in the dappled shade of the only tree and watched. The new recruits were all dressed alike in the jumpsuits that would constitute their uniform until they won the right to wear the red imperial tri-lozenge. Except for wide variations in coloring, they looked much the same. They were young, lithe, tall, and eager. The eagerness made Ki smile. He remembered his own well, and sometimes felt it still.

But the arrogance he was catching was a different and dangerous thing. The cub who gave in to that would think himself invincible, and Ki wore the case-hardened proof that no one was invulnerable. He rubbed his metallic left hand with his right, remembering, then dropped it to his side and pulled the digits across the palm in an unconscious motion, not really feeling the bumps and ridges of the hand as his "fingers" crossed them.

The arrogant one was not hard to find. He was showing off. While the rest of his group worked hard just to maintain the pace Lieutenant Mikal Lawwnum set for them during dueling practice, the arrogant one ran ahead, adding fillips and flourishes to passes that were intended to be clean and simple.

Ki rested his back against the rough bark of the tree and watched for a time, satisfying himself as to the quality of Mikal's leadership. His instructions were excellent. He judged the recruits well, and gave them enough to challenge,

but not so much as to discourage. The recruits
were a good group, too, working hard, trying for
perfection, taking instruction well. Except for
one.

The commander rumbled deep in his throat
while musing, then nodded to himself. It was
time for them to meet the boss. He clasped his
hands behind his back, and strode out onto the
field.

Mikal had been aware of the commander's attendance for some time. He had not been born
into the same pride and trained by the same
men as Colonel Ki himself for nothing. And the
commander's presence brought with it something akin to panic. Mikal never understood
why the colonel's presence did that to him,
bringing him to the edge of losing control. It
was certainly nothing about Ki personally. But
every time Colonel Ki looked in on Mikal, the
same thought recurred: *Oh Mmumna! Don't let
me mess up now!* He ran his eyes over the group,
trying to assess them the way the commander
would. They were good, and they would become
excellent. Except for one, there would be no difficulties. And he would be no difficulty either, if
his course could be changed from one of cocky
display to one of quiet excellence.

Mikal turned as he heard the commander's
step behind him. "Awwmuum!" he called, and
was gratified that all activity came to an instant
halt.

Though the men stood still at attention, there
was a kind of ripple that passed through them
as they recognized the Lionman who had joined
the group.

Mikal asked politely as the commander approached, "Would you like to see how this group is coming along, sir?"

Ki nodded once.

"Bakim!" Mikal barked, and the organized disorder of a swordsmanship practice resumed.

Ki walked among the men, slipping between the mock battles as if he were made of air. He knew he was being carefully and surreptitiously watched. He also knew his visual impression was a powerful one, his white face and hair floating over the black-fleck-on-black of his rank's mantle, demonic even, enhanced by the facial tattoos of his pride, pale red slashes up across the eyes, trailing down into an open swirl on each cheek. It was an unsettling appearance Ki worked hard to maintain. He sneered a bit, squinting his eyes slightly, to enhance the fierceness of his appearance. A first impression of a ferocious commander would be a deep and lasting one, one Ki chose to cultivate.

He stopped a little aside of the mock battle involving the braggart and watched for a time, aware always of the sounds and motions at his sides and back. It would not do to have the commander sent sprawling by an errant blow from a raw recruit. He waited, making an effort to keep the dust from the hard-packed field from clogging his nostrils. When he was certain the attention of all the others was on their own forays, he turned to the new man.

"Your name?"

"Leenoww, sir!"

"You have been having some success with the sword, I see. Would you care to try me?"

Leenoww looked startled for a moment, but then a gleam of impious glee came into his eye.

What a chance to show the commander what he could do! With luck he might even beat him!

Ki knew that look and understood perfectly what it meant. He also understood its foolishness. This recruit had to learn there was always someone better near at hand.

"Strike at me, hard, whenever you feel you are ready," Ki ordered.

"But...But, sir..." Leenoww stammered, disconcerted. The commander had no boken, or practice sword.

"Strike!"

With a ragged smile, Leenoww raised the wooden weapon to strike, and held onto the thought that he was the best in his group. Beating Commander Ki Lawwnum was not out of the question.

Almost before Leenoww knew he'd made the decision to strike, Ki saw the muscles of the man's shoulders begin to bunch under the form-fitting fatigues. The colonel waited until he knew where the blow was aimed, then flashed his hands outward to where the sword would be in a microsecond. Clapping his hands together over the blade, he made a twisting motion with both wrists. The boken came out of Leenoww's hands as if it had the ability of motion in its own right. The recruit would have looked down at his empty hands, but Ki moved again, and before the man's eyes could follow his brain's direction, Ki had the boken at the recruit's throat.

"It would seem you have a thing or two to learn yet, cub," Ki said softly as he slid the boken along Leenoww's throat in what would have been a fatal stroke had the blade been steel. He held the blade there momentarily, then dropped the point.

"You have the makings of an excellent swordsman," Ki said heartily, not allowing any room for resentment to grow. "Just the kind I need under me." He returned the boken and brushed the dust from his hands. Dust in his artificial hand was most annoying, grating and rubbing and slowing its reaction time.

A look of incipient hero worship washed across Leenoww's very young brown face. "I must learn that move!"

Ki laughed. "That move is a dangerous one, cub." He held up his left hand. "And not always successful." He turned away.

Mikal regretted he was not close enough to hear what the conversation had been. He had seen the gesture of the raised hand, and was eminently curious. He had never had the nerve to ask the commander how he'd lost the hand. The question had always seemed extremely impertinent. And he wanted to know how the situation had been handled. Somehow the colonel always knew exactly the right words, a trick Mikal had never mastered.

"Is there something on your mind, Lieutenant?" Ki asked in response to the dissatisfied frown on Mikal's face. "You seem most thoughtful. Come, walk with me a way and we'll speak of it." Ki took Mikal by the arm and spun him toward the palace. "Are you displeased because I interrupted?"

"No, sir!" Mikal responded, shocked.

"I felt it was time I meet this group. I suppose the story will make the rounds." Ki said it almost with a sigh, thinking of the next wave of unlicked cubs who would want to try the commander.

"Yes, sir." Mikal hesitated, stopped, pulled himself to perfect attention. "Sir," Mikal began, choking on his own nerve, "did you tell that recruit how you came to lose your hand?" He cringed slightly now that he'd said it, wondering if he'd made the mistake of all time.

The commander smiled a very wicked, mischievous smile. "Let's say the story told at dinner will be an interesting fairy tale."

Mikal was swept with a mixture of relief that the colonel was not angered by his question and regret bordering on sheer frustration that he still did not know the truth. But his wildly raging hero worship colored his face and he could not question further. "Thank you, Commander," he said, lowering his eyes.

Ki smiled indulgently, and patiently began to explain something he thought Mikal had missed. "I think I have done myself a favor. That man will be good with a sword in time. Perhaps very good. That is the kind of man I want and need under me. After all, Mikal, I may find him at my side one day. And, Mikal," he said, turning slightly so he was facing the lieutenant squarely, "I saw your awareness of Leenoww's problem. Though I tried my own solution, I'm certain yours would have been as effective. I have much confidence in you."

Mikal positively glowed under the praise, and he looked with unabashed pride at the commander. His affection for Ki was great, and he could never understand the irrational nerves that struck every time the commander came near. He had known Ki almost as long as he could remember, though time spent together had been necessarily brief. Ki's duties had kept him off Nide most of the time, and when he had returned his business had been with the adults. But there had usually been a moment for the cub who wanted to be in the Imperial Guard. Mikal had the right to call Ki "Uncle," as they were of the same pride and the same marital line, though Ki was not in fact his father's brother, and that had given Mikal some trouble as he'd come up through the ranks. As a result, Mikal worked twice as hard as any other man. And praise from his boyhood hero was twice as sweet.

Ki nodded as he watched the emotions flying over Mikal's face. "Return to your men now, Mikal. I think this is a good group. Work with them."

"Yes, sir!" Mikal saluted, and turned back to the practice field.

Ki watched him for a moment, then continued on his way into the palace. The empress would understand a brief delay, but she would not tolerate one moment wasted.

The training session had been an unexpected one. Ki took the lengthy walk back to his apartments, and for once regretted his quarters were not in the barracks with the rest of the Guard. He wiped his face and neck with a towel, thinking fondly of a hot tub, all the while realizing it would have to wait. He put his hand to his privacy lock and opened the door, then stopped.

Just inside the door on the floor was a small parcel, no bigger than one could hold comfortably in one hand. But there had been no package when he'd left. That meant someone had been in his apartments. He dropped the towel and stooped down to get a good look at the box. Wrapped like a gift, it looked totally harmless, but with the situation being what it was in the empire with a rebellion aborning, he was cautious. Certainly the death of the commander of the famous Lionman Guard would be a welcome coup, and if this was indeed a bomb, it certainly was not the first ever to make its way into the palace in spite of all security precautions. It would, however, be the first directed at Ki.

He heard nothing from the package, so he leaned slightly closer to see if he could get a hint of an identifying odor of whoever had handled the package. He sniffed. He knew exactly who had left the package. There could be no mistake.

Reaching out, he pulled a cushion from his sofa. Gingerly he settled the parcel on the pillow, and lifted it. Then he stood, slowly. Without tipping the box, he examined it from each side. It appeared quite ordinary. He held it closer to his face, and breathed deeply, hoping to discover whatever was inside. But nothing came to him but the scent of the culprit. He paused, considering. Then he shrugged. He put another pillow over the top of the box, and tore the paper and pulled off the lid. He half expected a very loud bang, and discovered he'd closed his eyes. When he peeked, he inhaled sharply.

For once, the princess had not been playing games. Inside, resting on a small brown velvet cushion, sat a nicely striated rock, alternating bands of black and white and grays that had been geologically folded at some point to form a fascinating swirl a little off center in the piece. With some polish it just might become a true thing of beauty. Also inside the box was a note in the princess's own not-quite-mature hand that said, *For your garden*. He smiled, knowing exactly where he'd put it, and padded softly out the double French doors that led onto the lawn, hoping the empress would not miss him just yet.

In actuality the garden was not his, as several of the apartments in this wing opened onto it. In practice, however, it was his private place of refuge. One of the apartments was not occupied, and the tenants of the others never entered, preferring the larger, more elaborate gardens, or staying indoors entirely. And even though there was an entrance to the garden from a hallway, the place was so little known, and in such a restricted section of the palace, strangers were an extreme rarity. Gradually, therefore, the garden had taken on the personality Ki chose for it.

It was a mingling of the carefully tended and planned gardens of old Japan and the wild freedom of Nide. A small patch of lawn ran up to Ki's doors, across the way to another set of doors, then jumped the small stream that trickled through the garden to end in a riot of flowers native to Ki's planet. The stream, though small, provided the sound of running water as it splashed down over a small waterfall of rocks. It then dropped away over the open wall at the end of the garden that overlooked the city of Osaka. As this palace stood on a promontory that had once held a medieval castle, the view into the city was magnificent, and Ki frequently watched the sunrise over the small wall.

For the second time in an hour he was taken unaware, for he was not alone. He could see someone standing near the patch of wildflowers.

Her back was to him, and, as she was stooped to admire the flowers, all Ki could really see was a robe of a soft golden color with full skirts. He was curious as to the identity of his visitor and was about to speak, then decided instead to quietly withdraw. He should be in attendance on the empress, at any rate. But as he began to move, the visitor shifted and turned toward him, startled.

Ki gasped. Never in all his experience had he seen anything as lovely. She was, quite literally, a live treasure. They looked at each other for several heartbeats before Ki found his voice.

"I'm sorry to disturb you. I'll go."

"No. Pleassse ssstay."

Quite taken by the sound of the waves in her voice, Ki acquiesced, forgetting appointments and stuffing the now-unimportant rock into his sleeve to be retrieved later. "Please. Won't you sit with me?" he asked her.

Slowly, gracefully, she nodded. "I will."

She began to walk carefully over the tiny bridge that crossed the stream halfway between the waterfall and the wall. Her robe was held together at her breast with one hand. The full skirts parted as she walked, and Ki saw her delicate fingers were the only fastening on her only piece of clothing. She hovered over the bench for a moment, then sank delicately.

"You are not like the others?" she asked.

Ki was puzzled. What others? "I'm afraid I don't understand."

"The other people in this place. You are not like them?"

A breeze wafted across her directly into Ki's face. He was struck by the extraordinary nature of her scent. It differed very little from the stream in the garden—water and minerals, though the mineral smell was somehow accented. Altogether welcome and fresh after the rancid sweat of humans.

"No, I am not like most of the people in the palace. I have a different homeworld. But there are others of my kind here. Have you not seen them?"

She shook her head, and her crystalline hair gave off a shower of reflections. "No. I have not seen them. But I am new here. I also have a different homeworld. Here they call me Opal."

"I am Ki Lawwnum," he said, giving his name the full Nidean accent, a harsh rumbling yowl.

She shivered, reacting much the way Aubin always did. Then she asked, "You have two names?"

"Yes. The first is my given name, referring to me only. The second is my pride name, and refers to me and all the members of my pride."

"I have never heard the word 'pride' used this way. Please what is 'pride'?"

Ki eyed her, wondering if she was making polite conversation or if she was truly interested. But she sat forward slightly, lips barely parted, her expression one of full attention.

"On my planet, Nide, a family consists of a father, mother, and children. But each family belongs to an extended family that we call a pride. The pride takes care of the young and old, sees to it that the laws are kept, watches to see that none marry who are too close in blood. A very large family."

She nodded once more, and Ki was distracted by the slight rattling sound that came from her hair. He looked at it intently.

She pointed directly into his face. "Is that coloring natural? Are those colors like mine?"

"No. It's a tattoo. It tells the rest of the people of my world to which pride I belong. They are granted when a boy becomes a man or when a woman marries."

"Tattoo? What is that?"

"Coloring or dye is inserted under the skin."

"Isn't that painful?"

"It can be."

"Your people go through much to be able to tell each other apart." She brushed lightly at his face. "But at least with the colors you can see, not like the rest here. They are all the same."

Ki understood that feeling, and sat silently musing on it. The companionable quiet stretched out.

She broke it finally. "I saw this garden as I walked down the hall from where I belong. The door was open, but I carefully closed it behind me as I was taught. I saw the growing things. Are those what are called flowers? I didn't know carbon could do that. Where do you belong?"

It registered with Ki that "down the hall" had to imply the seraglio. In answer to her question, though, he lifted his right hand and pointed. "Those doors lead into my apartment."

She gasped, a tiny cry strangling in her throat, and recoiled; the hand that had been grasping her gown was now outstretched in a warding-off gesture. She was thoroughly terrified.

"Have I done something?" Ki asked, totally dumbfounded, and stricken by the look on her face.

Still drawn away from him, breathing hard,

she tried to speak, discovered she couldn't, swallowed, and tried again. "Is it common practice here to kill babies?" Her voice was thin and forced.

"No. It most definitely is not common practice." Ki was almost snarling, his voice a flat rumble.

"Then, why did you?" She pointed at his hand.

He looked where she was pointing, but made no connection. *My hand?* he thought. *My sleeve?* Then he understood. "My ring!"

The above-average-sized opals set there winked and gleamed in the sun. "This was never alive. These stones are found here and elsewhere in the empire on and in the ground."

She relaxed slightly, but remained bent away from him. "You are quite certain? They are found on the ground? You have seen this for yourself?"

"No, I have not seen this for myself. I have never looked for these stones. I do have it on good authority, however, that they are mined from the dirt."

Resuming her upright posture, slowly her breathing returned to its previous languid rate. Ki noticed his heartbeat had speeded up some at the thought of killing babies, and carefully restored it to normal.

"If it offends, I'll remove it," he offered quietly, closing his metallic hand over the ring.

She moved slightly closer as curiosity grabbed her. "May I see?"

After a moment's hesitation caused by the pain of sharing his prized gift, Ki began the twisting motion necessary to remove the ring, but she stopped him.

"Pleasse. I do not wish to touch them."

He extended his hand for her examination. She studied the stones carefully, realizing the totally smooth texture was all wrong, and the transparency went too deep for there ever to have been internal organs there.

"Thank you. I have learned another new thing." Though her thanks were genuine, relief far and away dominated her emotions.

The door that led from the garden to the corridor banged heavily against the wall, and Opal jumped. Ki was on his feet in a slight crouch, hand on the hilt of his sword, ready to fight. They had both been so intent on their conversation that everything else had ceased to exist, and this reintroduction of the world had startled them. Ki did not react pleasantly to being startled. A seraglio attendant rushed in, panting and perspiring heavily, extremely unpleasant on a girl of her tender age.

"There you are! At last! Mama-san has been frantic. She has everyone out looking for you!"

Opal glanced at Ki, then regretfully lowered her head and stood hesitantly. "I come."

Ki stood as well, and watched as she glided slowly, slowly from the garden. He watched until the attendant shut the door soundly behind her. Then he sat once more, replaying in his mind his meeting with Opal, seeing it all again in the reflections on the water as it sparkled by. "It shines," he mumbled to himself, "almost as much as she." He crossed his arms, and found something hard and cold stuffed into his sleeve. He pulled out, totally forgotten, the princess's gift. Musing, he turned it this way and that, saying softly, "So this is why I came here."

* * *

The weapons range was a busy place just now. The junior Lionmen were attempting to move up their ratings. The quiet *pffuft* of the weapons was coming repeatedly, as were the blinding flashes of harsh white light. Mikal Lawwnum, Ki's marital-line nephew, had long ago found he no longer heard the sound, but the light still disturbed him, partly because it was so intense, and partly because it always reminded him of the brilliance of Nide's sun. He continued to walk the line, stopping at each man, watching, correcting, checking, making certain they would be ready for Captain Res's inspection. Most had improved markedly. The rest would probably never improve. But even at their current stage they were better than you'd find anywhere else in the empire. Of course, Mikal realized, that would not be good enough for the commander. He would keep them at it till most of them would be able to hit their mark dead center ninety-nine times out of a hundred, and then push them for the extra one. And if Ki didn't, he, Mikal, would.

"Aallaard Lawwnum."

Mikal had been watching a young Nidean ready his weapon. He responded automatically with "Det," then looked up, surprised at being addressed in Nidean.

"Aallaard Lawwnum, why do we practice with these...things," asked Private Leenoww very formally while he held the small box that was the energy weapon extended on the palm of his hand. "There is no honor bound to this thing. Only a sword has honor."

Mikal considered his answer carefully, wanting very much to say the right thing for once. "Private," he answered in common, "the sword is the more elegant weapon, and certainly the sword is more useful than that"—he gestured disdainfully at the energy weapon—"in a ship where one shot with one of those can rupture the hull and kill all aboard. But you must understand that these can kill too, and at long range. There will be times when you will be asked to use them. Certainly you must understand them. But I will never ask you to give them the respect you give your blade."

The young private considered what the lieutenant had said, then nodded sagely. "As you say, Lieutenant. It is good to practice."

Mikal was elated. This time, it seemed, he'd said exactly the right thing.

The empress, dressed most delicately in a blue floor-length dress that sparkled when she moved, stood watching her husband's Lionmen from a balcony, guarded and accompanied only by Commander Ki. She frequently reviewed the men from this perch, which was located on the rear side of the palace and ran in an L around two walls, one facing the weapons range, the other an enclosed drill field. It gave her the opportunity to be alone (except for the company of Commander Ki, of course, but he could be as talkative or as still as she wished) if she so desired. Today she was tired of everyone with whom she had regular contact, and worried, very worried. Too many things preyed on her mind, too many things happened much too quickly. She wanted very much to hear Ki's voice so full of quiet confidence. But instead of asking him to talk, to tell her of the goings-on in the palace to which an empress is never privy, she spoke.

"Take care of the princess," she said as she

pulled a small square of silk from her sash. It was the very one Ki had used to wipe his sword at Natanha's birth. The blood of the princess and the empress still stained it.

Standing fully and correctly erect, Ki answered, "You know I have sworn to do so." Then he leaned down to put his elbow on the railing so that his face would be more on a level with Elena's, and so she would know they were now speaking as friend to friend. "Afraid of rebels?"

Elena sighed heavily, and grabbed the ornate cast-iron rail with both hands. She stood looking out over the firing range for some time without speaking. Then she shook a fold of her skirt and smoothed it. Finally she turned to Ki. "We live in interesting times, my friend."

"Indeed." Ki noticed the deepening mauve circles under her eyes. They vaguely resembled the markings of the Didentaar, a pride that had special attachments to the Lawwnum. Where Ki had found the markings beautiful on Nideans, they were wrong, even ugly, on Elena. And there were tiny lines around her mouth that told she had been frowning a great deal. He hoped she would say more, but she merely continued to stare out at the bright white flashes beneath her. Sensing that more than anything she wanted to be truly alone, he said, "I will leave you, Highness. Your guard will be outside the door. You know I am yours to command," and he withdrew.

Ki left Elena feeling very uneasy. It was obvious to any who cared to look that she was worried. It was in every aspect of her: her sleepy-looking eyes, her mouth, her very stance. And that had never been like Elena. Even when she had first come here, hardly more than a child, as soon as she saw that Ozenscebo did not see to his duties, she stepped in and worked at making things right. Had she stopped working? Stopped fighting? It was a question that plagued him as he walked down the hall on the way · to the emperor's audience chamber. Though it was time to find out what Ozenscebo was up to, it was Elena who worried him. He wished he knew what was going on.

"Is something troubling you?" Aubin's light voice rang in Ki's ear.

"Mmmmmm," Ki rumbled, and then laughed as the hair on Aubin's arm stood at attention. "Yes, I'm troubled, but not so much as you are by my speech."

"Ki, you do that to me on purpose, and you know it. And if you didn't already look down-in-the-mouth, as if you could look anything else with those barbaric marks on your face, I would chew you out for it."

Ki halted in midstride, snarled "Barbaric!" before he realized Aubin had baited him. Then he let it pass, and continued with Aubin down the hall. "Yes, I'm worried. I'm concerned about the empress."

"Ahhh. Now, there's a lady who lives in interesting times."

Ki sighed. "Again?" he asked of the wind, thinking of what the empress had said just a few moments earlier.

"I beg your pardon?" asked Aubin, not understanding the reference.

"It's not important," Ki answered as they drew near the audience chamber. "You have business here today?"

"Unfortunately, yes. Ozenscebo has called several of the envoys together to discuss, in the

most disguised of terms, of course—we dare not
even admit that rebels exist—how to deal with
the rebels. I had hoped I wouldn't be found
down in the recesses of the law library, but I
didn't hide well enough."

Ki opened the door quietly, and the two
stepped through. Several men and women were
near the front of the room, packed as closely as
they dared to get to the emperor, hanging on his
every word. One figure, however, stood in the
very back of the hall. She was tall, taller even
than Ki, with the broad nose and leonine features of his race. Her white hair was close-
cropped, however, and stranger still, she wore
no facial markings except for the lines of great
age. She was swathed in the deep-desert robes
of her planet, wrapped as if to protect her from
the cold, and she kept them pulled closely about
her with her crossed arms. The only jewelry she
wore was an amulet hanging from her belt that
bore the pride markings of the Didentaar. An
unmarried woman, then, a person of no standing in her own pride, and yet Nide's ambassador
to Homeworld.

Ki greeted her, "Learaa Maaeve, waarrsho nu
Mmumna," in the traditional way, her name
first, then "Mmumna hold you," the "in the circle of her claws" part being understood.

She nodded to Ki respectfully, totally ignored
Aubin even though he was Luna's envoy, and
turned back to the proceedings at the front of
the hall.

Aubin stared at her curiously. Though he had
spent much time in the same room with her on
numerous occasions, she was still a total
stranger. She was odd, always at the back of
things, never saying a word, always watching,

listening, this woman who was the only ambassador at the emperor's court. Nide was an affiliate by choice, not a conquered world. *And I'll bet she misses nothing,* Aubin thought. *I imagine her reports to Nide are fascinating. Probably more complete than anyone else's. I'll bet she has a better overall picture of what goes on in this empire than I do.* He tilted his head, considering her unmarked face. If he understood Ki correctly, that meant she had never married. But it also meant she was still a child, regarded as a nonperson. She must be quite a woman, rising above a total lack of status to become ambassador.

But in spite of his open stare, Maaeve still did not acknowledge Aubin, so he made his way forward to listen, and Ki edged around the side of the group so that he might see the emperor.

The usual gathering of servants scurried about like ants, carrying wine, or more likely roed, to the emperor and his audience, passing among them with little sweetmeats, holding out fresh transcriber disks. But though it was usual, it was also unusual. Ki stiffened as he smelled it—fear, far and away more than the usual discomfiture of servants who waited on an uneven master. Trouble. Somewhere in this room a very frightened human was contemplating trouble.

"We have to consolidate the empire," Ozenscebo was saying. "We must find a way to bring the worlds closer together."

Ki edged closer to the group of envoys. No. The fear scent did not rise from them. From the servants then. It had to be. He turned like a dancer, lightly, on the balls of his feet, ready to change direction with the smallest of notice. His head turned, and he sniffed again. A nondescript servant approached the emperor with a goblet. But there was already a goblet at Ozenscebo's hand, and the servant hid his face. There was a blur of motion that was Ki and a sliding, savage sword that moved into an eerie, dreamlike lack of sound, and the servant's head skipped down among the envoys, spraying blood among them as it rolled. They stared at it like dumb cattle, the silence holding until some started to scream.

The emperor looked away from the ball-shaped object that had been a head, and directly at Ki. There was only mind surprise on his jaded face. "Amusing. But why?"

"I could not permit him to kill." Ki resheathed his blade, blood and all, and stooped over the body. From somewhere inside the fashionably full gown the emperor had ordered as costume of the day for his servants, Ki removed a high-carbon plastic needle—strong, sharp, and totally invisible to metal detectors. He sniffed the end of the unlikely weapon. "It's been poisoned," he said over his shoulder to the emperor. "It probably appeared as a stay on the security monitors."

The emperor suddenly realized what his danger had been, and his face turned snow white, drained of all color. He looked pasty and sick at the thought of his own death. Ki, realizing a sick emperor is not a sight for everyone, took charge, dismissing the envoys, who were only too happy to go, and calling for Lionmen to clear away the debris. The emperor, still somewhat dazed, looked down at his iridescent green robes. They were spattered with blood. Ki expected an outburst of some sort, rage at the spoiled finery, and was repulsed and revolted by what he got instead.

"It's ruined, of course," mumbled Ozenscebo as he fumbled with a golden-green sleeve, "but the blood is such a lovely color. Rich. A lovely color."

Ki was grateful when the emperor decided to leave as well. Seeing that everything was as he ordered, Ki wanted nothing so much as to leave the carnage behind. As he walked toward the back of the hall, he noticed two people remained behind. One was Aubin, the other Ambassador Maaeve. As Ki approached, she bowed to him, deeply, and departed, never having said a word. Aubin stood and stared as if he were some sort of bumpkin who had never seen a Lionman before. Ki began to walk out the door, expecting Aubin to follow, but Aubin only turned his head and continued to stare, unable to absorb what he had seen. Ki retraced his steps, took Aubin by the arm, and led him down the corridor until Aubin shook him loose. Aubin did not speak, either. Their course led in no particular direction, but they continued to walk at the pace Ki set.

At last Ki asked, "Why are you so quiet, my friend?"

Aubin stumbled slightly, awkward with emotion. "I've walked half my life with you and I never suspected. The man who moved like that is not the man I know."

Ki sneered, somewhat offended. "You've always known what I am."

"Yes. But there's knowing and there's seeing."

"Do you find me distasteful?"

Though Ki's voice was cold and deadly even, Aubin was certain he heard sadness in the question.

"No," Aubin answered thoughtfully. "Merely interesting. Interesting times need interesting men."

"And yet again," Ki mumbled with a grimace.

They walked on a way in silence, each alone with his thoughts. But they had, by unspoken mutual consent, taken the turn toward Aubin's quarters.

"I'd like to examine that sword sometime," Aubin said quietly, with a hint of shyness. "It is apparently something I do not understand as well as I should."

"When it's clean."

They entered Aubin's apartment as two old friends standing now on shaky ground. Aubin headed for his liquor cabinet while Ki disappeared into the bathroom. While he waited, Aubin looked at himself carefully in the mirrored wall behind the bar. He was getting old. His shoulders were no longer so straight, and his hair, which had once been brown and rich and wavy, was no longer so full or so dark. His sleepy brown eyes reflected his deep weariness, and his body sagged with a little excess weight. His hand shook slightly as he raised the glass, reaction to the fear fountaining inside him. This day had been too full. Ki was gone for some time, and Aubin was achingly certain he had lost his friend as well as his youth. The wait was a sad and long one for him, full of interior terrors, and yet he was startled when Ki at last reappeared.

"It's clean," Ki said of the naked blade he held. He extended it to Aubin, hilt first. "Don't touch the blade. The acid in your skin will etch it, and your fingerprints will become a permanent part of the edge. This hoj has been in my pride for four generations. See? Each of these stones set here in the pommel represents a man who has kept the blade. Another shanshen gem will be added for me when the blade goes to Mikal. It was made by the master swordsmith Kaanshaar." He ran his long, thick, slightly pointed nail along the steel, and it hissed its response, sending a chill running down Aubin's human spine. "If you look at the pattern, you will see his handiwork. The wave-and-ruffle pattern of the folded metal is his signature."

Aubin was a jumble of emotion, and still hesitated to take the proffered sword. He looked at the gleaming steel blue of the killing surface and the hilt covered with gray-blue stuff like shark-skin. At last he took it in his hands, awed by the purpose for which it had been used such a short time ago, and found to his surprise he quickly drifted deeper and deeper into a flow that followed the wave pattern on the edge.

Very quietly, Ki said, "Usually the only ones who are permitted a close inspection of a hoj are pride members and those who feel its cutting edge. Please keep this to yourself."

Ki waited, watching Aubin lose himself in the pattern, seeing the beginnings of real understanding of what the blade meant to Ki dawning in Aubin's face. He flexed his left hand, feeling the lightness that meant the sword was not part of him at the moment. He waited what he felt was a reasonable time, longer than he wanted to, a small eternity, then extended his hand to take the blade back. Aubin released it slowly. In spite of its intended purpose, it was a thing of delicate luster and deep pattern, and Aubin found he was entranced.

Ki took the blade to himself like a lost lover.

He held it quietly for a moment, then slid his thumb along the cutting edge hard enough to draw blood in order to satisfy the steel. It sighed as he replaced it in its scabbard.

Chapter Four

LONI WAS DRESSED in her idea of street clothes —a pink suede jumpsuit, tight in all the right places, low-cut in front, with black high-heeled boots that brought the top of her head almost to Colwin's shoulder. Her long dark hair swung in fancy braids down her back.

They walked along the broad avenues of the center of the empire's capital. The streets had been planned with royal processions in mind, and were bright with plantings along either side. Set back off deep walkways were the most elegant shops in the entire empire. They were the bottom floors of flashing new ceramic highrises, but most displayed only single-window shops of rich opulence to the passing throng. Over all, at the head of the street, lurked the palace like the bleached skeleton of some long-extinct behemoth, visible from almost anywhere, and cold.

It was a glorious day, one of those rare occasions when Loni found herself free to do whatever she pleased. She had originally planned to sleep late, have breakfast in bed and a good hot bath, generally pampering herself as she usually did her customers, but it had just so happened Colwin was free today also, and that was too good to miss. In spite of the boy's youth, there was a lot to admire—especially from the rear.

"Where the hell is this place? Shayton?" Colwin asked as he was led through yet another busy shopping section of Osaka, through the crowd, mostly ladies, a few wearing traditional kimono, most not, but all carrying packages from expensive shops as if they were badges of honor.

"I promise you," Loni answered laughingly, "it is nowhere near that dreary place."

"It's not dreary," Colwin grumbled.

"No? Then, why'd you leave? Come on. Enjoy the walk. You haven't seen sunshine in weeks, and the pallor of your skin proves it."

He brushed the soft golden brown hair away from his baby blues, looked carefully around the crowd to see if they were being particularly noticed, and leaned close to Loni's ear so she would be the only one to hear. "Rebels don't usually hold maneuvers in the light of day in the middle of Capitol Center."

"No, they don't," she responded, "but they do go for walks on beautiful afternoons with their best girls."

"Only if their 'best girls' happen to be paying their salaries and know the only place in town to get an energy weapon repaired with no questions asked."

Loni sighed theatrically, which was appropriate since they were now entering the theater district. Crowds were thinner here, as it was not yet time for matinees to begin, but the streets were still busy with people crossing to other places. Loni pictured the old district, and the flavor of it all, from her childhood readings, and regretted the blown-concrete structures that had replaced the ancient wood. No matter how necessary after the destruction, when the Ring of Fire had blown the cap off civilization and thereby allowed the empire to spring up in its place, it was a loss. "Colwin, you have no romance in your soul."

He groaned, and she laughed.

"Oh, look! Kabuki!" She pointed to a traditionally clad hostess attempting to draw passersby to the performance. The kimono she wore was rich in color and heavy of fabric, and Loni thought it must be old. She wanted to touch it. "There's a performance this afternoon. Maybe we can still get tickets." She started toward the hostess eagerly.

Colwin held back. "Do we have to? I don't want to spend four hours listening to a language I don't understand. Besides. They never did learn how to sing."

"Colwin, these people were singing beautifully centuries before your people even were people. And *I* understand the language. You forget I was raised in Osaka."

"You serious?" Colwin looked at Loni, bewildered. "You are. You really want to go. You understand this stuff and, worse yet, you like it."

"Yes, I like it." Loni's eyes went all far away, no longer seeing the skyscrapers and theater billboards. She was no longer hearing the babel of voices in a hundred different languages. "My mother used to take me to the theater when I was a little girl. Even though we came from a not-so-nice part of town, she said I had to be educated if I was going to get anywhere. I thought it was the most wonderful time ever, for what my mother would have said were all the wrong reasons. I had my mom all to myself for the afternoon, and there were the colorful costumes and the sad stories and the white faces and the demons." She drew a deep breath and came back to the present. "What little girl could ask for more?"

"You're a big girl now. What do *they* ask for?"

She pinched his ass. "Give you one guess."

"Loni!" he almost screamed as he pushed her hand away. "Behave yourself! You're old enough to be my mother."

She giggled girlishly, thoroughly enjoying his discomfiture. "You really know how to hurt a girl. I'm only forty-seven. You make it sound like I was around for the first emperor." She was trying to be stern, but laughter still crinkled her eyes. "I didn't get started that young!"

They left the rows of theaters behind, and went into a street that was much quieter than the one they'd just left. Mostly residential, the houses turned blank faces or walled gates to the street. They were only one or two stories tall, a real oddity in this city where up was the only way anyone could afford to go. Narrower than the norm, therefore dark and cool, the street took Colwin by surprise.

"I didn't think any of this survived after Fuji blew. This place should be in a museum." He looked around intently. "Those gardens back there?" He pointed to a solid fence, taller than he, and white, that enclosed what appeared to be an open area.

"Probably."

"Loni, nobody can afford to pay the land taxes. Ain't possible."

"Colwin, these homes have been in the same families for generation upon generation. They'd starve before they'd lose their gardens. A few of them have," she added acidly.

Like a small child, Colwin jumped as high as he could in an effort to see over the wall.

Loni caught his sleeve. "Colwin, you're embarrassing me. Privacy is very important to these people. You're being incredibly rude."

Seeing something new in Loni, Colwin asked, "Since when does rude bother you? You deal with it every day."

"In my place of business, yes. There it goes with the territory. Sometimes the rubes don't know any better, and with a little gentle prodding you can move them. Sometimes they don't care, and then you can bounce them. But here, Colwin, here ... These are people's homes. Their little private hearts. Here I won't abide rudeness. Besides, if you can hold on for just a little longer, the gunsmith has a garden, very tiny, but exquisite, and I know he'd be proud to show it to you. Now be a good boy and come along."

Colwin went into an instant sulk. She'd done it again. She'd treated him like a kid. He kicked at a stone. How did she manage? Not two minutes ago she was playing sexy, grown-up games with him, and now he was a naughty little boy with no manners.

"Loni! Loni!" another voice called from behind them. "Loni, did you hear?" The young man puffed heavily. He was obviously in good shape, so he must have run some distance.

"Hear what, Anka?" She put a hand on his fuzzy blue arm. "Take a deep breath, then tell me."

He did as he was ordered, almost rocking Loni

off her feet when he pulled back his arms in order to fill his lungs expansively.

"The bodies," he panted. "Seven of them. Thrown from the palace walls. And only one of them was one of us." He wheezed. "But our guy ...his head was cut clean off."

Colwin flashed past Loni and pinned the large man to the wall with his forearm crushing Anka's throat. "Shut up!" he breathed. "Do you want the entire blasted empire to know who we are?" It took Colwin a moment to realize he was causing Anka pain. Sheepishly he released Anka, regretting he'd overreacted because Loni had treated him like a child and he'd been angry. Now he deserved to be treated like a child. He'd lost control. Again. Colwin turned to Loni, expecting she would have wasps on her tongue. But Loni just stood there, her face looking very waxy under her makeup.

"Loni?" Colwin tried to get her attention, but she did not respond. He turned to Anka. "Get outta my sight. And keep that big blue mouth of yours shut!" Colwin did not even wait to see if Anka fled. He turned back to Loni. "Sara Korlon," he sniped, "wake up. You knew this would happen sooner or later." This time the barbs were on Colwin's tongue, and Loni blinked. "He knew the risks." Colwin spat into the street.

"It isn't time yet. What a waste!" she wailed.

"He knew the risks," Colwin repeated even more viciously, grabbing her arm and giving her a savage little shake.

That hit home with her, and she blinked. "His life was wasted, and I've seen too much of that. And the others...They were wasted, too. And for no damned reason." Color flooded back into Loni's cheeks, an angry, fiery red. "I don't like waste, and I won't accept any more of it!" she said, ice crystals exploding frigidly in her voice. "No more death!"

It was very cool, and the air was dead still and damp with dew. The trees in the garden and on the ground far below the palace walls sat perfectly still in true wooden fashion, as if carved, waiting for the breeze that would signal the beginning of the day. The dark had begun to fade, but barely. The stars still winked, but Ki could feel that very soon they would dim and disappear.

This was the only time of day when the entire palace was still. The men on guard were not stirring yet, restless to be relieved. The men who would do the relieving had not yet awakened. The serving staff was still abed as well. And the residents of this place, the cream of society, would not stir until well into the day.

Every morning without fail, duty permitting, rain, snow, or sleet notwithstanding, Ki sat in his garden. He would rise very early and work out, hard, in the gym when he had the place totally to himself. Then he would shower. With his mane still wet, he would come to the garden to listen to it dry. He would get down on his knees, place his swords in front of him within easy reach, sit on his heels and rest his hands on his thighs. It was ritual with him, this time for reflection and peace. The only thing that would change from day to day was the position of his head. At times, if things were well within him, he would watch the sky as the stars died and the sun was born. If he needed to see inside Ki, he would lower his head till his chin touched his breast. Then there was nothing to see but himself.

This morning, though disturbed by the events of the day before, he watched the sun come up. His mind was too jumbled even to begin a logical process of thought. He would need time to sort through the events and the emotions they evoked in him. There had been the kill. Clean, swift, it should have been satisfying, but it was not. It left too many questions and too few answers. Then there was Aubin. He had seen the hoj, held it naked in his frail human hand, and he did not bear the tattoo of an adult Nidean male of the Lawwnum pride. Did that mean Ki, without pride consent, had conferred member status on Aubin? The way he, Ki, interpreted the legend, it did. His mouth turned up at the corners, smiling at what Mikal would say to that. Then the smile broadened as he tried to picture Aubin wearing pride tattoos. The smile fled. The empress. She was tired, so tired her fragile human beauty was beginning to fade. Her husband's excesses had finally begun to take their toll even on her. And those excesses had moved into the realm of murder. The corners of his mouth turned down all the way into a frown. Seven men had died yesterday, only one with cause. They had died because Ozenscebo needed revenge for the threat against him, and the perpetrator of the threat was already dead. So he had pointed at six of the servants, quite randomly, and had declared them traitors. Lionmen had executed them as ordered, but it left a bad taste in everyone's mouth. More than that, it was a waste.

As the sky began to lighten, faint bands of pink appearing where the sun would soon be, Ki

realized he, too, was tired. He needed Nide and
a good rest, something he had denied himself for
too long. Perhaps he would invite Aubin to join
him there, to instruct him, subtly, of course, in
the ways of the Lionmen now that he was an
unofficial member of the pride. It would not
hurt that hedonist to toughen up a bit. Vaguely
he wondered what the response of his people
would be to a Nidean bringing a human home
to a planet that did not have a single foreigner
anywhere on it outside of the emperor's em-
bassy compound. Would they resent Aubin as
ferociously as only a Nidean could resent?
Would they harass him openly? It was conceiv-
able they would accept Aubin with open arms
while rejecting Ki for enlisting him without
pride consent. He sighed. He needed to go home,
with or without Aubin. If only he could talk to
Ambassador Maaeve. Her reaction would reflect
all the others'...

At last his thoughts drifted off, leaving him in
quiet peace. Finally he could lose himself in the
sound of the running water, broken only by his
own breath. His heart beat loudly in his ears, a
drum to accompany the beginning fluting of the
birds.

He left his drifting in the split second it took
to recognize the sound. Someone was at his
door, the exterior door that joined his apartment to the public hallway. Though he did not
appear to have moved, his muscles, which had
been slack, were now tensed, ready for whatever
came through his door.

It opened, then shut carefully, quietly. The
steps were hesitant, furtive, the culprit obvious
and loud in his caution. Ki's right hand edged

down his thigh closer to his knee, that much closer to the swords which rested just in front of him. He attempted to catch the scent of the intruder, and was frustrated by the ventilation system that kept the air constantly moving out of his quarters to be replenished with fresh. When he finally caught the scent, well known, the hand crept back to its original position. The sounds changed again. The maker was attempting to sneak up on him. The effort at stealth was clumsy at best, but Ki waited.

"Beautiful sunrise, is it not?" Ki asked the intruder.

About three feet behind him, the princess stamped her foot in disgust. "How? I thought I'd caught you with your back to a door. How did you know it was me?"

"I heard you, I heard you, I smelled you, I heard you."

"I beg your pardon?" Natanha said as she came around to sit by his side. "I don't understand."

"I heard you at the door. Quite noisy. I heard you moving about the room, I suppose attempting to find out where I was. Then I caught your scent. You are quite distinct, you know, different even from your mother. Then I heard you again when you tried to sneak up on me. You are as quiet as a herd of imlowwn."

Natanha's balled fist hit her leg in a cute little gesture of frustration. "One of these days I'll catch you. One day you'll be dreaming, and I'll catch you."

He turned his head away from the sunrise and to Natanha for the first time. He studied her face, so much like her mother's, the determination there, and raised an eyebrow. It was the only response such a statement deserved.

She was about to insist, then changed her mind. "Where's the rock? Did you like it? Did you like it?"

Ki raised his left hand, causing a glint on the metal, and pointed to the water.

"Where," she demanded. "I don't see it."

"It's at the base of the waterfall. The water is polishing it. When the time is right, I'll take it out." Ki was suddenly intensely aware of the similarity of Natanha and her cherished bit of earth. She too would be ready for public viewing only after she'd been polished. He only hoped the process would not be too painful.

"No one can see it at the bottom of the waterfall," she pouted.

"I know it's there, as do you. Who else needs to?"

Natanha subsided, and found herself regarding the sun rising over her father's capital. In this light, delicate, fragile, none too sharp, the city was wonderful. The tall towers picked up the pinks and yellows of the dawn and threw them back at her. She could not see from here the hovels that had grown up at the edges of the city, filled with squatters who could not pay the land tax. From here it was golden, warm, exciting. She imagined the people beginning to get ready for the day, soon to fill the streets with writhing snakes made of people, patchy snakes with colors from all over the empire. The low residential districts lost their bone whiteness in this light, becoming fragile pink roses almost lost in the high canes of the skyscrapers. Where the 'scrapers left their shadows there were dark pools of blue, deep, deep, like the lake that filled Fuji's crater.

After a time, she found her voice and the courage to speak of what had brought her here.

"They tried to kill Daddy yesterday."

"Yes," Ki answered, aware of where this line of questioning was likely to go.

"Will they try to kill Mama, too?"

"Probably."

Natanha paused. This next was the heart of the matter. "Am I going to die?"

Ki was relieved that she had brought this question to him. He did not want another to answer it, to frighten her, or, worse yet, to lie to her. "Eventually. We all do."

She was frustrated. "*You* know! Are the rebels going to kill Mama and me?"

"No."

"How do you know?"

Ki opened his right hand, slowly turned it palm up, and extended it gracefully to Natanha. It was answer enough. He would never permit it. She put her small hand in his, feeling safe now, and returned to watching the sunrise.

"Scarlet and cadmium yellow going into violets contrast nicely with the oranges in the highlights in the blue shadows, right ...?" She was showing off for him.

He turned his face toward her, his eyes open wide, and this time raised both eyebrows. Softly, she withdrew her hand from his.

"Yes." She sighed. "Mama says I talk too much, too." And, as if Mama had reminded her, she smoothed her skirt in unconscious imitation. Then she looked at Ki. His back was straight, his hands on his thighs, relaxed, his face to the new morning. She shifted her weight, straightened her back, too, and placed her hands. Then she checked Ki again, to see that she'd done it correctly, and went back to watching her father's city come to life.

Ki smiled indulgently.

Chapter Five

———◆———

MIKAL STOOD AT the entrance to the audience hall, looking very imperious. He was in charge of the morning's security precautions, and it was a job that suited him perfectly. He felt he was ready for command, and wanted every opportunity available to prove it. Captain Res had turned security over to him, with firm and detailed instructions. Mikal felt he had obeyed them to the letter, and that was good. But. Mikal was learning there was also something very disturbing about being in charge. It rested heavily in his belly, this feeling, whirling there like a confined tornado. He had to do this thing correctly. The emperor's life and the lives of countless others rested on it—and there would be no second chance. He would never be able to explain a mistake now, not to Captain Res, nor himself, nor, Mmumna forbid, to Commander Ki. But he dare not let the men see this hesitancy, this uncertainty, either. Hence, the impe-

rious face turned to the world. It was Mikal's
natural defense.

There were small mirrored panels on either
side of the huge doors opening onto the audience chamber. Mikal turned and studied himself
in one of these. He knew the commander would
be by soon, and everything, every hair, must be
perfect. His mane was satisfactory. The large
frond around his face was smooth and gently
rounded. The long fall that ran down his back to
his knees had been brushed and brushed into
total submission. It hung straight and clean in a
brown-black mane down his back. His sidelocks,
with more red glinting in them, formed perfect
tapers as they hung down his chest to frame his
face. The dark gray of his mantle, the badge of
his rank, did not really suit his golden-brown
coloring, but he wore the uniform with pride,
regardless, hoping soon to exchange it for the
blue of a captain. That day could not come soon
enough. It would be very pleasant to see himself
in the blue, and it would suit. He would look
even better in the black of the commander, he
thought, and he sighed wistfully. Long, hard
hours of work had gone into each promotion,
and Mikal hoped for more advances. He wanted
to be commander one day, bringing yet more
honor to his pride. He knew Captain Res would
probably be the next commander after Ki re-
tired some long years from now, but there was
no reason why he, Mikal, could not be the one
after that—as long as he made no mistakes. He
straightened his red sash and adjusted the
swords to a slightly more rakish angle. He
flexed his knees, making certain he moved freely
in the dark gray hakama. Satisfied there was

nothing more he could perfect, he turned back to the hallway.

His men were beginning to leave the audience chamber. Captain Res had gone over the hall the night before, completely, and even though Mikal did not doubt the thoroughness of the job, he had had his people go over it again. Even an hour was enough for something to change. He entered the hall proper. This room had never appealed to him, and he shrugged, thinking he must be too Nidean to appreciate it. There was nothing wild or free about this place. Everything here was contrived. This was a smaller room than the throne room, but, if it was possible, it was even more gaudy. Mirrors were everywhere, walls, ceiling, tiny chips in the floor, throwing back the light from the hundreds of tiny bulbs buried in the ceiling to simulate stars. Drapes had been cut so they hung away from the windows as mere ornament, allowing even more light to enter from the beveled glass wall running the length of the chamber. Hidden fixtures threw light from the window wall even if the sun was down. And, if one was very observant, one might notice the mirrors were tilted in such a way that all the light reflected back to the head of the chamber where Ozenscebo would be seated. It was clever, and totally artificial.

One by one Mikal placed his men. He knew them well, and each had certain capabilities. One had a nose every bit as capable as Commander Ki's. He was stationed near the head of the hall, within arm's reach of where the emperor would be. Another had eyes like an eagle. He was put at the back, to watch for anything that did not look right. Another was quick of mind, and Mikal put him near the center of the room where he might hear something that would be important. Then he stationed himself at the outer door. From there he would know all who entered, all who left, and would have an overview of the entire room. There would not be a repeat of the assassination attempt of yesterday. Mikal would not permit it.

Mikal took one more look inside just to make sure everything was as he'd ordered, then settled himself into the comfortable stance he could hold for hours if necessary. A group of three courtiers came down the hall. Mikal recognized them, and fervently wished them to pass him by as if he did not exist, which was the lot of Lionmen most of the time. He had encountered these three before, and knew them to be haughty, cruel, and as artificial as Nidean paper money. "Mmumna, please don't make me deal with these turds!" he mumbled to himself.

"Why, look! There's Lieutenant Lawwnum!" one of the group said just a trifle too loudly with just a bit too much surprise. "Perhaps he can tell us what's happening!"

Mikal felt a rumble grow in his throat, and had to work hard to squelch it. Seda Paschasia was one of the emperor's entourage who turned Mikal's stomach. She was too slick. If she said good-morning, one had better check the sun to see what time of day it really was. He closed his eyes as Paschasia sidled up, all black feathery gown and perfume, both, Mikal guessed, supposed to be sexy and feminine, camouflaging the real, unctuous reptile. In fact, the bad cut of the gown did nothing to compliment her, and the feathers looked like reptilian scales from a distance. He opened his eyes in time to

see her smile at him with crooked crocodile teeth.
She wore too much makeup. It creased around
her eyes, reinforcing the idea that she had something to hide. At her waist she wore a dagger, all
gold and rosewood, a mere toy. One of Seda's
fantasies was to be the feminine warrior, but
Mikal knew she couldn't use the dagger, and she
certainly couldn't be compared with the female
members of the Lionmen Guard. They handled
both their weapons and their femininity better
than Seda Paschasia used hers.

"Lieutenant, what was all that fracas about
yesterday? Did Commander Ki really behead
somebody? Was there really blood?" she asked
in her midrange yet squeaky voice.

Unwillingly, Mikal nodded assent, wondering
what it was this crocodile was after. Surely
she'd heard all the details by now.

Mercer Parry hung back behind the two
women. Inwardly, he groaned. *Paschasia, you
cow, you could have phrased that more delicately,*
he thought. *Do you want to give us all away with
your ramblings? Next time I choose a confederate,
it will be someone with some brains, even if that
does make them harder to direct!*

"Oooooh! Did you hear that, Jad?" Seda
gushed. "He really did! He cut off someone's
head!"

Jad Templa, accompanied by Mercer Parry,
approached Mikal. Jad looked bored by the entire world. Mikal noticed her sneaky dark eyes
darted everywhere, yet, somehow, she didn't
seem to be really a part of what was happening
here and now. A strange and thoroughly discon-
certing combination to Mikal, who was used to
Nideans who, to him at least, were always what
they seemed. She wore her long hair up and

away from her face, which gave her a boyish look that matched her choice of clothing.

What a pair, Mikal thought. *One thinks she's an Amazon, the other thinks she's a male. Mmumna protect all Nide from the likes of these!*

Jad examined the back of her hand. "We knew Lawwnum killed someone. We knew that yesterday," she said, trying to cover for Paschasia. "Why don't you ask him something we don't know?" She addressed Paschasia, but refused to look at her.

Seda poked her head around Mikal to glimpse the inside of the audience chamber. "Is the emperor really going to have an audience today? In spite of what happened yesterday?"

Mikal nodded.

"Oooh. The security must be awfully tight. Did you know, Mercer"—she swished her black-feathered skirts as she turned to him—"this morning they wouldn't let me into the throne room? I had all those papers and they still wouldn't let me in." She turned back to Mikal. "Will you let me in for the audience? Is everyone being allowed in?"

Mikal took a paper from his sash. "Is your name on my list?" he asked as politely as he could without choking.

"See, Mercer? Tight security." Seda nodded sagely to herself.

Mikal destroyed that theory. "If your name isn't here, I can add it. Do you wish to have it added?"

Mercer, recognizing the fool Paschasia was getting nowhere, asked boldly, "Is security tight all over the palace? Is there any place that's restricted?"

"Security is always tight in the palace. Com-

mander Lawwnum would not have it any other
way." Mikal had taken a distinct dislike to this
vein of questioning.

Parry ground his teeth in frustration. This
was getting them exactly nowhere, and, if it
continued, might make the lieutenant suspi-
cious. "Come, ladies. Let's leave the man to his
work. He'll take good care of our emperor, I'm
sure." He shepherded them around a corner.

Seda Paschasia stopped when she was certain
she was out of Mikal's hearing. "Why did you do
that, Parry?" She pouted. "We might have
learned something if you'd let us continue."

Parry threw up his hands. "Seda, what kind of
an ass are you? If you had asked one more question, you practically would have told the lieutenant what we are about! You don't want to
find out what kind of entertainments Ozenscebo
can dream up just for you, do you?"

She stamped her foot, which ruffled her
feathers and made her look like a scratching
hen. "Don't you say things like that to me,
Mercer Parry!" she snapped. "I don't frighten as
easily as *some* people around here." She looked
pointedly at Jad Templa, who was busy ignoring
them both.

Parry felt the frustration rising to a killing
pitch. He would do the bitch in himself right
here and now if he didn't need her to do his
dirty work. He hadn't been this angry since
those damned Lionmen had put down the
Avoyan uprising! And if his planet were not relying on him to find a way to get rid of that tire-
some empress so they could lead the emperor
around by the nose, how he'd relish a long, slow
death for this...this bitch!

He took a deep breath and put a tight lid on

his anger. Until they were rid of the empress, he needed Seda. "We did learn one thing..."

Seda tossed her head. "I told you I would get you some information!"

"We know we didn't send that assassin. The meeting yesterday was about the rebels. If we strike right now, no one would dream of looking inside the palace for us! It would be assumed the rebels had tried again!"

Jad nodded. "That is a reasonable assessment. Assuming Paschasia can keep her mouth shut about what we decide to do," she added in her precise fashion.

Seda started off down the hall in a huff. "Well! If that's what you think, you can damn well do this all by yourselves!"

Parry rolled his eyes. "Wait, Seda! We have to work together!" he called as he started out after her. He could not afford to let her run around loose.

Jad watched for a moment or two, sighed heavily, and followed. No matter what they did now, they were all in this up to their necks, regrettably, together.

Although Elena had been sitting on the throne for only a few moments, she was already uncomfortable. She had not slept well last night, and she ached everywhere. She shifted, and smoothed her rust-colored heavy velvet skirts. Her hips were particularly painful. *That, no doubt, is from sitting on this beastly chair for so many years,* she griped inwardly, though the small smile of polite attention she wore never wavered. Because she was tired from not sleeping, she also felt cold. She always did when she

wasn't in the best of shape. She motioned to Ki,
who stood to her left near the family entrance.
Though he had not been looking in her direction, he began to approach her at once. *Un-
canny,* she thought. *I would have sworn he didn't
see me.*

"Ki," she said when he arrived at her side, "is
it colder in here than usual?" A shiver ran down
her, and her feet danced slightly where they
hung a few inches above the floor. "This room is
always so cold it's hard for me to tell."

He frowned. "Yes. And that should not be. I
can see you are uncomfortable. I'll have someone take care of it."

"Thank you," she said, and, as the envoy who
had been speaking had stopped when Ki had
approached, she turned back to him apologetic-
ally.

Ki started the order for more heat down the
chain, and resumed his place by the family door.
Natanha sat on her mother's right, dressed
today in white lace with blue ribbons wound
through it, looking like something out of a Vic-
torian picture book. She sat still, with her hands
folded in her lap, paying strict attention to the
goings-on. In sharp contrast, Magnus was sliding over the floor like a rat, playing some game
in his child's mind. He was dirty again, and not
occupied in a way Elena would approve, but he
had the sly good sense to stay out of her line of
vision.

When the heat came up, the motion of the air
brought a whole new wave of scents in Ki's direction. He sorted through them, more to avoid
boredom than from any real need. The emperor,
who had been scheduled to meet with his
envoys this morning, had at the last moment

gone off on some wild-goose chase with Mercer Parry. That was unfortunate from the standpoint that his absence could be misconstrued as cowardice. Ozenscebo had not reacted particularly well to the assassination attempt, and there were seven dead bodies piled up at the bottom of the palace walls to prove it. *But then again,* Ki thought, reconsidering, *perhaps it is better to have him a coward than a libertine. It would be difficult to say which is the more harmful.* His absence meant this meeting was likely to go smoothly. Ki understood from the way Elena was holding her head, tilted slightly to the left and slightly back, that she had made up her mind about the tax issue at last, and, in this instance at least, there would be very little dissension—especially after Elena's comment about keeping fewer advisers. Ki had enjoyed Natanha's version of that story, full of her own viewpoint and useless asides that made it all her own. No Nidean child would wander so in a telling, but Natanha was not trained to an oral tradition. He wrinkled his nose in distaste. He cared very little for the perfumes of most of the women and some of the men, and they were coming to him strongly. They were heavy, musky scents that on Nide one would never consider appealing. At home a light grassy, floral scent would be preferred, or at most a light amber. He blinked. He had caught something ...He exhaled heavily to clear his nose and breathed in deeply, looking for the something odd. He had it! Somewhere in the consular group someone was in a state of high agitation bordering on panic. All casual ease feel off him, and he began searching the room for any visual signs of such seething.

Jad Templa looked more like a boy than usual today. Her long hair was hidden under a peaked cap, and she wore tight-fitting pants that disappeared into high boots. A long shirt was gathered at her waist in great folds that hid any pretention to roundness. She had been watching the commander from her spot near the public door, and had seen him stiffen. Although she did not believe all the stories about him and his fabled abilities, she was not willing to test their truth today. She had also felt the heat come up. She tugged at Seda Paschasia's sleeve.

"Seda, it's time for us to go."

For once, Seda did not argue with her supposed friend, and the two slid out the door like ghosts, blending smoothly with a group of several other envoys who were off on various missions.

Ki continued to search the room, but he could not pin down the elusive agitation. None of the envoys seemed any more upset than usual, and the retainers went about their jobs with oiled precision. The scent hung in the air for a short time, blown about by the ventilation, then faded into nothingness. Though he tried once or twice to pick it up again, the scent was gone.

He edged a little further to Elena's left so that he might have a larger view of the group facing the empress. There seemed to be absolutely nothing odd about them, if one overlooked the fact that some had begun to guess that Elena was not going to give them their new tax and were therefore not very happy. Otherwise . . . He put his back up against the wall and felt the cold seeping out of the marble. He did not like this feeling of not knowing what was going on around the empress and his princess. He folded his arms and let his head fall slightly forward as an uneasy, restless feeling crept into him along with the marble's cold. *Someone must have found whatever they lost,* he thought, but realized he did not believe it.

He stood against the wall, listening with only half an ear. Other ears were in the room to listen, and the men attached to them would report anything of interest to him later. He seemed to have picked up the empress's malaise, and he decided it must be the cold. She was absolutely correct—this room was never comfortable, and lately he had come to appreciate comfort the way Ki as a youngling never had. He sighed lightly, thinking perhaps it really was nearly time for him to retire. But then there was Natanha to consider, and he sighed again. He really didn't trust anyone else to care for her properly—anyone except the empress, of course. But the empress could not swing a sword. Retirement would have to wait until Natanha came into her own, hopefully as heir to the throne. She would make a much finer ruler than her brother.

The ventilation system continued to blow warm air into the high-ceilinged throne room with something of a vague background hum, and Ki began to find it mesmerizing. He lifted his head to look out across the group in front of Elena. They were all paying strict attention to the empress's wishes, and she was being very specific about something, detailing it point by point. Natanha still sat like a statue at Elena's right and Ki smiled a little. No Nidean cub would be so still for so long, but then again, none of them were likely to rule the empire, either. He was proud Natanha behaved so well—at least in

public—and understood so much. It even
pleased him that she was not afraid to question what she did not understand. She had a
quick mind, and when something was explained to her in terms she could comprehend,
she grasped things very thoroughly, often
showing Elena and Ki nuances they had
missed. Perhaps it was only her fresh, childish
perspective, but Ki, fondly, preferred to think
of her as intelligent.

A new scent came across his sleepy nose. *Oranges*, he thought. *Must be the kitchens.*

Exactly one heartbeat later he was fully erect
and striding in great haste toward Elena. This
ventilation system did not connect with the one
from the kitchens. The scent of oranges when no
food was present could be only one thing.

As he strode quickly toward the throne, he
grabbed Magnus up from the floor in an eagle's
one-clawed swoop and tucked him like a
squirming piglet under one arm, totally ignoring the bites and kicks and squeals the prince
administered. As Elena turned her head to see
what was causing the commotion, Ki reached
her side.

"Quickly, Your Majesty. Out," he said as he
reached her side, pitching his voice for her
alone. His first duty was to Elena and the children. He would warn the others and try to avoid
panic if he could, after he was certain the family
was safe.

"Mama, what's wrong?" Natanha had seen Ki
approach Elena unbidden, something he rarely
did in public, and he certainly never grabbed
Magnus that way. But by the time Natanha finished the sentence, Elena had her by the wrist
and was dragging her toward the doorway be-

hind the throne that only one of the royal family's or Ki's palm print would open.

The two guards posted at the door were shocked, and looked at each other in total disbelief. Ki was manhandling the prince in a most unfriendly manner. Never had they seen or heard of such behavior from their commander. Totally off balance, one Guardsman stepped between Ki and the door as Ki approached it almost at a run. The other was in such shock he did not move.

"Commander," she said, "have you gone mad? I respectfully request you put down the prince."

Ki did not bother to answer her, but hit the lock to open the door. *There may not be time for niceties*, he thought, and he slammed into her chest full force, sending her sprawling into the royal family's waiting room beyond. The floor was polished marble, and slick, and she fell to her seat and slid like a child who has misjudged the ice. Ki hefted the prince like a hurling stone after her, and the prince got quite a ride down the length of the room, sprawling, bouncing, and turning, his dirty silks flapping and twisting.

Elena caught up and ran through the door, a bewildered Natanha in tow. She did not stop at the entrance, but headed straight for the other door at the far side of the room that gave onto the royal apartments, and she did not release her grip on her daughter's wrist. She slowed only to grasp at one of Magnus's outspread arms as she passed his spread-eagled form.

Ki saw Elena heading for the other door, and was gratified she understood enough of the situation to do exactly the right thing, heading out and away from the throne room. He began to

turn back to the door to the throne room to
make sure it was closed behind them when he
realized the Guardsman he had sent sliding was
now on her feet and drawing her sword. He had
to make a choice. He could either defend himself
or close the door. If the door was closed, it
would be another buffer between the empress
and his princess and the blast. The door had to
be closed. He turned his back on the Lionman
and hit the lock.

The door slid from its pocket in the wall and
started across its track to the other side of its
frame. It seemed to take an achingly long time,
but actually Ki did not even have time to finish
the turn he was making preparatory to protect-
ing himself. The door almost closed, but not
quite, and the blast sent him flying.

Amazingly, he saw everything as it happened
with vivid clarity. He saw himself lifted from
the floor a few inches and pushed forward as if
by a puff of giant's breath. He saw the Lionman
begin to turn into a swing of the hoj she held
before she too was taken off balance by the
blast. He saw his arm drawn down to his side
and saw the edge of the sword meet his chest
and upper arm, though he felt nothing at that
moment. He felt nothing, in fact, until the giant
stopped breathing and dropped him to the floor
on top of his Guardsman.

Then the pain began. Ki twisted over and
looked down at himself. Blood was already
staining his clothes, and Ki knew the wound he
bore across arm and shoulder was more than a
scratch. He could feel his blood, warm and
sticky, inching thickly across his chest and down
his dangling arm. He picked himself up unsteadily, rocking badly as he held himself up

with only his undamaged arm, and realized he'd had to swallow twice before he could hear. The female who had been beneath him was out cold, though she looked otherwise uninjured. There was, at least, no blood on her other than what appeared to be Ki's. Ki did not try to stoop to aid her—he would have blacked out. He moved toward the mangled remains of the door that had tried to save him from the blast, and was sick at heart at the sight in what was left of the throne room. The Guardsman who had been on the other side of the door was no longer visible, though Ki could see pieces of his hoj and shar spread across the floor. Many of the courtiers had taken the cue of Elena's hasty retreat and left the room as well, but many had not, and there were bodies and pieces of bodies mixed into the rubble. A large section of wall was completely gone, and with it a matching section of floor. Windows had blown out, taking their frames with them. Broken pipes poured rivers of water down shattered walls and on into the gaping hole to flow over the floor two stories down. It was terrible. And there was no sign of any of the Lionmen who had been on guard. None, except for the broken pieces of sword.

Ki leaned against the wall as a wave of dizziness washed over him. *Terrible. This is worse than war,* he thought as he sank down along the wall into unconsciousness.

It didn't take long for word of the explosion to reach the outside world. The rebels had known of the attempt even before the dust had begun to settle. Colwin shifted uncomfortably, and shivered. He was scared. There were too many things he didn't know about what had happened. He had been stretched out on his belly on this hill across from the palace for two hours now, watching the activity in and about the palace, trying to piece together exactly what had happened from what he heard and what he saw. Apparently there had been considerable damage. Several Lionmen, seven that they could account for, had disappeared in the blast. Reports had it that Commander Ki Lawwnum himself had been damaged, though reports as to how badly differed widely. Workmen had been summoned immediately, and some of their apprentices were rebel. Colwin knew the floor and a section of the wall had been blown out, that several people on the floor below the throne room and uncounted servants in the next room over, not to mention all the courtiers who had not departed when the empress had, were dead. Though he was tired of the damp earth and the insects, he was fascinated by the activity across from him. His eyes rarely left his field glasses, even when reports were being poured into his ear by his fellows.

Suddenly a brand-new activity caught his eye, and he shifted so he could see clearly down into the courtyard that usually served as a recreational area for the Lionmen. Quite a few of the Guardsmen had entered the courtyard, but they were not in uniform. At least it was not a uniform Colwin had seen before. They were dressed all in white, stark and vivid against the damp stone of the palace. One carried something white, and placed it gently against the wall separating the yard from the rest of the residence. Another large group of Guardsmen followed, likewise dressed in hard white, and a few more folded bundles kept the first company. This group of Lionmen was followed by more and more. Some few of the new arrivals put swords and other small, personal things in prominent places. Gradually the Lionmen sifted themselves into orderly ranks, and stooped quietly in the hunting crouch they could hold for hours, generally with their heads bowed. It stunned Colwin to see so many of them in one place. He had never seen more than a handful of them together before. He looked carefully, and found that he could just make out their facial markings. They looked sad.

Ki stood just outside the courtyard in the shadow of the barracks watching his men assemble. He would not enter until every one of them was present. Those who were on duty were represented by their ceremonially folded kimono, placed carefully in the ranks, usually by the Guardsman's closest comrade. Those who would never be returning, the ones this ceremony was held for, were represented by a personal belonging placed in full view of the gathering as a remembrance. It was a painful gathering, the most painful that Ki had attended since the Avoyan uprising. This was even more difficult, however, since, at the time of the uprising, his only job had been to stand quietly in the ranks. This time it was his duty to offer the respects, for now it was he who commanded. His shoulder was flaming with pain. His left arm was heavy and useless, also alight, his phantom hand burning with torment, something he had not been plagued with for years. And he hated the sling the medics had forced on him. It reminded him too much of another time and another injury. He had refused any kind of

pain-killer. He wanted to know he would do his
men the honor they deserved without being
lulled to sleep. He swayed slightly, and rested
his intact shoulder against the wall to steady
himself. At least Elena and Natanha were safe.
The worst they had suffered had been a bad
scare. It was a good thing he had realized when
he had that the smell of oranges had to be explosives. Now he understood, of course. The
room had been cold because the explosive went
off when it reached a normal room temperature.
The orange scent, though not built in on purpose, had served many an explosives man as a
warning that his material was too warm to handle. If he had been a moment slower... He
ground his teeth and promised the rebel who
had planted that stuff a slow and agonizing
death.

He moved just enough to look into the courtyard. It appeared all were present, but it would
not do to hurry this, so he leaned once more
against the wall. He closed his eyes. He would
join them in just a few more moments... Sharp
agony ran down to his phantom hand and made
him clench his mechanical replacement. His
mind sped back, unbidden and unwelcome, to
the day he'd lost it to an Avoyan rebel. The
planet had tried to secede from the empire.
Even then, just after he had taken the throne,
Ozenscebo could not stand for anything to be
taken from him, and he had sent his Lionmen to
quell the uprising. A much younger and badly
inexperienced Ki had turned to guard himself
with an empty hand, and come away with no
hand at all, lost to the blast of an energy
weapon at close range. At least it had had the
kindness to cauterize as it cut. Ki had not bled

to death. When he had come out of shock he had promised himself it would be the last mistake he'd make. Sometimes he wondered if such a promise was capable of being kept.

"Commander?"

Ki's eyes snapped open, and he winced as he jerked his head around, surprised he had not been aware of her approach. Before him stood one of his Lionmen Guards, dressed like himself and all the others in stark white. *I should know her*, he thought. *She's important.*

"Commander, I respectfully request permission to commit seppuku."

Ki was too tired and in too much pain to show surprise, even at the thought of ritual suicide. "Why?"

"I threatened and attacked my commanding officer. That act endangered the empress and her children. My fellows are dead, but I am alive. That is not right."

Now he knew why she was important. She was the one who had tried to stop him from manhandling the prince. He shook his head. "I do not grant permission. You performed your duty correctly, and I forbid seppuku. Dismissed."

She bowed, deeply, and held it for a long while. Ki returned it respectfully, and watched her as she moved dazedly to take her place in the ranks. When she was in place, Ki entered the yard.

The Guardsmen had been in a deep-kneed crouch that was good for hunting, or ambushing an enemy, or just waiting. There was a slight rustle behind Ki as he took his place at the front of the men. He stood there for just a moment, tense and tired and sad, and then dropped his head into an attitude of mourning. When his

head moved forward, the men behind him came
to attention. After that, there was no movement,
no sound, except for the slight breeze ruffling
the hems of the white kimono. Together they remembered.

Colwin had watched the ranks form, and
wondered what this gathering was for. When
Commander Ki Lawwnum took his place at the
head of the ranks, Colwin found he was both relieved and angered. In a way it was too bad the
rebels were not rid of the bastard, but in another way it was more challenging to do battle
with a worthy opponent. He thought the ceremony, for such it must be, would last a few moments. But those moments slid by, and still the
Guardsmen stood at attention. The sun began to
set, and still they stood. The white of their kimono took on the bloody coloring of the dying
sun, and still they remained. The reds changed
to violets, and then to blues as the light gave
way to night, and still they stood, though Colwin thought he saw the commander waver once
or twice. But there was no other motion until
the stars had begun to shine. At last, long after
Colwin found that their stillness infected him
with an intense desire to motion, nervous,
twitchy action, he saw them dismissed.

The formal gear and the sling had been removed, but the miasma of weary pain still lingered. Ki bent his knees to reach the note on the
tabletop, having learned most painfully that in-
clining his head was likely to send waves of dizziness over him. He knew the note was from
Aubin—Aubin was one of the few who had access to his quarters, and his handwriting was

unmistakable. Though he had seen the note when he'd first returned to his quarters, he had not opened it. He'd wanted a shower before he faced another problem, and he had a feeling any communication from Aubin on this night had to be a problem.

It was now considerably past the middle of the night, and Ki was more tired than he remembered being for quite a while. He had found the ceremony for the dead Guardsmen difficult to suffer through. At one point he'd actually felt himself swaying. That had been followed by the most thorough security check he'd ever run. Almost every man he had under him was activated. The entire palace had been swept, and Ki had followed his nose around a large portion of it just to be sure the job was being done correctly.

They had found exactly nothing. The crew sifting through the wreckage of the throne room had found the same, except for a few tiny fragments that told the experts what type of explosive had been used.

Ki snorted. "I know what kind of explosive they used!" he said to himself. "I smelled it. I told them what kind it was!" He began to swing his arm down toward the tabletop, ready to hit it in utter frustration, then realized what the jarring would do to his body and managed to stop the swing with only a minimum of discomfort.

He sighed, then sat in the nearest chair, lifting his left arm gingerly to avoid hitting the armrest. Clumsily he managed to hold the note in his left hand while he opened it with his right. Then he set his mechanical hand into his lap most carefully, and read.

See me, the note said. There was not even a signature.

"See me?" Ki said angrily to the walls. "See me? It's almost dawn, I've been hacked at and blown up, I've peeked into every dark corner in this palace, and this human says, 'See me'?" He would have liked to have taken a bite out of something, preferably something alive, like Aubin.

"Well," he said, "in spite of my weariness I'm nowhere near ready for sleep. I might just as well find out what Aubin wants."

He stood, slowly, making certain of his balance before he moved off to find his clothes, groaning softly as he went.

As he walked down the hallway to Aubin's quarters, his eyes found the Guardsmen at their posts and noted their behavior. Every last one of them looked personally offended that someone had gotten into the palace. Some were obviously in the depths of mourning as well, but all were alert and efficient. Ki's mind would not leave his planned precautions no matter how he tried to turn it. The royal family was now out of reach of anyone save Lionmen. Guardsmen were even cooking and serving meals and changing linens. The female serving the empress was not happy. Though her male counterparts were in the same boat, she seemed to take offense at her duties, probably, Ki realized, because it was more difficult for a female to manage a promotion. Nidean females were respected as warriors, but very few were ever fully accepted as leaders. She would have to be replaced as soon as possible. Morale would suffer soon enough under such circumstances—it did not need to be pushed.

Aubin's door was open when Ki arrived, but he did not walk in. He stopped at the threshold and rang the buzzer. He was tired, and not at all in the mood for Aubin's human games.

Aubin's head popped around the corner from the kitchen. "Come in! Don't stand out in the corridor like a stranger."

"I am not in the habit of intruding into private quarters without an invitation like some I could name," Ki taunted. *I am tired*, he thought. *I sound like Seda Paschasia.*

"Sit," Aubin invited, gesturing vaguely to the chairs spread about his sitting room. His attention was really in the kitchen, where he had been cooking a midnight "snack" that would have successfully fed four—if they were very hungry.

"Thank you, I prefer to stand," Ki answered icily. He was not in the mood for foolishness. "Exactly why have I been summoned?"

Aubin recognized when he heard the tone of Ki's voice that by being distracted he had possibly made a mistake. Ki was hard and formal, something he always fell back on when he was very tired, very angry, or very tense. Aubin guessed that tonight Ki was all three, plus sore and mournful. But Aubin knew what to do about that.

"Sit!" he exclaimed forcefully, and he grabbed Ki by his right shoulder and pushed him down into a chair.

Ki's upper lip was twitching. He was ready to bare his fangs. This human had laid hands on him! He was inflating, breathing deeply, ready to fight—but he suddenly collapsed. *I really am tired, tired,* wandered through his mind over and over.

Aubin saw it, all of it. He knew that if Ki had been in top form, he, Aubin, would probably be minus a head right now. It was only too painfully obvious that Ki was not in top form. The way he had deflated worried Aubin considerably. He bent down slightly to look carefully at Ki's marked face.

"It's a good thing you're you, my friend," Ki said quietly. "No one else would have gotten away with that."

Aubin nodded, then turned to walk to his liquor cabinet.

"You would turn your back on me? That is not wise, Aubin."

The envoy smiled into the mirrors over the bar, his eyes meeting Ki's in the glass. "Perhaps not, Commander, but I don't believe I'm in any danger. I am, after all, Aubin Tabber, your best friend."

Ki winced at the thought of a human being his best friend, but it was probably true. Command here did not leave one open to Nidean friendships. Some of the tension seeped out of Ki, but he was still tightly wound.

Aubin returned with a drink and handed it to Ki, who promptly set it aside.

"You really should drink that," Aubin urged.

"I don't drink in public."

"You forget. I am not the public. And you really do need that."

"What makes you think I need anything from you?" Ki was tense again, and wanting badly to fight, to strike out at someone. Aubin, unfortunately, was handy.

Aubin mumbled quietly under his breath, "I knew this wouldn't be easy," then said to Ki, "Because, my dear old friend, you look like shit."

Both of Ki's eyebrows went right into his hairline. Aubin had completely shocked him. Ki hadn't realized the human could be so stupid. He began to rub the fingers of his left hand across his metallic palm. They made a slight squeaking noise as they bumped over joints and rivets. *I will not show any irritation,* Ki told himself forcefully. *Aubin would enjoy it too much.*

Aubin walked away from Ki toward a pedestal that was the central focus of his sitting room. On it sat a small bronze, something Aubin could have held in his two hands, which he did on occasion just because he wanted to be a physical part of it. It was a sculpture by Rodin, *The Caryatid Who Has Fallen Under Her Load.* He had bought it from a very disreputable black-market dealer years and years ago. The man had told some tale about rescuing it from the now-sunken Art Institute in Chicago, America, but Aubin doubted the entire story. Oh, it was a fact that the Art Institute was now under water. Most of the lakeshore, extended and built out with fill, had turned to liquid muck during the earthquakes of the Destruction and returned Lake Michigan to its true proportions. Even the relatively innocuous New Madrid Fault had taken back some of its own when the Ring of Fire blew. Fuji had not been alone in that. But Aubin could not see the extremely fat and greasy man climbing into a wet suit to rescue objects d'art. More likely he'd bought it himself from someone who'd told exactly the same story. Aubin didn't really care. All he cared about was that the lady was his. He loved her, and he didn't care who knew it.

He stroked her lovingly, and said, without

turning around, "You're going to hurt yourself if you keep doing that."

"Doing what?" Ki asked in surprise.

"You're going to wear out your hand and pull every last muscle in your back. You're too tense." He gave his lady a last pat, and turned to face Ki. "You're drawn. You're not going to be any good to anybody if you don't relax."

Ki paused for a moment, his hand wavering over the glass Aubin had set at his side. How he hated it when Aubin was right! But he could feel the tension, and now that Aubin had pointed it out to him, he knew about half the pain he was feeling was only tension exacerbating little ills. He picked up the glass and sipped lightly at its amber contents. Liquid warmth ran down his throat, and spread instantly to all the reaches of his body. As alcohol rarely affected him, Ki was surprised. He was surprised, too, at Aubin's perspicacity—it bordered almost on precognition. How had the human known he would need a fight, a drink, and a friend?

"If I didn't know better, I'd swear you were a Nidean in disguise," Ki said, meaning it in all kindness.

"Bite your tongue!" Aubin cried in anguish. "I wouldn't want to be a Lionman. You people don't know how to have fun. You all walk around like that young lieutenant all the time, with a steel rod up—"

"I get the picture," Ki said, raising his right hand to stop Aubin's graphic description. Cautiously, he took another sip of his drink.

Aubin walked over to the sofa across from Ki's chair, thinking as he walked, *Good! He's taken another drink. Better not make a big deal out of it,*

*though, or he'll never take another. I've got to be
careful now. I've finally got his attention.*

Ki cut across his thoughts. "What did you put
in this?" He waved the drink at Aubin.

"Just good old-fashioned bourbon whiskey.
Why?"

"Alcohol doesn't usually affect me this
quickly."

Aubin nodded knowingly. "You're very tired.
You're very tense. And if I know you, you
haven't made time to eat. When did you eat
last? You aren't Superman, you know."

"Who?"

"A perfect strong man out of mythology."
Aubin downed the rest of his drink, set the glass
aside, and slapped his knees. "Food! How do you
like your meat?"

Suddenly feeling his weariness, Ki answered,
"Don't bother."

"How do you like your meat?" Aubin asked
again, a little annoyed. "I'm going to assume
rare. And I was fixing a snack when you came
in, anyway." He vanished into the kitchen, and
Ki heard pots rattling. Then Aubin's head made
a reappearance around the corner. "But is that
rare or *rare?* Warm or still bloody? Will beef suffice?"

"It will do," Ki answered, and Aubin disappeared once more. The lack of conversation settled heavily on Ki. It seemed everything
bothered him tonight—or was it this morning?
He looked around Aubin's apartment as if it
were the first time he'd been in it. The colors
were soft and sandy, neutral, almost like the
browns and pale oranges of the desert. The lines
of the furnishings were clean and uncluttered,
the curves soft. Ki looked over at the sculpture

that fascinated Aubin so, and shook his head. That he did not understand. A woman could never support a building, so of course she had fallen under the load. What was the fascination of someone trying to be something they weren't? There was an aesthetic there he did not understand. Behind the bronze was a print, quite large, of a massive set of gates. Aubin had said the bronze had been a study for part of these *Gates of Hell*. Ki found that though he did not understand the various pieces, they worked together well, energetically, and he could take something away from the writhing mass. The other print gracing Aubin's walls hung, on Ki's right, on the division between the sitting room and kitchen. That was pure fantasy, and Ki had always enjoyed it enormously, though, of course, he could never say so to Aubin. It was old, by a twentieth-century artist, and it showed big, puffy clouds that were really polar bears rollicking over a flat landscape. Aubin called it *Polar Bears over Iowa*. Someday he would have to find out from Aubin where Iowa was. He somehow doubted the bears belonged there, but they were having so much fun that even Ki could understand. He began to relax slightly, and suddenly the glass seemed very heavy. He set it aside, and it clinked as he set it down.

"I heard that!" sailed out from the kitchen. "Finish your drink or you get no yummies!"

This man is insane! Ki thought, and the tension started to build again like a roller coaster climbing another hill. *Why do I trust him?* Ki could feel the liquor pounding in the fingertips of his right hand. *What was I thinking? Why do I let him order me around?* The Nidean stood, picked up the glass, and started for the kitchen.

I command the Lionman Guard. He set the glass down heavily, noisily, angrily, on a kitchen countertop.

Aubin looked up from his fussing. "You didn't finish that."

Ki shifted his stance so that his feet were shoulder width apart, his back arrow straight, a ready stance if ever there was one. He crossed his arms deliberately.

Oh, shit! is what ran through Aubin's mind as the change in Ki's attitude registered.

"Just what are you up to, Aubin Tabber?" Ki rumbled.

Aubin set his cooking utensils aside. A look of stern intensity wiped out all facetiousness. "Time to be straight. I've seen too many like you, Ki. Take every responsibility and burn themselves out. When I was very young I had to learn a trick I call 'putting things in a box.' When a problem is unsolvable, when there's nothing to be done, put it away. That leaves you with enough energy for the things that can be dealt with. You're getting tired—too tired. When you make a mistake you're going to walk into that courtyard and slit your belly open. I haven't enough people who I care about that I can let that happen without protest."

Suddenly Aubin was shaking, really shaking, quivering like jelly. *Now I've said it,* he told himself. *He'll either leave now—or hit me. I'm not sure I want to face either one.*

Ki had been staring at Aubin all during Aubin's speech. His gaze never wavered. He didn't drop it now. But slowly he loosened his arms and uncrossed them. He reached across for his drink, and leaned as casually as he was able in his current state against the doorjamb. He raised the glass in salute to Aubin.

"Definitely a Nidean."

Ozenscebo hated the tight security. His valet had not been in to dress him, and the Guardsman who had tried had been all thumbs. Why, he'd ended up fastening his own robe! Imagine! Not only that, but there were Lionmen everywhere! There was nowhere he could go to escape them.

Out of boredom and frustration, he'd decided to attend his sitting anyway. He was having his portrait painted for the gallery. All the other monarchs of his line were there, and he should be too. He was, of course, the best of the lot. He would have the children painted as well. Magnus would be emperor one day, after all. Between his teeth he said, "I suppose I'll have to have Elena done, too. But she certainly won't add anything to the show."

The sittings were at least interesting, in a way. Though he never cared much for sitting still, it was fun to think of his face growing on the canvas, larger than life. It was probably the only way to do him justice.

A Lionman opened the door to the gallery, and Ozenscebo stepped on him as he went by. "Damned Lionmen! They're even underfoot!" he said to himself angrily as he took his seat.

The artist was a nondescript little man, though the emperor had been told he was the finest portrait artist available. He looked nothing like what Ozenscebo thought an artist should look like. He had both his ears, for one thing. And no hair. And he was short. Somehow the emperor had always pictured artists as dashing creatures in fantastic clothes. And here was this fellow, boring.

"Good morning, Your Majesty," he said in his nasal twang.

Ozenscebo answered with, "Bah!"

Unruffled, the artist requested the emperor to take his seat, and refreshed His Royal Majesty's memory as to his pose.

Though he sat quietly, Ozenscebo was very unsettled. He was bothered by so many Lionmen being around at one time. There seemed to be more than he could control easily. And he did miss his little pleasures. How was a Guardsman to know how he liked his tea in the morning? His valet knew—sweet, with a glass of roed on the side.

They tried to kill my son, was the thought that kept recurring to him. *They tried to kill my son. My wife and daughter, too, incidently, but they tried to kill my son.*

"Would Your Majesty be so good as to turn slightly, like so?" the artist asked.

Ozenscebo shifted, but the request barely registered. *I'll have to reward him, of course. Ki kept them from killing my son. But what do I give him? A woman? Do Lionmen like women? Yes, yes, certainly they do. Otherwise there wouldn't be any little Lionmen. Wasn't Ki married? I'll have to find out.*

The emperor was stiffening up already. Although it had been two days since he last sat, it felt as if his muscles were locked in this position and would never shift again. He twisted his head to relieve a crick in his neck.

"Now, Majesty, I must have you just so," the little man said, and he fussed over the emperor again, arranging his arms and head and the full skirts of his gown.

Ozenscebo frowned, but the artist caught him at it. "Remember, Your Majesty, we're looking stern for this portrait, not unhappy."

The emperor was bored by the gnome, so he went back to his musings. *I have to get him something. A mouse? Cats like mice. No, that won't do. The old boy never did have a sense of humor. A promotion? No. My great-grandfather was smart to recognize how dangerous they can be. They really did try to kill my son. I can't get over it. The nerve! My heir! Yes. He will be my heir. I'll have to make it official soon. This week. Ki saved my heir. I'll have to give him something...I know. I'll have Elena choose. She's good at that sort of thing.*

In spite of all instructions, a smile nudged the edges of Ozenscebo's mouth. *We'll keep it a secret. Surprise him. Might get a reaction out of old Stoneface. I wonder if he can smile? And if it's not the proper gift, I'll have Elena punished.*

"You!" The emperor came out of his musings violently. "I want to see it!"

The little man was buried in his work, miles away from what the emperor was saying. He was trying to capture that glint in the eye, the one that made Ozenscebo look as only the emperor could..."One moment, please, Your Majesty."

"Now!"

It was the slight rustling among the guards that woke the little man, bringing him back to his surroundings, making him realize who he was talking to. He turned the portrait, half-finished, so that the emperor could see it.

"I don't like it. Start over."

"I'm sorry you're not pleased, Majesty," the artist whimpered, very much aware of the Guardsmen at his back. "Can you tell me what's wrong? Perhaps I can fix it."

"What's wrong is I don't like it! How dare you question me!" the emperor roared. Challenging him! This little man was a nuisance!

The look of anger on the emperor's face made the room become suddenly cold and clammy for the poor artist. Wondering who'd hated him enough to recommend him for this commission, he took the portrait from the easel and crossed the room to his box of supplies. From this he took a small knife, and poised it over the canvas.

Everywhere in the room hands went to sword hilts. It was obvious the Guardsmen were edgy after yesterday's attempt.

"What are you doing?" Ozenscebo bellowed.

"I'm...I'm just going to take the canvas out so I can reuse the stretcher, Your Majesty."

"Don't you dare cut my face! I'll keep that. You're dismissed! Now get out!" Ozenscebo was yelling, venting a lot of the impotent anger he'd been storing up since yesterday. It felt good, he discovered, to let it run. And run it did. The emperor raged, knocking over the easel, spilling paint, breaking porcelain paint cups. He enjoyed his display. It felt good, so good, to destroy.

The artist, only too happy to abandon all, was escorted quickly out.

The rage did not sustain itself very long. After all, that took energy. When it ran down, Ozenscebo stood very still, breathing heavily. He looked down at the floor and saw the broken paint cups covered with oil paints of various colors swirling together. Light hitting the surface of the oils and thinner reflected iridescent rainbow hues, and Opal leapt to mind.

"I'll visit Opal now," he whispered to himself, but instead of leaving he got on his hands and knees to look closely at the whirling mess he'd made. Covered with all the shades of paint, the porcelain looked just like thin shards of opal.

The Guardsmen were totally nonplussed. Never in any of their collective experiences had this emperor gotten on the floor. They looked at one another questioningly.

"Is he all right?"

"What should we do?"

"Is he ill?" crossed the large room in stage whispers, loud enough to finally capture Ozenscebo's attention.

"I'm fine," he said as he struggled to get up off the floor. "I'm fine. Take me to the seraglio."

The interior of Parry's quarters did not suit him at all. He supposed that was why he spent so little time here. The rest of the palace was lush, rich, and wonderful to behold—in short, the perfect surroundings for a hedonist. But here, in the Avoyan envoy's private apartments, there was none of that grandeur. Parry frowned heavily as he looked around. The gold of the public rooms was here unadorned plastic, and simply fashioned at that. Mercer ran his hand along the slick back of a dowdy chair and grimaced. Nothing. That was what Ozenscebo had left Avoy after the uprising. Not a trace of anything, not even self-respect. The planet could not afford, not even now, thirty-nine years after the attempted secession, to properly outfit its own envoy to the court. Much of the poor furnishings that surrounded him had come from Parry's own very limited resources. He had to be very careful. He counted every penny he spent, his own or Avoy's. He needed to be able to maintain some sort of standing in the envoy circles, making some expenditures necessary. But with Avoy ready to rid itself of the choking grasp of the empress, he had to be frugal to the point of miserliness with Avoy's funds. Assassinations were very expensive.

Avoy had not intended originally to rid itself of the empress. Avoy remembered the things Ozenscebo had ordered, and was searching for a way to rid itself of the hated monster. It had not been until Parry had come here as envoy and seen for himself that the empire spun on Elena's word that their new plan had come into being. It may have been Ozenscebo who had ordered their original humiliation, but it was Elena who saw that it continued. Ozenscebo had become a slug, totally derelict in his duties, a man who could be twisted easily to fit the Avoyan idea of how the empire should be run. Elena, on the other hand, was a voice of reason and sagacity screaming into the emperor's void. Now it was she who must be eliminated so that Ozenscebo could be controlled in the fashion the Avoyans chose. And Parry, who had been the first to see the possibilities, intended to have a great deal to do with the pulling of the puppet's strings. Many promises had been wrung from the powers that ran his home planet.

Parry sat on the unyielding plastic and slid into a position that was as comfortable as could be attained. He rested his head on the heels of his hands, and his thick shock of brown hair fell forward over his face. Drawing his hands over his eyes, he began to rub at the long, thin, bird-like nose that dominated his face, remembering how it had been. Mercer kept the boy of seven who had seen the uprising alive in his memory to remind him why he had to control the empire, even if it meant dealing daily with Ozenscebo.

On Ozenscebo's orders, the Lionmen had been turned loose on Avoy. On his orders the Guardsmen had pillaged and destroyed wildly. Anything of value had been turned in to the Royal Treasury. Anything denoting power—buildings, generators, news facilities—was turned to rubble. Parry shook his head. He had been a child then, and the destruction both fascinated and repelled him. But the thing that had fascinated him the most had been the Lionmen. They had been thorough. So thorough, in fact, Avoy had had planetwide famine for two Earth/Solar years before Ozenscebo could be convinced to have mercy and allow shipments in. But in all that time, and during the years of occupation that followed, Parry had never seen a Lionman with anything of value. Though they took anything they found, they never kept it. They turned it over to the emperor. Even as a child Mercer had not understood it. There had not been a single souvenir. He had never witnessed, before or since, such total stupidity. They had risked their lives and not profited. It was an example Parry never intended to follow. There would be great reward for him in the wake of the risks he was running. And he intended to keep his life in spite of Seda Paschasia and Jad Templa.

The knock at the door caused Parry to jump and tense. He was not in the habit of having visitors. There was no sense in allowing his penury to become common knowledge. *Lionmen!* he thought. *They've found me out!* He balled his hands into fists, forcing himself to calm. Of course they hadn't found anything. There was no way they could.

"Parry! Open up!" announced Parry's two fellow conspirators. He hesitated. He knew it was them, but he did not relish admitting their stupidities into his own quarters, so he did not move. When the knock came again, this time more insistently, he managed to shrug off some of the anger and vengefulness—yes, and fear— that had inhabited his musings and rouse himself.

The smile he presented to the two women was gracious and worldly. "Come in!" he said with a sweep of his arm. "My place is yours."

Seda Paschasia sniffed loudly. "Don't be cute, Mercer. We know you don't invite people in any more often than is absolutely necessary." She looked around haughtily. "I can't say I blame you." She looked at the chair Parry had occupied earlier and wrinkled her nose. "Ashamed, I suppose. Still, Mercer, it doesn't do to lie to us. We're the closest thing to friends you've got."

The smile faded entirely from Mercer's brown eyes, though his mouth still turned up at the corners. "I enjoy my privacy, Seda, and I advise you to remember that," he said coldly.

Though there was a hint of real danger under Mercer's words, Seda did not find it. "Oh, don't be so sensitive. Really, Mercer, if we're going to pull this off, you're going to have to learn to hide your feelings."

Parry wanted badly to smash her in the crooked-toothed grin. "You're right, Seda. I'll work on it," he said most humbly while he thought of ripping out the woman's tongue with a pair of tongs. At least then she could no longer babble just to hear herself talk.

Jad Templa, dressed today in a man's hunting outfit of tightly fitted breeches and knee-high boots, pushed past Seda and swooped on into the room. When she reached the other side, she said, "I don't think this is the kind of conversation that should go on with the door open. Or have you two decided you like the idea of suicide?"

Mercer nodded, and nudged Seda out of the way so the door could be fastened. Even though he disliked them both and trusted them less, Jad at least had some common sense.

"Of course, Mercer, you 'swept' the room. You know for a fact we're not being overheard?" Jad kept to the other side of the room, as if she were afraid of coming in contact with the others.

Seda swirled her full black skirts in a huge arc as she seated herself on Mercer's sofa, the only luxury he had allowed himself. "Of course he has, Jad. We all do," she said preemptorily as she arranged herself in an exaggerated pose that looked like something out of an early twentieth-century movie.

Behind her, out of her line of sight, he nodded reassuringly to Jad. She deserved that much—but not a whole lot more.

Mercer walked around the sofa and sat on the hard plastic chair he had occupied earlier. It gave him a good look at Seda's face. There were bags under her eyes as if she hadn't slept, and she kept glancing over her shoulder. Mercer shrugged inwardly. He'd known it would happen. She was getting twitchy.

"What's the matter, Seda?"

She leaned forward eagerly. "Mercer, it's going to happen. I know it will. Sooner or later they're going to realize it had to be someone inside the palace who set the bomb. And when they do, they'll come looking for us!" She looked back once more, just to be sure.

Mercer settled himself a little more firmly in the chair, and watched her carefully. If she was going to crack open like an overripe melon, he had to be rid of her now. If she was only nervous, it was possible he could make further use of her.

"Now, Seda. You know no one's even considered that the bomb was set by anyone other than the rebels," he said soothingly. "It would take quite an intuitive leap for them to realize it came from inside."

Some of the nervousness leapt out of Seda with one reflexive jerk, leaving her more still than before. "Do you think so? Do you really think they're still looking for rebels?"

"I know they are. I heard Ozie's guards talking about it only this morning. Seems they're looking very hard for the hole in their screening system that let the explosive in. They won't find it."

"Are you sure?" Seda asked pleadingly. "Really, really sure?"

"Yes," Parry answered, and this time he was able to put the real conviction of the truth behind the statement. He knew exactly how the explosive had come in, and he would know if anyone discovered it. He didn't think they would, seeing as how he had tapped Ozenscebo's own stores.

Jad watched Seda beg for, and Mercer give, reassurance. She saw that Seda ate up everything Mercer said, and was smugly revolted. She didn't fall for it. They were nowhere near as safe as Mercer wanted Seda to believe. And she could see just how nervous Seda was becoming. Jad felt herself becoming more nervous, too, but for different reasons. She was learning to trust Mercer less and less. He was too sure in the way he soothed Seda. He hadn't said a wrong word yet. And if he was that good at manipulating Seda, was he any less so when it was Jad's turn? *Perhaps it would be wisest,* she thought, *to give them both a wide berth.*

Seda had obviously taken in everything Mercer said. "Come here, Jad. Join us. Mercer says everything is just fine. Together we can do anything. I'm sure of it now."

Jad walked toward the sofa, quaking inwardly. She was going to have to find a way out of this. Soon.

Chapter Six

———◆———

KI FOUND HIMSELF once more striding down a hallway in formal gear. This day was an important one for the empire. This was the day Ki's special charge, Natanha, would be made heir. And even though he was unhappy at being once more part of a formal pageant, for Natanha's naming he felt he could stand it.

What an empress she'll make! he thought happily to himself. *She has all of her mother's intelligence and diligence, and all the restraint and*

*patience I could teach her. She'll be wise and kind
and gentle, and her subjects will love her,* he
thought. *There will be none of the horrors Magnus
would incur.*

Magnus!

Ki's stride lost all its spring, and slowed to a
creeping shuffle. *He wouldn't!* Ki screamed to
himself. *Surely even Ozenscebo can see what a
disaster Magnus would be!* His left hand clicked
coldly as he ran his mechanical fingers back and
forth across his steel thumb and palm. *Not even
Ozenscebo,* he reassured himself, and continued
down the hall.

Everyone said Natanha would be the heir. It
was common knowledge. Even Aubin had said
Natanha was the only choice. So why was there
a cold lump in his gut?

He approached the doorway that would admit
him to the public area of the palace and paused.
He checked himself over in the ever-present
mirrors banking the doorway. Aside from looking very tired, he was presentable. He had prepared himself with Natanha in mind. He had
even polished his hand, which still clicked with
the motion across the palm as was his habit
when uneasy, unhappy, angry, or even lost in
thought. He stood there for a few long moments,
wondering, then finally drew a deep breath and
opened the door to the room that would hold
the overflow from the audience chamber and
shouldered his way between the twin Guardsmen who blocked the door.

It was full of people. The banners and flowers
that had appeared overnight appealed to Ki.
The lights and warmth brought a festive atmosphere to the place. The people were milling like
imlowwn, but they were so happy it was impos-

sible to take them badly, in spite of their intense, overpoweringly human smell.

"Surely Natanha will be the one," Ki heard as he crossed the threshold, and he nodded to himself. Common knowledge. And a hearty wish.

"Look! Commander Lawwnum!" rippled with awe through the crowd as Ki made his way into its heart.

"Commander! It is Natanha, isn't it?" was asked of him a dozen times as he worked his way through the crowd partly by pushing, partly by intimidation, and partly by courtesy. He never answered the question. He couldn't.

He was still some way from the audience chamber itself, and time was running short. He had lost too much to musing. *I should have come the back way,* he thought, though he knew he did not want to miss mixing with Natanha's people. *I must not be late.* He dropped his hand to the hilt of his hoj, brought his eyebrows together in an angry scowl, and began a low rumble in his chest. Though the sound was regarded as a lullaby, a monotonous soother of infants among his people, he had discovered quite by accident it had another effect altogether on adult humans. The crowd opened a path, parents hauling children out of harm's way, though the children inevitably looked up at Ki and smiled. They understood.

As he walked his now-clear path, Ki realized he rather liked the colors. It warmed the place, giving it life and happiness. It took some of the cold out of the stone, even if Ozenscebo had been himself and overdone it all. The enclosed space was not really meant to hold so many people. The throne room was really the place for this kind of gathering, but it was still under re-

pair. This large enclosed courtyard was merely
the overflow for the audience chamber, but anyone who could make the ceremony with any reasonable expectation of being admitted had
arrived early this morning. Only a relatively
small number would be allowed to view the ac-
tual ceremony in the audience chamber with
the royal family. Still, they were present. Ki
wondered at their numbers. The babble of their
voices rang off the walls and bounced down
from the high, rounded ceiling, amplifying the
sound to a deafening roar. *I'm going to have a
headache before long,* he thought, but dismissed
the discomfort with a shrug. *I wouldn't miss
this. I've waited a long time for my princess to
come of age. She'll come into her own now, and
Elena will be so proud of her.*

At last he made it to the door of the audience
chamber proper. He squeezed into the room behind a very fat man who was sweating profusely
and rancidly through his many layers of fancy
clothes, and started to make his way to the front
of the room to his customary spot behind
Elena's shoulder. He could see how the chairs on
the dais had been arranged. The largest was, of
course, for Ozenscebo. But this time Elena's
chair occupied the same level. There were two
rather small and plain seats also on the same
level, between the places meant for emperor
and empress. This was the first time the children had been given this kind of recognition. It
would not be long before the emperor made his
entrance, and Ki was not yet in his customary
place.

As if the thought brought the act, the doors
opened to a deafening fanfare and Ozenscebo
escorted Elena on his arm into the room. They

were both in white, stark and dazzling. Their robes matched, being fitted at the waist, cinched with gold cord, and full-skirted, which suited Elena but not Ozenscebo. The children came behind, also in white, Natanha dressed like her mother, Magnus in knee-length tight pants, full-sleeved shirt, and vest. He had been eating something gooey-sticky and was no longer white. In spite of her son's state, Elena looked very calm. Her charm radiated, and she never failed to capture her audience. Ozenscebo grinned. He tapped his hands together as he took his throne, almost as if he were clapping his hands in sheer glee. Ki recognized the signs. The emperor was keeping a secret.

Ki headed toward the guard that flanked the emperor's chair, thinking to take a place there since he could no longer approach the empress unobtrusively.

"Excuse me, sir."

Ki looked up, surprised to be addressed by one of the Guardsmen. They did not generally speak when on duty unless ordered to do so.

"You're supposed to sit there," the Lionman said as he gestured across the room to a bank of chairs where several notables were seated.

"Sit?" He never sat during a ceremony. It limited his field of vision.

Somewhat nonplussed, but not wishing to cause a stir, Ki obeyed and headed for the indicated seat. Ozenscebo was still taking the plaudits of his crowd, so Ki passed with relatively little notice taken of him. As soon as he sat, however, a herald stepped forward. Silence fell like a feather quilt, thick and heavy.

"We hereby state," Ozenscebo said into the silence, "that the traitor in our midst will be found and dealt with. This traitor has committed the unpardonable crime of trying to assassinate Us and Our Royal Heir, but this foul plan was foiled by Our own Colonel Ki Lawwnum of the Imperial Lionman Guard." Spontaneous applause broke into the emperor's speech. Ordinarily this would have outraged him, but today he smiled, pleased. "It had been Our intention to reward him with promotion, but, as he has already reached the highest rank allowed to Lionmen by law, We will give him a small token of Our appreciation. We searched very long and hard . . ."

Ki shifted uncomfortably. The emperor never worked at anything. If his hand was truly in this gift, it was likely to be a viper in the bosom.

" . . . to find something appropriate. Come forward, Colonel Lawwnum."

Ki clenched his left hand, and stood, his face a stone mask. He was preparing himself to be embarrassed publicly. Ozenscebo had no taste and no shame. Ki moved to the center of the dais and stopped two steps below Ozenscebo. He bowed to the emperor correctly, but without affection.

A large orange silk cushion, thick and heavily tasseled, covered with a large square of matching fabric, was brought to the emperor's side. With a theatrical flourish, Ozenscebo pulled the covering away to reveal a scabbarded sword, shorter than Ki's though showing about the same type of curve. The furniture was exquisitely wrought, the deep golden color of shikudo, an ancient Japanese alloy of copper and gold. Dragons twined down the grip, which was covered with ray skin, crossed over with black-and-gold-braided silk cording. The scabbard was black with silver flecks, ringed round with bands of silvery metal. It also bore a motif of crossed hawk feathers near the open end. Ki was washed with a need to reach out and take the blade, its singular beauty touched him so. It was delicate, gentle, and he longed to see the killing edge. It was with difficulty that he restrained himself.

"This sword was made by Shigehide, and carried by an old family. It was made during the Edo period of old Japan. Receive this from Our hand with Our thanks."

Ki's pause looked like only a moment to the audience, but to Ki's burning fingers it was an eternity. At last he reached out to grasp the sword, wondering still if the thing of beauty was rigged in some way to make a fool of him.

"My thanks, Your Majesty," Ki said with a deep bow. "But I merely did my duty."

Ki turned back to the place assigned him, aflame to draw the blade and examine it closely. The balance of the thing was fine, drawn down to a hair. So much he could already feel. If this was a joke, it was an elaborate and expensive one. Suddenly a thought occurred to him. He changed the sword to his metallic left hand and raised his right, which had been holding the prize, to his face as if to rub it. Instead, he inhaled deeply. There was his own scent, of course, strong in the moisture of his hand. And there was Ozenscebo's deeply woody perfume and his innate papery odor of age. But there was also something more. Something fragile and days old. But he no longer feared the gift. Just a trace of Elena's fragrance lingered.

Ki took his place and looked at the emperor questioningly. He had never seen Ozenscebo so solicitous of his family and those who served him. It was wrong somehow, out of place. And there was still that secret glee shining from the emperor's eyes.

The speech continued, but Ki's attention had wandered back to the thing in his hand. It was both heavy and light, having substantial weight of its own, but being much lighter than his hoj. It was warm under his hand, and cool if he shifted it. This was a thing requiring study, and he wanted badly to leave this room overfull of people and draw the blade.

So deeply was Ki's attention riveted on his new blade that he did not hear the rest of Ozenscebo's speech. He heard nothing, in fact, until the emperor ended with, "...my heir, my son."

After that, he heard and saw nothing of the interminable ceremony. He was in shock.

Natanha paced the length of her mother's room again. It was late, much, much later than a young princess should be up. But Natanha was determined to talk to her mother if she had to wait until the breaking of dawn, or noon, or the next night. This was important, she knew that somehow, and it was strange. So strange it was beyond her understanding.

She stopped in front of her mother's dressing table and played with some of the articles on it, straightening them, moving them over, then picking up the brush and running it unthinkingly through her fine hair. Then she slammed the brush down, hard, on the tabletop, frustrated at the length of her wait.

Ashamed at her outburst, she sat down deflatedly on the tiny bench in front of the mirror.

"Shame on you, Natanha," she said to her image. "What would Ki say about that? He'd tell you you're spoiled and you have no control over yourself." She sighed. "And I guess he'd be right."

She stood again and paced some more, touching her mother's things as she went by them, gathering something of a sense of the empress's presence from them.

Ki looked bad, she thought. Natanha had never seen him look so tired. She remembered vaguely when last he'd been gone from Homeworld for a long time. She'd been a mere toddler, and it was only some time later that she surmised he had been away on some campaign or other. He'd been tired when he'd come back that time, and lonely. She remembered how he loved to play with her and make her laugh right after that. But even then he did not look so... empty, so hollow. And he was so busy! She would have accepted him as confidant in place of her mother, but he was still off dealing with business.

She yawned. The ceremony had been incredibly long. She had not understood the vast majority of it. The only interesting things had been the look on Ki's face when he'd taken the gift Mama had found for him, and the reaction of the people when Papa had said Magnus was his heir. She had not foreseen that. She had assumed everyone knew that Magnus, Papa's pride and joy, would, of course, be heir. That anyone had thought it might be her was simply silly. She had not been surprised.

But Magnus was strange, and his strangeness was beginning to upset her. Natanha crawled up on her mother's bed and knelt in an approximation of the posture Ki assumed when he needed to think, then smoothed her thick French velvet skirts.

It had been after the ceremony. She had wanted to ask Mama something or other, and had looked for her in Magnus's room. He had been the star of the show, after all, and perhaps Mama had business there. But she was not there. Magnus had been alone, Natanha assumed after having frightened off his nurse. He was on his belly on the floor not far from a birdcage that rested, door open, in the center of the tiles.

"Get down!" he hissed at her. "Be quiet!"

Creeping out of the corner of the room came a small black cat with white boots and white chest that Natanha had never seen before. It was none too clean, and had something of a feral look about it. Hungry, it was stalking, slinking along one paw at a time, toward the birdcage.

Now that Natanha was on the floor, she could see the cage was occupied. In it was a tiny blue and green parrot-type feathered creature that occupied one of the palace gardens. They were known for the beauty of their songs, but this one was not singing. It was frantically jumping from perch to swing to bottom of the cage to perch. It was aware it was being stalked, but it was not smart enough to realize safety lay outside the cage door.

The cat came closer, lifting its velvety paws in exaggerated care. It made not a sound, and Natanha was fascinated. She had never seen a wild thing hunt its prey. The stealth of the feline totally engaged her attention until the tiniest cheep escaped the panicked bird.

"Stop it, Magnus," she'd whispered. She'd suddenly realized what was about to occur. "Don't let it get the bird!"

"Be quiet, Nat. I want to see what happens!" His voice was thick with anticipation.

Natanha had started to shift. "If you won't stop this, I will!"

Magnus had grabbed her arm painfully hard, digging his nails into her flesh. "Be still, Nat!" he'd yapped. "If you stop this, I'll tell Daddy!"

Now horrified, Natanha had stared. The cat approached the cage carefully, watching the children with sly twists of its large golden eyes. When it reached the cage it paused, waiting for some inner signal. Then its paw swept out, arcing accurately through the door of the cage. As it moved, the claws sprang into position and ripped into the bird's breast, knocking it forcefully into the wall of the cage before pulling it out toward the cat's bared teeth. Tiny welts of blood sprang up around the embedded claws, and smeared the white stocking. Magnus let out a whoop of victory and ran to pick up the cat. The cat did not want to be parted from its prey, and scratched the one who was poaching. Magnus let out a yell, and drew back a bloodied hand. Shock, anger, and fear crossed his face in rapid succession. Then he cocked his foot and kicked the cat with all his might.

Natanha heard an audible snap when Magnus connected, and the cat dropped the bird and let out a yowl of pain and sped past her on three legs to hide behind a large toy chest in the corner of the nursery. Magnus took out after the cat, but halted when he passed his sister.

"Get out! Now!" he'd yelled, and Natanha, not

wanting to know what would happen next, revolted, scared, had fled.

She trembled a little now as she thought about it, and left her kneeling position to curl up on top of the covers, wrapping her arms about herself.

"Mama must be very busy," she said softly to the room. "But I wish she'd hurry."

A very long time passed, and Natanha was almost asleep when the empress finally made it back to her room. Elena was still in her heavy court garb, and she had only just now gotten away from the frenetic goings-on. She removed her earrings, and began to remove her rings before she realized Natanha was curled up on her bed. She smiled at her daughter.

"Do you know what time it is?" she asked quietly.

Natanha yawned widely and sat up. "It's two thirty-seven, but I have to talk to you."

Elena was facing her dressing table now, her back to her daughter, and she smiled. Natanha's time sense was unnerving to those who had never experienced it before. Elena moved so that she could see her princess in the mirror, and was surprised at how grown-up Natanha looked and sounded. *I thought children were supposed to look vulnerable when they were sleepy,* she said inside her head, then she leaned forward toward the mirror to look at her daughter again. Of necessity Natanha was an odd mixture of child and adult, and Elena regretted Natanha's forced maturity.

The empress rose from her seat at her dressing table and crossed to her velvet-covered sofa. She sat herself delicately, and then raised her hem to kick off her shoes. She ran her hand down her skirts, rearranging the folds, then opened her arms to her daughter. Elena was tired. Very, very tired. She had wanted a hot bath more than anything, but judging by the expression on Natanha's face as she crossed to her from the bed, this was serious business.

As the child sat, Elena said, "Now that you have my undivided attention, what's troubling you so much that you're still awake?" She settled back with a knowing "mama smile," the one Natanha hated, but it disappeared quickly as Natanha told her what had transpired in Magnus's room. It was replaced with an expression of severe determination.

"You're thirteen now," the empress told her daughter. "Because you are also princess royal you must be a grown woman, too." Elena paused, thinking back. "I wasn't much older than you when I was married to your father. You have reached a point where you must face some difficult things." Elena turned to face her daughter, and took Natanha's shoulders in her hands. "Magnus is your brother and my son, but he is also an abomination. Your father has seen to that. As you were firstborn, I had hoped you'd be declared heir. I've trained you for it from your birth. But since your father has decided to inflict Magnus on the empire, we're forced to make some modifications in our lifestyle." She dropped her hands, placing them together in her lap, and her expression became very serious. "First, child, avoid Magnus whenever possible. Do not trust him. There's a storm coming, and Magnus and your father will be the center of it. If we're not very careful, we may be swept away. Secondly, should anything happen to me . . ."

Natanha stifled the cry that came involuntar-

ily by stuffing her fist into her mouth. Her eyes
became very large, and reflected her fear perfectly.

Elena tried to smile. "I'm not expecting anything to happen, but if it should, you hide. Disappear. Stay out of sight. Make your way to the
port as soon as you are able, and take passage to
Midron. My family is still there, and they will
care for you."

Natanha was still chewing on her fist. Elena
did not want to scare her too badly. Natanha
was going to need to be able to think if this
thing came to pass. Still, she had to be prepared.

"Now, child, I'm glad you came to me and I'm
glad we had this talk. But there's nothing more
we can do right now except worry, and worrying
only uses up precious energy needed elsewhere.
So go to sleep now and put this aside." She
touched her daughter's hair tenderly. "You may
sleep with me if you like."

Slowly Natanha rose and began to disrobe.
Elena noticed that her child's figure was just
beginning to blossom into that of a woman.
She's old enough, Elena mused. *I wonder what
kind of marriage I could arrange to get her away
from here.*

Ki made his morning rounds as usual, even
though he still felt drained and tired after yesterday's long and pompous ceremony. His medi-
tations had not been as restoring as usual. He
had, in fact, almost drifted off to sleep, something he had never done in all his life. The shock
and disappointment of yesterday had taken
their toll.

Perhaps I'm getting old, he thought, and raised his right hand into his line of sight. His skin had the color change associated in his people with age. But he still felt young, and his step was still firm. He sighed.

What a mess. I dare not leave Natanha, especially now that Magnus has been declared heir. I must see she is safe. I can understand Ozenscebo wishing his son to be his heir. After all, that is the way of my people also. All things pass to the male children. A woman-child does not even take her place in the pride until she is married, and then she joins her husband's. But in this case... Natanha is really better suited to the position, even if she is female. My people would have understood that.

He passed one of his Guardsmen and gave him a quick but encompassing glance. All was as it should be. Mikal would have seen to it.

Mikal is working hard. Maybe too hard. I wonder how much hazing he takes from the others. His position is not a comfortable one. But he is the next highest in rank of my pride. The honor blade will be his, and along with it will go the responsibility for the honor of our pride. So much incumbent on one so young. I hope—I feel —he will do it justice. Much of our history and too much of our blood is tied to it.

Our blood and the royal family's. Did I not cut the umbilical that tied Elena and Natanha with this very blade? He automatically moved to rest his left hand on its reassuring hilt, but felt the lightness of the emperor's gift instead of the comfortable weight of his familiar hoj. *But where do I go from here?* He dropped his hand and began flexing it, then ran the fingers crosswise against the palm, feeling the little ridges left by joints. *I have reached the highest rank allowed to anyone of my race. It is thus decreed by law. The humans have been terrified of us ever since they failed to conquer Nide. Even though we have vowed to serve the empire, and have done so faithfully, the fact that we have never been a conquered people cannot be forgotten. There has been too much pain, both given and taken. It's time to retire.*

He passed his men at their posts, and every last one of them managed to glance greedily at the new sword the commander wore. Ki could feel the curiosity pouring from them. There was not a one who wouldn't have liked to have asked about it. But they wouldn't. It would not be polite.

I'll have to practice with it. It's not as long or as heavy or as wide as my hoj, but it is longer than my shar by just a little. It sits well in my hand, however, and the balance is exquisite.

He turned into the seraglio to check on his men there. Pink light came in through the tinted skylight and danced off the droplets of the fountain to splash across the pink marble and pink furniture. It was almost like entering an alien world where all color was one atmosphere that a body floated through. The terrazzo floor felt hard beneath his feet, however, and Ki knew this world from of old, having spent his share of time standing guard in one of the tiny alcoves. As he checked in at each hiding place, Ki realized Ozenscebo's personal guard was present. Either he's getting an early start, or he's had a long night, Ki thought with a hint of a sneer.

Mama-san's heavy floral scent assailed him before she herself rounded the corner.

"Good morning, Commander Ki," she said as

graciously as she was able before she'd had her morning roed. "You're here early."

"Yes," he agreed, even though he was almost two hours later than normal. "Tell me, which chamber is the emperor occupying?"

Shocked, Mama-san asked, "Don't you know?" She curled her upper lip into a sneer. "You're supposed to know everything."

"I don't live in the seraglio," he answered coldly, then realized open warfare with Mama-san would not be beneficial. "Please," he asked as pleasantly as he could. "Where is the emperor?"

Mama-san answered him shortly, then started off after her roed. She had not been served in bed this morning as was her custom, and she was unhappy. And when she was not happy, neither was anyone else in her domain.

Ki stood for a moment watching the tempest recede down the hallway, then turned in the direction of the emperor's chamber. He had not gone four steps before Opal came regally into view, dressed in a gown of the sheerest of white syn-silk which slid invitingly off her shoulders. She hesitated, nodded to Ki, then moved on slowly in her exquisitely languid fashion.

"A moment please," he asked before he knew he was going to speak.

She stopped and turned gradually back to him. "Yesss?"

"You have not been back to the garden. Have you lost your interest in carbon's colors?"

She lowered her head, and the peridot crystals that were her crown clinked together softly. She raised her shoulder to shift her gown, and as it slid down, Ki could see more of her delicately colored skin. It warmed his to a blush.

"Mama-ssan ssaid it would be improper for me to return." She hesitated, then timidly raised her eyes to meet his. "My interesst remainss."

Ki found for the first time in ages he was feeling somewhat shy himself. Opal was totally disarming. But he nonetheless reached into his sleeve and withdrew a small deep-blue velvet box, no bigger than an inch on a side. He had stashed it there earlier this morning, as he had for several mornings, just in case their paths should cross. "Then, here's another piece of carbon for you to study."

Her hand floated delicately above Ki's for some time while she decided to take the box. Then, lightly, she took it, her fingertips just brushing his. He resisted an urge to quiver. She looked the box over carefully, then gently, slowly, opened it as if wishing the surprise to last as long as possible. A stone sparkled there, clear, with rainbow flashes, a marquise diamond.

"Move to a light," Ki suggested, and followed closely when she did so, breathing deeply of her fresh-water scent.

She was delighted by the flashes of color that rewarded her motions. She laughed lightly, and her hair answered with a chorus of its own. She looked at him, their eyes touching, and looked as if she was about to speak, but then she stepped back.

"Thank you. It's time now for my mineral bath."

She moved away, and Ki watched her go, forcing his hands to remain quietly at his sides instead of calling her back.

"Pretty thing, isn't she?" Ozenscebo asked coldly from behind Ki's left shoulder.

Ki started. He had been totally unaware of the emperor's presence. *How long has he been standing there?* he wondered. *And how engrossed was I that I didn't even smell him?*

"She must have her mineral baths, you know. Otherwise, I'm told, she becomes quite rigid. Interesting, isn't it?"

The emperor moved on, and his guard caught up with him, leaving Ki standing in the empty corridor.

"That lovely creature has a weakness, and Ozenscebo knows what it is," he whispered to himself. "That scares me."

A new artist was at work in the gallery sitting room. A dropcloth had been spread under him, and he worked on the backgrounds of the large painting currently on his easel. He was young for this kind of commission, in his early twenties. But there were reasons he'd won the job. First of all, none of the portrait artists of the older generation wanted to touch this commission, especially after what had happened to his predecessor, and secondly, he was good. If he managed to please the emperor, his career was probably made. The sycophants who abounded at court would all want their portraits painted by the same man who'd done the emperor. Although he detested the people, the steady income would be a wonderful relief.

His curly blond head bent over his palette, and he swept together the colors he wished for his brush. His frosty blue eyes studied the painting for a heartbeat before he put the brush into motion. He worked intently, back and forth between palette and easel, totally involved. He did not hear the commotion behind him when the emperor entered followed by his Guardsmen. So enrapt was he that he jumped when the emperor's hand fell heavily on his shoulder.

"Are you ready for me?" Ozenscebo asked, expecting, of course, a positive reply.

"Your Majesty!" panted the artist as he bowed deeply. "You startled me! I thought you were to be in audience today, and I was not to be graced with your presence."

"I've changed my mind. I do not feel like sitting there listening to the din those dogs create. Let Elena handle such things!"

The young man, taken aback, bowed once more. "As you wish, Your Majesty." He busied himself at moving the chair for Ozenscebo, then the easel. "Will you be good enough to sit, Your Majesty?"

Ozenscebo complied, amused at the youngster's obvious nervousness. He was so amused, he sat quietly while the young man posed him until he was perfectly positioned. Then he did something he rarely did. He relaxed. None of his courtiers were present. Elena, the bitch, was busy elsewhere. And it was pleasant to sit here in the sun and be immortalized.

There was a large crystal vase sitting in the window embrasure. It was filled with glorious flowers from the palace's various gardens. But the wild array of colors from the flowers did not appeal to Ozenscebo as much as the rainbows spilled on the pale blue carpets from the crystal. They were breathtaking. But even they could not compare with the skin of his lovely Opal. How she gleamed in the sunlight! Rose and lavender and the most hot, electric blue the emperor had ever seen jumped from her to his eye.

The emperor looked up. He was seeing the back of the canvas, but even that made him smile. His portrait was bigger than any other in the gallery. He'd made certain of it. And Magnus's was just as large. Elena's was as small as he felt he could get away with. But his whole household should be represented. After all, he had the finest in the empire! That meant Natanha would have to be painted, too. But there should be more...

"You!" he said explosively to the artist. "Have you ever painted a Lionman?"

"No, Sire. Never."

"Then, I have a new experience in store for you. You will paint the commander of my Lionman Guard as well."

The artist's face lit up. "I thank Your Majesty! It will be a real privilege to paint Colonel Lawwnum."

Some of the wind went out of Ozenscebo's sails. It was unfair that overgrown mouser should have such respect and admiration. But still, a portrait of him would round out the grouping nicely. He liked the idea.

He went back to watching the sunflares on the vase. How beautiful it was, and how delicate. One hand was all it would take to smash it.

"Have you ever done any sculpture?" the emperor asked the artist eagerly as an idea began to take shape in the back of his mind.

"Yes, Sire. Some."

"Have you worked in metals?"

"Yes."

"Any good?"

"I've been told I am," he answered humbly,

wondering where in the world this line of questioning was going.

"Then, I have a commission for you." Ozenscebo got up from his chair and began to pace excitedly, sending the dragons embroidered on his full-skirted robe dancing in circles. "I want six gold hammers, each with a differently shaped head. They must be perfectly balanced, and fit most comfortably into the hand. Is that understood?"

"Yes, Sire."

"Good. Have them ready in one week."

The young artist's eyes started out of his head. "That's imposs..." He clamped his teeth together over his protest when he saw the thundercloud gather on Ozenscebo's brow. "Yes, Sire. One week." But *Oh my God* kept running through his head.

"I suggest," the emperor said coldly, "that you remember what happened to your predecessor. One week!"

Ozenscebo's gaze danced lightly over the vase, and examined it closely, his wonderful idea erasing the annoyance of the artist.

A young page, no more than six, dressed in the royal livery quietly entered the room. The Lionman at the door looked down at him, and smiled in recognition—and encouragement. Elena was an exacting mistress, but kind. The emperor was explosive. Heartened, the youngster approached his master.

"Your Majesty," the boy said as he bowed deeply. He held the pose while waiting for recognition.

"Yes?"

"The empress wishes to inquire whether or

not you will be joining her in the audience chamber?"

Ozenscebo whirled, and raised his hand preparing to swing on the child. The Lionman at the door stiffened. He would not interfere with his emperor, but he would not forget an unkindness to a child, either. But the emperor restrained himself, and satisfied his urge for destruction by knocking the vase off its pedestal. It shattered, spilling water and flowers and shards in a moist cascade.

"You tell Her Majesty..." the furious emperor began. "No. Never mind. I'll remind that bitch myself who's the emperor here!"

He stormed off, leaving in his wake an amazed gathering of subjects.

Lionmen threw open the heavy doors to the audience chamber. The ornately carved wood flew weightily against the walls and thudded there, reverberating. A stream of Guardsmen followed their fellows into the room and formed an expanding wedge that pressed the courtiers against the walls. Into this wedge strode Ozenscebo, raging.

"What is the meaning of this, Elena?" he bellowed as he tore down the aisle opened by his troops. "Have you spent so much time messing in my business you've forgotten who's the emperor here?" He bore down on his wife like an avenging angel, his wrath, righteous in his own eyes, flaming.

Elena's delicate flower-blue eyes opened widely at Ozenscebo's entrance, though to a casual observer she never lost her serene expression. She was startled, not by the outburst—there had been enough of those lately—but by the violence of it. It took her a moment to comprehend what was happening. Then she stood, and taking the first move of any good mother, she protected her young. She dropped her right hand behind the folds of her full royal-blue velvet skirts where it would not be visible to her bellowing husband and motioned to Natanha. The princess moved quickly and quietly behind her mother, dropping her head and pulling in as much as possible on herself. The idea was to be as invisible as possible. As much as she wanted to, Elena did not turn to see what Natanha had done. If her daughter had not understood, she was in grave danger, but to turn to her was to fix the emperor's wrath in a direction Elena did not wish it to go.

I've got to act fast, the empress thought to herself while she struggled to fight down surprise and panic. *If I don't, I'll lose control totally.* She dropped a tiny curtsy to her husband, and bowed her head in humble, if feigned, contrition.

"Forgive me, Your Majesty. I meant no insult. I was merely concerned lest the empire suffer for lack of your wise counsel."

Ozenscebo had been about to mount the steps to throw his wife off his new throne, bodily if necessary. But now he paused, one foot on the riser, and considered. It was not often he heard good things from Elena, and here she was being publicly contrite. He turned enough to catch a glimpse of his courtiers standing along the wall. They were agog, many with mouths hanging open, some looking hungry for blood. It was enough. The emperor was not in the mood to entertain the masses. "You're quite right, Elena, my love," he said facetiously. "We have business here."

Elena stepped to her right, keeping her back to the throne, and, still keeping it behind her out of sight of her husband, put out a hand to Natanha, who took it eagerly. The empress pressed down firmly on her child's hand, keeping her close behind her skirts, while she retreated from the emperor's reach.

"Now that you have arrived, Your Majesty, you no longer need my poor woman's advice. With your permission, I will retire and leave you to the work at hand so you may handle it properly and without my distracting you."

Ozenscebo beamed. That was the way a woman should behave! Humbly! His anger had had one good effect, at least. He waved languidly at his wife. "By all means," he said as he sprawled across his throne. "Withdraw."

Elena did not hesitate. She spun and headed for the family entrance as quickly as she could without running, drawing Natanha to her side, and then pushing her through the door first. Then she palmed the lock without even breaking her stride so it would close the door behind her.

Mercer Parry had been watching the episode with something bordering on glee. He had hoped this time Elena had pushed her royal slug of a husband too far. When Elena managed to leave the killing grounds without so much as a scratch, he was severely disappointed.

Damn you, bitch! he screamed inwardly. *You always manage to slither out of trouble!*

There had to be a way to get rid of Elena! He turned and walked thoughtfully out of the chamber. The emperor would now have to deal

with the business of the empire and would not
be free to play for hours. He would not look for
Parry until then.

But his anger! That is fascinating! Parry mused
as he walked down the hallway alone. *Perhaps!
Perhaps there is a way to get rid of the whore?* He
chuckled warmly as the glimmer of an idea
fleshed itself out. *If I can manage to turn Elena
into an annoyance for Ozenscebo, to make her
look bad, to see to it she distracts and disturbs
him, there is a chance, a small but perfect chance,
that the maggot will do my work for me!* Parry
hummed a snatch of a popular tune as the sheer
elegance of his idea took hold. *And I won't even
have to find a way to blame it on the rebels!*

Parry was so happy he could hardly contain
himself. He hummed and whistled as he made
his way through the endless maze of corridors
toward his chambers. He was so happy even the
thought of spending the afternoon with his plain
plastic furniture was not depressing.

No! he thought gleefully. *Not alone! My lover,
my beautiful lover will be waiting for me! It's
strange to think there's someone waiting for me
today,* he reflected as he hummed. *I'm glad we
decided to share my apartment.*

Things were going so well Parry could hardly
stand it. His lover had just moved in with him,
he'd seen Elena have to swallow her pride, and,
even more amusingly, flee, and Ozie, the bastard, was getting angrier and sloppier by the
day. Why, he, Mercer, had even figured out a
way to get rid of that bitch of an empress without having to raise a hand! Wonderful! The only
thing that stood in the way of the plan was that

damned Lionman. But he could be dealt with. If nothing else, he could send one of those fools, Paschasia or Templa, to Lawwnum with a gift. Of course, the gift would immediately explode before that pussy Lawwnum had time to figure it out. If the gift took the fool, too, so much the better. It would be one less idiot to tolerate, one less link to the envoy Mercer Parry. But he was forgetting. After today there would not be so many fools in this world. Another nice turn.

When he opened his door he was smiling broadly. Today was one of those rare days when everything went right. He was feeling so good he immediately went for a glass of roed. He could afford it today. And if his plans came together the way they should, he'd never have to do without this costly luxury again. He sipped appreciatively. His darling had remembered to ice it down for him. Parry took another sip and threw back his head to savor it. He could almost see the colors brighten. He walked to the sound system and programmed some low, sensual music, then turned to the ventilation system for a scent of something pleasant.

"Lilies of the valley?" he questioned himself. "Tarasti?" The aroma of the bittersweet herb was one of his favorites. "No! I have it! Perfect! Oranges!" He hummed along tunelessly with the music he had playing, and set the controls for oranges. "How close we came!" he exclaimed. "We almost had the whole damned lot." He raised his glass in a toast. "Here's to death, explosives, and oranges!"

A complete change came over his face. "I wonder where my beauty is? The roed was iced, so my darling can't be far..." He walked to the bedroom door and quietly opened it. The bed-chamber lights were down. The form sprawled on top of the covers was limned with the bright-ness from the sitting room.

"Gorgeous!" Mercer breathed, awed by the sight of the relaxed body that was now all his. "Lovely!"

"Darling," he whispered as he walked closer. There was not a stir from the bed. He sat down softly on the edge to get a better look at the prone form of his lover. Thomas was not tall, something that caused the boy some problems. But he was exquisitely muscled. The bright white light from the sitting room haloed him, giving every ripple, every rise, a hot highlight and deep black shadow. Every contour was pal-pably visible to Mercer's roed-steeped eyes.

The envoy reached out to touch Thomas's dark hair, then stopped, wishing to enjoy a little longer the carefree perfection of his sleeping nude. The broad shoulders rose and fell gently with each indrawn breath, and the finely-drawn muscles moved irregularly with the sleep rhythms. The dark long hair fell across them and down around the square, full chin of his side-turned face. Thomas's mouth, with its deeply pink wide lips, was slightly open, reveal-ing his even, pink-white teeth. His thick, per-fectly rounded leg was extended, bent at the knee, and covered with a heavy pelt of dark hair. His impeccably rounded buttocks called for Mercer's caress.

Though he waited as long as he could, pro-longing his visual pleasure, Mercer could re-strain himself no more. He leaned forward and dripped the dregs of his roed on Thomas's sleeping shoulder. There was the slightest quiver of golden flesh, but no more. The boy did not wake.

"Thomas," Mercer called, impatient now that the roed had him in its full grasp. "Thomas, wake up."

The young man turned over, propped himself unsteadily on one still-sleepy elbow, and slit open his chocolaty-rich brown eyes. "Mercer?" he asked through a yawn. "I thought you'd be with the emperor for hours yet."

"He won't be needing me, so I came directly to you." He smiled with as much sincerity as he could muster. "It's been a good day for me. I feel exceptionally fine." He ran his finger down the boy's breastbone, and on down his stomach past his hips. "I want you to please me some more."

Thomas's long black lashes fluttered over his eyes, and his hand met and intertwined with the envoy's. "Tell me, Mercer. Just what happened to make you feel so good?"

Parry launched into a full description of the day's events, not forgetting to glorify himself in the process. In his telling, every turn of events had been directed personally by his hand.

Thomas sat and watched as Parry spoke, his big eyes, opened wide, supposedly at Parry's cleverness.

Parry's hand curled gently in Thomas's hair, and pulled the boy's face close to his own. "Enough talk!" he exclaimed huskily.

Thomas gave in to his embrace, and closed his eyes. But he separated his mind from his body's activities. *Eight weeks!* he said to himself. *For eight long weeks I've put up with you, you pervert!*

*But I've finally got you. I can't wait to get back to
Loni with this!*

Early the next morning there was a pounding
on Mercer Parry's door. He lifted his head
slightly from the pillow, and dropped it heavily
again. He was hung over. Too much roed, too
much sensuality. He was wiped out, and with no
hope of immediate recovery. But the pounding
continued until Thomas crawled from under
him and answered the door.

Thomas returned to the bedroom. "It was a
page. The emperor wants to see you."

Parry put out his hand to Thomas in an invit-
ing gesture. "Let him wait. Come back to bed
now."

But Thomas avoided his grasp and went to
the closet and began pulling out clothes. "You
know Ozenscebo has no patience. You'd better
hurry."

Parry groaned, but picked his head up off the
pillow again. "I'm going. Make sure the shower
is hot, will you?"

A small shudder ran through Mercer as he
watched Thomas head off for the bath. Just
what was it that the emperor wanted at this
hour of the morning?

Ozenscebo jumped off the throne the moment
he saw Parry. "Wait till you see!" he exclaimed
excitedly. "Just wait!" He grabbed Parry by the
arm, motioned his questioning guard to stay behind, and began leading the envoy through the

corridors of the palace, down belowground into rooms not generally seen by the public.

"Just look at this!" the emperor exclaimed as he opened the door where he'd at last stopped.

Mercer drew in a sharp breath when he followed the emperor into the glaringly lit room. There, strapped painfully to extremely awkwardly shaped restraints, were Jad Templa and Seda Paschasia. They had been stripped of all their finery, and now, except for the fact that Seda was still taller than Jad, it was difficult to tell them apart. Jad was bent over backward at a sharp angle in a flexible table, the top of her head resting in a congealing pool of her own blood on what had been an immaculately clean tiled floor. Seda's lips kissed her shins, her doubled abdomen resting on a knife-edged support that swung lazily from the ceiling. They were both sweaty, dirty, and damaged, their faces puffy with a beating, and discolored all over.

"Your Majesty! How nice of you to join us!" exclaimed a little man who emerged from behind a stack of unpleasant chrome-plated sharp surgical implements. "They're prepared just the way you requested."

Ozenscebo patted the man's tiny shoulder. "Thank you, Doctor." He turned to Parry. "They've been implicating you. Isn't that ridiculous?"

Parry, unsure of where the emperor was leading and just how much he already knew, merely nodded, being currently incapable of speech. Of course they would implicate him. Wasn't it he who had dropped the hints in the right ears, indicating that Jad and Seda were guilty of the explosion in the throne room?

But the emperor continued, blind to Parry's hesitation and obvious worry. "The doctor has given them roed, so they are exquisitely aware of his ministrations. Look how nicely he's prepared them for us."

Morbidly fascinated, Mercer walked over to get a better look at his cronies while the emperor took a chair. Both of Jad's eyes were so swollen she could not open them. Seda's mouth was torn up so he could see where she was missing teeth. Blood and saliva dribbled moistly down her chin. Both of them had large gashes under each small breast where burning incense had been inserted. Even Mercer, cruel as he was, felt a little sick. It took a moment or two for him to arrange his face into a careless mask before he turned back to Ozenscebo.

The doctor had brought a bowl of fruit and some wine and roed for the emperor, and placed it on a small table at the arm of Ozenscebo's chair. His Majesty picked up a ripe fruit, bit into it hungrily, and wiped away the juices that dribbled down his chin with the sleeve of his silk gown. Then he cocked his head to one side and frowned slightly.

"But they're only moaning," he complained. "I want them to scream. I love screams."

"Yes, Majesty, yes," the doctor said, and pulled two hot irons out of a brazier. He applied them quickly, one to each prisoner, and they sang loudly if not sweetly. They quickly subsided to moans as soon as he stopped, however. Both of them were too worn out for sustained arias.

"More, Doctor," said the emperor with an excited wave of his hand.

The little man reached for a glistening implement with long thin hands covered with dark hair, thick, like fur, and held up a flensing knife.

"No, no. Too delicate." Ozenscebo stood, and wiped his hands down the sides of his full skirts. "Let me show you what I had in mind." There was a coal scuttle on the floor next to the brazier. In it rested a supply of charcoal and a large scoop for filling the brazier. The emperor picked up the scoop and looked at it, appraising. Then he turned it in his hand so he held the front edge of the scoop with the handle pointing outward. He walked to Jad, whose thigh was not much larger around than the scoop, forced her legs apart, and rammed the handle between her legs, shoving the scoop higher and higher into her until blood ran down his arms and her legs in red rivers. "You tried to kill my heir," he mumbled over and over again as he wrenched the scoop viciously sideways.

Parry swayed. It was only by force of will that he stayed on his feet. He was next! This was what Ozie had in store for him! This, or something less pleasant.

The emperor dropped the scoop and picked up the hem of his skirts to wipe his hands, corrupting the baby-blue silks. He turned to Parry with a sickening smile, panting.

My God! the envoy thought. *Now he's ready for me!*

But Ozenscebo missed the fear in his playmate's eyes. "Wasn't that fun?" he asked happily. He advanced on Parry, but it did not register that the envoy backed for every step he took. "I want to thank you for your loyalty. I want you to know you will be rewarded." He grasped Parry's shoulder in a friendly fashion.

"Excuse me, Sire," the little doctor broke in. "What about the other one."

The emperor turned away from Parry to consider. "Mmmm. I've had enough for today. Amuse yourself."

Chapter Seven

———◆———

KI ENTERED HIS APARTMENT, and paused. There was something in the air. Something...

"Mmumna take this blasted ventilator!" he rumbled as it pulled the scent away from him once more.

He sniffed again. Perfume. Yes, that was it. Perfume. Strong and heavily floral. And, oddly enough, coming from the garden.

Ki dropped his mechanical hand so it rested on the hilt of the katana. He had been practicing with it and it was no longer a stranger, but it did not have the reach and feel of his hoj. At times he regretted that. Like now.

He walked to his French doors, opened them, and stepped out. It took only a moment for his eyes to search the entire garden. Mama-san stood in the farthest sunny corner. She held a goblet of delicate crystal full of roed. Next to her on an almost-level rock sat a beaker that had been full of the rosy fluid.

"About time, asshole," she said acidly.

Ki's hand clenched the raspy wrappings of the

sword tightly. He did not take her opening comment well. "To what do I owe the...honor of your presence?" he asked in an equally acid tone.

Mama-san did not reply immediately. His calmness was not what she had expected after her opening gambit. When she noticed she had paused, she tried to cover it up by imbibing more of her roed, then she stooped to fill her glass from the beaker. It rocked slightly as she replaced it on the uneven boulder.

Ki felt the sun on his shoulders, soaked up by his mantle, and relished it. It was always cool here compared to Nide, and no matter how long he spent on Earth, he never quite got used to it. But though the sun was pleasant and welcome, he could not breathe well. Mama-san's choking perfume forbade him that simple comfort. Her scent was so strong he could not even smell the rest of his garden. *She probably did that on purpose*, he thought. *She's been waiting for me.*

Mama-san's face was red and puffy with anger. She was furious, and she wanted Ki to know it. "What in the name of all that's holy do you think you're doing?"

"Specify," he answered coldly. He was not in the mood for twenty questions, especially from an overly fragrant madam.

She sneered at him. "If you want to damn yourself, that's fine. If you want to damn yourself *and* Opal, that's fine, too. But not me. You stay away from me. I don't want your help in that or any other department."

Genuinely nonplussed, Ki said, "I don't understand."

Mama-san pulled a small box out of her sash. Though she held it as if she wished it were a weapon, the look on her face was one that could have led someone to believe she held a particularly repulsive reptile. "This!" she spat, and she threw the box at Ki's head.

In a motion as smooth as Mama-san's silk kimono, Ki grabbed the box out of the air. The weight of the missile was negligible. The box itself would crush if he closed his fingers. He looked up at Mama-san curiously. Full of roed and too much emotion—a potentially dangerous mixture, as the roed enhanced every emotion and sense—she was reeling. Ki looked away, disgusted by her display, yet forced by the demands of etiquette not to notice. He opened the box.

"Where did you get this?" he asked when the magnificent marquise winked at him in the brilliant sunlight.

"From that goddamned tramp!" Mama-san answered angrily, and put a hand to her head as her anger began to affect her seriously. She adjusted her balance with the elaborate care of a drunk, then dropped her hand to look at Ki. "Don't you realize what kind of danger you're putting us in?" she asked him almost pleadingly.

"I assure you, I'm not—"

"The hell you're not!" she screamed. Her lips pulled back from her teeth in a terrible grimace. "I've got eyes, Ki Lawwnum, and so does the emperor. He's got more eyes than even you suspect. How do you think he'd react to one of his goddamned Lionmen, the commander of his goddamned precious Guard, no less, messing around with his current favorite?" She was breathing hard, and sheer fury made her voice high and thin.

For more than two heartbeats Ki did not

move. Then he dropped his hand from his sword, and clenched it with a tight, mechanical clink. He looked down at the diamond, watching its heart warm in the sun, then closed the box and tucked it carefully into his sleeve. He pulled down the edge of his sleeve into proper alignment, then met Mama-san's eye.

"You are correct. The gift was inappropriate." He turned back to his apartment, never having closed with his adversary, yet feeling defeated.

A shriek reverberated off his back. "I'm not finished yet!" the madam roared. She had waited nearly an hour for this, working herself up the whole time. She had a lot more yet to say.

Ki opened his door before he paused. The hand holding the knob was white at the knuckles, so strong was the hold he had on his anger and embarrassment. He did not turn to look at her.

"Yes, you are," he rumbled as he disappeared into the solitude of his own quarters, leaving the sunshine to an unappreciative Mama-san.

Elena's back was to Natanha. Though the empress was facing the mirror of her dressing table, she tried not to let her daughter see her reflection. There was a fierce blue and red bruise crawling up the side of Elena's face, and that upset her daughter greatly. Involuntarily, Elena winced as she applied heavy pancake makeup to cover the snaking bruise.

"Mama, I don't understand what's happening," Natanha complained, and her mother could hear the fear in her daughter's voice. "Daddy's been angry for almost two weeks."

Elena sighed, and nodded. Ozenscebo had

been on the warpath ever since, as he phrased it, Elena had summoned him. For some reason he insisted she was trying to preempt him, when in fact all she was trying to do was run his empire with some sort of discipline. Something had to stand between the Grand Imperium Alligantia and anarchy, even if it was only a very tired, very scared woman.

Natanha's skirt of colorful, cheerful ribbons did not suit her unhappy face, but it rustled happily anyway as the princess came to stand behind her mother and put her arms around the empress's neck for reassurance.

"Mama," she repeated sadly, "I don't understand. Daddy's always been difficult, but you and I could always find a way to get what we wanted. When I was little all I had to do was promise to stay out of his way. But now we can't do anything right. And he hit you in public!"

Thinking only that she was grateful Ozenscebo's rings had not laid open her cheek, Elena put down her makeup sponge and reached up to take one of the small, dainty hands that were clasped over her bosom. Holding it gently, she turned slowly so that she faced her daughter squarely. "He is the emperor. I am his wife. He may do with me as he wishes."

"But all you did was suggest beef for dinner—" she whined.

Elena cut her off. "No, child. He is the emperor." The empress tugged softly on her daughter's hand so that the child knelt in front of her mother. Their eyes were now on a level as Elena sat in the tiny dressing-table chair. "Don't trust your father. And remember, if something happens to me, you are to do as I've explained. Do not attempt to resist the emperor."

Considering her next words carefully, Elena continued. "And this is going to be hard. You cannot trust the Lionmen, either. They take orders."

Natanha's eyes became very large and round as she began to take in the implications of her mother's instruction. She paused, trying to absorb the sense of it, then asked guilelessly, "Even Ki?"

Elena tried diligently to keep her voice even and level. "If something happens to me, it will be very difficult for him. Stay away from him. He may make the wrong decision." The empress could feel her throat closing as tears threatened. She could not afford to let Natanha see how upset she was. "Go and find my maid, child," she said as she turned back to her mirror. "That woman is useless. I can't find any of my jewelry."

Natanha obeyed, but she moved slowly and heavily. She had never considered she would be cut off from her beloved Ki, her teacher and special friend.

Elena watched her firstborn in her mirror and thought, *I've got to find out what Ozie is up to. I must keep Natanha safe.* She picked up the sponge and applied another layer of pancake to the bruise. *I must check again with Midron. They must be prepared to care for her. But how can I know what to do when there are so many things I can't find out?*

Parry stood at the glass wall of the garden that overlooked the Lionmen's courtyard and watched them practicing. The garden, with all of its delights, its rare fruit trees, delicate flowers, shimmering waterfalls, had disappeared for him. His concentration was devoted solely to the groups below. Each Lionman, even the ones still in the jumpsuits that denoted recruits, moved like water running over stones; there might be a ripple, but the major portion just flowed. They were exquisite, vicious, and ultimately in Parry's way.

Especially Lawwnum. The commander got in the envoy's way every time. It seemed no matter what sort of plan Parry conceived, no matter how elaborate or how simple, that pussy found a way to circumvent it before it could even begin. Even the ridiculous plots of Paschasia and Templa, as bizarre and subnormal as they could be, were frustrated by that— Parry could not find a word bad enough to explain how he felt about the commander.

And as stupid as Ozenscebo was, as easily led, he was absolutely stubborn about one thing. He would not part with his commander of the Lionman Guard.

"If he had to do one intelligent thing," Parry said to himself under his breath, "why did it have to be keeping Lawwnum?"

He sat down on a marble bench and flinched slightly as its coolness surprised him through his thin garb. His clothes had to be stylish, so he of course adopted the full-skirted gowns the emperor preferred. But where Ozenscebo's were heavy brocaded silks, Parry's were the thinnest, cheapest synthetics he could buy and still be presentable in court. He leaned forward to get a better view of the activity below him, and leaned his elbows on the metal rim holding the glass panels in place. A shiver ran down him as the glass and metal, cooled by the autumnal winds, chilled his skin.

He heard a footfall behind him, and found another reason to shiver. Exactly one pace behind him stood two Guardsmen in full regalia. They both wore the gray of a lieutenant, so these were not mere messengers. And he had not heard them approaching until they wanted him to.

"Yes?" Parry squeaked.

The Guardsman on Parry's left took hold of the envoy's arm. Parry felt the roughness of the man's palm through his thin gown, and felt the fingers curl completely around his unmuscled limb. The thick nail of the thumb pressed heavily into his soft flesh.

"The emperor wishes to see you, Envoy," the other Guardsman said in his rumbling way. "We have been sent to escort you."

The first Guardsman pulled Parry out from behind the bench. As the envoy emerged, the second grabbed his other arm, and Parry began to skip steps as they lightly held him above the floor to hurry him along. There would have been no other way for Parry to match their quick, long strides. Parry was panicking. He had been sent for many times, but Ozenscebo had always sent a page or one of his bevy of servants. Never before had Lionmen been dispatched for escort service. Unless he was being arrested?

"Where are you taking me?" he asked as they piled him into an elevator. He was thoroughly frightened when neither of them deigned to answer.

They reached the ground floor of the palace, and dragged Parry out into the pale sunshine of the main courtyard behind the front gate of the palace. A cold wind whistled by and stuck its frigid fingers under his finery. This time, however, he was held too rigidly to be allowed to shiver. The Guardsmen crossed the courtyard quickly, and entered the other side of the palace. This was not the public portion, and Parry had rarely been here, though his last visit had been very recent. He had never liked it. It was dark, and just like old movies; it looked damp and unkempt. It also smelled, something Parry could not abide at the best of times, and he gagged silently. He had never been able to figure out exactly what the smell was, but he associated it with age. He was beginning to think, however, he would never have a chance to smell that way himself as, since the Guardsmen were leading him deeper into the palace, he was about to die young.

Over and over again the envoy asked himself, *What did I do wrong? Where's my mistake?* He never found an answer. There should be absolutely nothing Ozenscebo could hang on him. Nothing. Unless Lawwnum ...

He looked around anxiously. He was deeper into the palace now than he had ever been before. The wood, metal, glass, and steel of the upper levels had been replaced with the stone of the mountain the palace stood on. He was inside the medieval fortress, which had been carved from the bones of the earth. That meant there was nothing below but interrogation rooms, those small cubicles where one would say anything to gain some peace, no matter how permanent.

The Guardsmen stopped in front of a heavy steel door, and one of them pounded upon it with a closed fist, then pushed it open. Parry struggled briefly, but was restrained by the simple expedient of being lifted off the floor and stretched between his escort. The three of them entered the cell, and when Parry opened his eyes enough to see, there was Ozenscebo enthroned in an ornately carved wooden chair upholstered with red velvet that was completely out of place in the blazingly lit room full of chains and machinery. The only other furniture was a stainless steel table, and an extremely large vat, about six feet across and three feet deep.

"Outside. I won't be needing you," the emperor said to his two Guardsmen.

They opened their hands eagerly, and dropped Parry into a heap on the stone floor. They turned their backs quickly as the envoy began to crawl toward the emperor, pleading for mercy in a broken, wet voice. Ozenscebo did not move until the door had been closed behind the Lionmen.

"Oh, stand up," he said deprecatingly to Parry. "You haven't done anything. It was just a joke." He looked his envoy up and down with a critical eye. "I must say you didn't play very well." Then he dismissed that as he recalled his purpose in having Parry brought to him. He turned eagerly toward the vat. "Come here. There's something I want you to see."

Parry grabbed the table and pulled himself weakly to his feet. Some joke! A man with a weaker heart would not have survived it. Parry wobbled, and grabbed the edge of the table for support. He almost hadn't survived it himself.

I want to kill this maggot right now, he thought, and began to reach for the poisoned steel pin that was always concealed in the heel of his boot. *I want him to know what it feels like to be a joke.* But then he stopped. One sound, no matter how slight, that did not feel right, one yell, and

the guards just outside the door would be on
him in a moment. *Another time, maggot,* Parry
promised himself. *I'll have you yet.* Then he
pulled himself together and walked to the edge
of the vat.

The tub was full of desiccant, the white crystals blinking dully in the extremely bright light
of the cell. Ozenscebo pushed a red button on
the wall, and machinery began humming. A
series of chains that hung down into the vat
went taut, then began to shift slightly as they
lifted a weight.

Parry watched with total disinterest, his attention still on his racing heartbeat, until he
saw a slender hand rising in an elegant arc,
fingers sweetly curved, from the desiccant. But
it was no human hand. Then there was a gleam
from a green crystal, and Parry was sure his
color was exactly the same shade. Opal was rising slowly from her dry tomb, completely rigid.
Her face was frozen in fear, and there had been
plenty of time for terror. One hand was extended a little, as if she were warding off a blow
that never came, or pleading for help that was
never given, and it was that hand that Parry had
seen first. But in spite of her current statuesque
bearing, she was still beautiful, and Parry, who
never felt anything, felt sad.

"What happened?" Parry just managed to
choke the question through his restricted throat.

"Don't ask so many questions," sniped a glee-
ful Ozenscebo. "Just watch. You'll enjoy this."

The statue was brought over the floor and
gently lowered till it stood of its own accord.

"Do you think she's still alive?" Parry asked.

The emperor cocked his head to one side, considering. "I don't really know, but I think she is.

I've heard it said her people can remain this way for quite some time before they die. Of course"—he chuckled—"most of them don't end up this way on purpose."

Ozenscebo moved just enough to pull the table out from under Parry and station it close to Opal. Mercer noticed for the first time the elegant leather box resting there. The emperor opened it eagerly. Inside rested six gold hammers, all of various sizes and shapes, each in its own satin nest. In the hard, white light they looked sickly yellow and sinister.

"Beautiful, aren't they?" the emperor asked as he took one from its case. "I had them specially made for me. See how they fit my hand?" He held the hammer up for Mercer's inspection, then set it down again. "Have you envoys managed any kind of a settlement in that Midron affair?" he asked as he took the smallest of the hammers and walked toward Opal. "I'm expecting something from you soon, you know," he said as he stooped, raised the hammer, and let fall a blow on Opal's little toe. There was a soft *plink*, and a chunk of opal rolled away.

For once in his life Mercer Parry was out of his depth. Here was a man who was more warped than even himself. But as the emperor continued to *tap, tap*, Mercer found his revulsion dissipating and being replaced, quickly, by an intense interest in the operation.

"She makes some nice sounds," Ozenscebo said when he saw Parry lean closer for a look. "You give me good advice. I think I'll appoint you prime minister." The little golden hammer fell again with another *plink*. "What do you think about that?" The emperor hit at Opal's extended hand, and a long fissure grew up her arm.

Now totally fascinated, Parry mumbled, "Honored, sir," and wished to know if Opal was feeling any of this. If she was, it was the most exquisite torture ever devised. Her silicon skin was fissuring deeply, sending spider webs of cracks all along her arm.

Ozenscebo picked up a larger hammer and hit again at the hand. A large crack developed at the forearm, and the hand fell to the floor, shattering into pieces. He went back to his chair to pick up the goblet of roed resting next to it on the cool floor, and sipped delicately as he walked back to his damaged Opal. "Join me?" he asked Parry. "There are plenty of hammers."

But Parry had regained some of his equilibrium, and he bowed slightly. "I wouldn't dream of depriving you, Sire."

Ozenscebo shrugged, and picked up another hammer with a rounded peen. He placed his hand behind Opal's damaged arm, and began circling her breast with light taps, eventually creating a connecting network of lacy lacerations encircling her breast entirely. Then he took the largest hammer again, and hit heavily above her nipple. The entire breast severed, and he caught it as it fell.

"They were so nice, weren't they, Parry? Mmmm. I think I'll make this into a doorstop." He chuckled wickedly. "Or maybe I should give it to Ki for his garden." He started to laugh, then stopped and wiped his eyes. "No, I don't think he'd appreciate the thought. But I do have another idea. Elena needs something nice. She's been moping ever since I hit her, and she's so difficult when she mopes. But this piece is too big, don't you think?" He stooped to pick up a piece of the hand that had shattered on the floor, set it neatly aside, and then ran to hit at her hair for a piece of peridot.

Parry could hear him mumbling, "Nice contrast."

Chapter Eight

LIGHT CREPT THROUGH the slatted blinds to throw a latticework pattern across the bed in the darkened room. Colwin stretched, and looked down at the girl at his side. She was attractive, beautiful even, with rich, glowing olive skin and black, black hair that flowed heavily to her waist. But Colwin hardly saw her, just as he had hardly felt her when he hadn't been able to give her what she wanted a little while ago. His mind was to full of what Loni had said for the allure of any woman to penetrate right now. Prime minister! They were going to make that slime Parry prime minister!

But how had Loni known that? There hadn't been any sort of formal announcement. Rumors of it hadn't even begun to filter down the grapevine. He made a fist and hit through the coverlet to his naked knee. *Damn that woman!* exploded in his angry mind. *She wouldn't tell me how she knew. We're going to have to keep a closer watch on her. If anything happens to her, we're all going to be lost.* He sighed heavily. *Let's face it. I'm worried about her.*

Small noises from the outside made themselves known to some part of his awareness as he picked absently at the comforter. He'd never been unable to perform before, and it bothered him, but not so much that he didn't hear the soft rumble of a room-service cart outside the door, or the horns honking far below the window. He had been raised on the streets; one thing you never did if you wanted to survive was stop listening. You might not consciously hear it, but you listened anyway, and catalogued every sound.

His frustration was building daily. He wanted to kill the emperor. Elena, too. She was some control on Ozie, but not nearly enough. And every day that goal seemed just as far away as the day before, no matter how hard they fought, or how thoroughly they schemed. They never got any closer to being rid of the scum.

His men were running into things they weren't expecting, too. Some of them weren't coming back. *But they can't be dead,* he told himself. *I couldn't handle that.*

But Lawwnum, that pussy bastard, him I want to see dead. Hell, I want to kill him myself. I want to be alone with that slat-eyed freak for five minutes. He'll never cut down another of my men like he did that day in the audience chamber.

He shifted uncomfortably. *But I understand when Loni says we'll be butchered if we attack the castle. We're good, but there's not enough of us.* Then he chuckled lightly. *Oh, hell, Loni keeps me in line just about as much as Elena keeps Ozie in line.*

But that thought brought him right back to

Parry. How had the worm gotten himself appointed P.M.?

His companion sighed in her sleep, and shifted, pulling her hand all unaware down his side. It tickled, and he shivered, but it was warm and tantalizing all the same. *Must have been that bastard Parry that kept me from showing this lady what a man is all about.*

Teresa felt him shift when her hand contacted flesh, and she opened her eyes, as if she'd been sleeping, heavily and slowly. "You awake, lover?" she asked huskily.

"Yeah."

She moved closer, her long fingernails playing with the hair on his chest, and just touching the skin underneath. "You ready to try again?" she asked sweetly, invitingly.

"What the hell," Colwin answered, and buried his face in the hollow between her breasts.

She twined her fingers in his hair, and stared up at the ceiling. Loni said he'd been acting funny ever since the explosion in the throne room, but not being able to please her was more than funny. Colwin was seriously worried about something. No wonder Loni wanted her to find out what the problem was. But she'd actually found out very little. Loni was not going to like that, but at the same time she'd appreciate that he didn't talk to every girl he took to bed. But now it was time to institute plan two: relax him.

She pushed him off her, and pinned his shoulders to the bed with small, delicate hands. She kissed him fiercely. "You just lay back, lover, and let Teresa handle this. We won't have any trouble this time," she said as she slid her hand down his chest, down his abdomen, and into his thick, curly pubic hair.

He laughed richly. "I can already feel that we won't," he said, and relaxed. She could be the master this time.

The old-style helicopter wove its way noisily over the city center, around and around and around. The sound of its engines could be heard even over the dampeners, and that made the loudspeaker announcements somewhat hard to understand. But repeated as often as they were, all day long, it was eventually understood by anyone not profoundly deaf.

Loni watched from one of the windows of her private office. Two or three times the copter had come very close to her building, giving her a better view of the two bodies hanging beneath than she really wanted. There was not much left of Seda Paschasia and Jad Templa. Both were so badly mangled their mothers would have had a hard time recognizing them. Loni was glad her office was totally soundproofed. She didn't want to hear over and over again how loyal citizens should turn in any other traitors. It would have driven her quite mad. But she couldn't seem to turn away from the window. There was something fascinating in a grisly fashion about how the emperor chose to show off his dead enemies. Loni thought things like that had gone out in the Middle Ages.

She looked down at the crowds on the sidewalks. They were not behaving the way they usually did. Some stood and stared at the sight. Some moved slowly, eyes down. The usual energy flowing around the downtown area was absent today, as if Ozenscebo had sucked it all away and kept it for himself.

Loni rested her head against the transparency and felt the coolness against her skin. She closed her eyes against all that was going on outside, and just listened to her building. Hers. All of it. All two hundred stories. This office was on the 197th story. Above it was her apartment. Below was the business empire it had taken all her life to build. The first fifteen or so floors of her small empire were devoted to the finest and most expensive shops in Osaka. In all of Capitol Center there was not a finer collection of things from anywhere in the empire. The rents from the stores paid for a large portion of the property taxes. The rest of the revenue came from the resort and bordello. Loni smiled to herself. The bordello was the best in the universe. The classiest. The richest. The prettiest. And she worked very hard to keep it that way. Even Ozenscebo would be jealous if he ever came to visit.

She was disturbed by Colwin and a few others entering her office. They went to the windows as if drawn by force, and stood silently watching the bodies being dangled over the heads of the crowds.

Loni's thoughts turned back to the events of the day. She was fairly certain the bomb had to have been planted by Parry. The two beneath the copter were his buddies, but they wouldn't have had the brains to figure out a plot all on their own. And it must have been meant for the empress. The emperor had been drawn away just before the bomb went off. It was too neat otherwise.

Colwin broke the silence. "Loni, what is that bastard Parry up to?"

Loni shrugged. The only thing that made sense was Parry wanting to control the empire himself. But surely even he could see he'd never get away with it. If he made even the tiniest mistake, Lawwnum would see to him in the blink of an eye.

She turned to look at Colwin. Something had happened there. He was more quiet, more composed, than he'd been in some time. Some relaxation must have been just what he needed. He was even useful again.

The copter swept by again, this time so close the windows of the office rattled. A chill swept over Loni. The two were so terribly mangled...

This place is soundproof, she decided, *but that's not enough. I don't want to die the way they did. If I have to go, I want it to be quick. I'm going to have some sort of device installed in here to insure that. Ozie will never drag my body around like that.*

Darkness was settling over the city finally. The crowds below were thinning as shoppers headed home. Soon the people who worked in the city would head out, too, leaving only those who stayed to play at night. Loni hoped darkness would put an end to Ozie's show. But at that instant, bright, hard, white lights came on under the helicopter. Once more the attention of all those on the street, and, Loni supposed, those in the buildings who watched as she did, returned to the gruesome duo. In the glare of those lights, with all eyes on them, the bodies were cut loose to drop into the river. One of them missed, however, and smacked hard on the concrete before falling finally into the cover of darkness and water. Loni shut her eyes.

Those two were only stooges, she said vehemently to herself. *I swear, if we manage to get rid of Ozie, Parry goes too.*

Chapter Nine

I SHOULD NOT be doing this. I should be taking care of security, overseeing my men.

It was not Ki's idea to have his portrait painted. He thought it was rather silly. After all, he had no place in the royal family. But the emperor thought he would make a ferocious addition to their grouping. Besides, he wanted to show off the sword he had so graciously presented to Ki. And what the emperor wanted...

At least this was supposed to be the last sitting. Hopefully, that would be the case. The artist seemed competent enough. Perhaps he'd had the good sense to be accurate. Ki didn't think he was in the mood for misjudgment today.

He took his place, and assumed the pose the artist had selected. The young man was shocked he did not need to adjust the colonel, but Ki only smiled. He knew what the position had been.

Then he lost himself to thought, totally blocking out the artist and the inanities of the few dilettantes who watched. He had much to think about. Why in Mmumna's name had he gotten such a cryptic note from Mama-san this morning? One word only: *bastard*. And the only signature was her perfume. There was no doubt Ki would recognize it, but why was he a bastard this time, and why no written signature? There was no reason he could decipher.

I shouldn't be sitting here idle like this. I should be doing something. I'm very restless today. That note, I suppose. I don't understand what she means. Maybe I should retire. After all, my skills as a historian are still good. With a little sharpening I could be acceptable as a puppeteer. And I miss Nide. Everything here is so wet. But if I do leave, much as I hate to admit it, I'll miss Aubin.

"Thank you, Commander. I'm finished now. You have been an excellent model. I've never had anyone remain so still."

Ki accepted the interruption and the compliment with a nod of his head, then started on his rounds without even bothering to look at the all-but-finished portrait. *If I do retire, Mikal can stop wetting his pants every time I appear.*

Almost as soon as he left the sitting, he ran into a green private, obviously on some errand. "Private!"

"Sir!" snapped the cub as he slammed to a halt and perfect attention.

Ki stepped closer. "Leenoww, isn't it? Where may I find Captain Res."

Leenoww swallowed. He was happy to be remembered—maybe. "I just left Captain Res in the throne room, sir."

Nodding, Ki asked, "Have you learned that move yet?"

Leenoww gave a hint of a smile. "No, sir. Not yet. But I will!"

Ki waved the youngster on, then went to find Res. After consulting his internal clock, he was glad Ozenscebo would not be in the throne room at this time of day. The emperor had been getting more and more extravagant. *And I have no desire to be the brunt of his jibes or his anger.*

The rebuilt throne room was garish. There was no other word for it. The floor had been re-poured, re-creating the old one almost exactly. But there were no other semblances. The walls were painted a Chinese red, and instead of paper, they were covered with millions of tiny chips of polished constanadium in a pattern. The destroyed ceiling had been replaced with a single vault, an architectural masterpiece completely spoiled by being hung with fine draperies resembling fishnets. Between the draperies were gold chandeliers. But their light was the harshest, purest white that could be obtained, and it glared blindingly off the constanadium. Even Ki, born to Nide's sun, had to squint. He guessed the humans found it outright painful.

Elena sat on the new throne. This one was even larger than the last, and looked even more uncomfortable for her. It was a jade feathered dragon, and the jewels in its serpentine twists would probably buy a planet. The throne was so massive it looked like it was consuming Elena, especially the way the arms curled around her tiny sides. But though she looked out of place, she was still the empress and managed to hold her own against the mighty beast.

Ki had not yet reached Res's side when the door to the family entrance opened and Ozenscebo charged in. Elena vacated the throne in one well-practiced motion, and the emperor whirled into it, his purple robes following the swirls of the dainty veil on his tiny ocherous hat.

Ki froze, unwilling to make himself a target. *There goes the neighborhood!* he sighed to himself. *Oh, Mmumna! I sound like Aubin! That human has contaminated me!*

Ozenscebo sat on the throne grinning like the proverbial cat, his jagged yellow teeth glaring against the purple.

Elena, uncomfortable with that grin, broke his silence. "My Lord, Chancellor Kashi and I were just discussing how well your plans for containing the epidemic have worked out. There have been no new outbreaks, and for all intents and purposes the emergency is over."

"How lovely." With an exaggeratedly delicate gesture, the emperor waved Kashi away. He sat back, smiling devilishly to himself, and clapped his hands daintily.

Three servants appeared at the back of the hall. The female who led them was dressed, if such was the proper word for her state of near nakedness, in gold tissue. She was followed by two extremely handsome young men, both dark, both with the well-formed muscles of hard use. They wore small loincloths of the same stuff as the girl's costume, and carried between them an ornately carved chest that even the girl could have carried easily.

Elena felt her fingers beginning to twist in the folds of her skirts, but she felt them as if they belonged to someone else. This little unexpected display scared her. With her husband dressing and acting so oddly, there was no telling what was in the box. It was obvious, however, she was supposed to ask.

"What is it?"

"I've gotten you a present," the emperor answered, and he just barely managed to keep the giggle out of his voice.

"That wasn't necessary," Elena said as meekly as she could, hoping against hope she could still turn this gift in another direction.

"I know it wasn't necessary. But when I saw it I knew I wanted you to have it."

The emperor gestured to the bearers, and they opened the chest, which unfolded like a blossoming flower. Inside, on wine-red velvet, rested a wildly baroque piece of jewelry. But, in spite of its being overdone, the pendant was beautiful. And set in it was the biggest opal Elena had ever seen. It seemed to hum with life. It flashed with exquisite warm red and orange flashes.

She had to admit it. "It's beautiful."

"Yes," the emperor answered amusedly. "Isn't she."

He stood so he could take the piece from the chest. "It's the only one of its kind. I've given its attendant"—he gestured absently to the girl, who bowed—"strict orders that when you're not wearing it, it must go back into its bath to keep it soft."

At that moment Elena realized what it had to be. She gagged, and struck out at the gruesome prize in horror. She succeeded in knocking it out of Ozenscebo's hands, and it fell to the floor.

Ki was thunderstruck. It couldn't be! But he couldn't move, not even to prevent himself from hearing the rest of this confrontation.

The emperor's eyes flashed, and he bared his

teeth. "What in the hell is wrong with you, woman? Are you refusing my gift?"

Elena, who was still gagging, was finding it hard to speak. "Was that—" she choked out.

"What difference does it make?" the emperor shouted. "It wasn't even human!"

Now Elena's rage took her past her trauma. "She was alive!" she screamed. "She was intelligent!" Elena was breathing heavily, anger spilling over her common sense.

Ozenscebo's frown deepened. "Go to your quarters," he said with low menace.

Elena lifted her head and her skirts, and started for the door.

The emperor, sensing this round had gone to his empress, picked up the necklace and threw it at her, hitting her squarely and painfully in the middle of her back. "You forgot your necklace, dear!" he raged. "Bitch!" he called after her before he realized this had all taken place in front of a room full of people. "Out!" he yelled. "Get out, you stupid cows!"

He pointed to the girl in the gold. "Not you. You stay. Where's my son?" he called. "Bring him to me now!"

Ki began to shuffle out with all the others, for once glad to be part of the crowd. He knew he should continue his rounds, but he found he couldn't. He was shaken, twisted all the way to his very soul. He needed to be alone for a while.

At last he arrived at his quarters. He went immediately to his bedroom and removed his ring-bracelet and placed it in its wallumnar-wood box, thinking it would be a very long time before he saw beauty in an opal again. Then he went to his garden. He sat in his customary place, and lowered his head. He saw his hand shaking like a quaking-aspen leaf. He automatically straightened his uniform, then set about purposefully to calm himself. He took a deep breath. Then another, and another.

Parry left the throne room as quickly as he could. He wanted to dance! To sing! He was so excited he could hardly contain himself. *She's done it! The bitch has finally done it!* he whooped to himself as he skipped down the corridor. *She's made the ultimate mistake! She won't last long now.*

He entered his new suite to find another pleasant surprise. Thomas had just finished working out. His muscles were puffed up with exercise, and he was covered with a slight sheen of sweat. Parry had never seen the boy look so appealing.

The setting was perfect, too. The new rooms were those designated for the prime minister. They were elegant. They were done in an old-fashioned French manner that appealed to Parry. The walls of the main reception room were painted a deep blue, with pale blue moldings and gold accents. The ceilings were high, and there were real crystal chandeliers that he suspected were quite old. The carpet was a dove gray with just a few blue overtones when the nap was run in the opposite direction, and thick enough to sink into. It was heaven! Or, rather, the master bedchamber was. It was done in apricot with dark wood wainscoting. A perfect setting for his little jewel, Thomas.

Thomas retched when Parry skipped in on him unexpectedly. He hated Mercer Parry more than he had known it was possible to hate be-

fore he'd taken this on, and he detested the way
Mercer insisted on showing up without warning. It meant there was never a time Thomas
could call his own. But with long practice, he
hid it well. He draped his towel across his heav-
ing shoulders and walked to the bar to pour
some roed for his keeper.

While he poured, Thomas stared at Mercer's
reflection in a small mirrored art piece flanking
the bar. Thomas knew he could kill Parry with
his bare hands, and that was probably the only
thing keeping Thomas sane on those nights
when Parry was amorous. The knowledge that
he outweighed Parry by fifty pounds of good,
solid muscle helped him to deal with the fact
that Parry liked to dominate men. Parry could
always die. Violently.

But not just now. He seemed to know something important, and he was jumping all over
the room, unable to contain it.

"Why are you so excited, Mercer?" Thomas
asked quietly as he handed him the drug.

"We've got her! He's got her! She won't last
long now! He'll have her, and soon! God, she
was stupid!"

Thomas poured himself a glass of water and
sat on the arm of the delicate, peach silk sofa.
"What are you talking about, Mercer?"

"God, she was stupid! She never should have
refused the gift! Even I was sickened, but I
would have taken it, then left the room before I
threw up! I've got to contact Avoy and let them
know!"

Mercer poured himself some more roed from
a decanter that sat on a side table in the reception room. The decanter matched the goblets
that had been used at the banquet. It was a spe-

cial mark of the emperor's favor, as was the un-limited roed Parry was making liberal use of.

And it caught him. He was so high his mouth overflowed. He knelt in front of Thomas and stroked the boy's thighs eagerly. "Thomas, just wait. Just wait a little while. When all this is over, I'm going to take you home to Avoy with me. All I have to do is deliver the empress to my people, and then we'll leave. They can control the emperor themselves. The rewards will be rich, Thomas. You just wait and you'll see. Our quarters then will make these look like a sty. We'll have anything we want. Nothing will be too good. I'll dress you only in silk. Not in syn-silk. Real silk. That suits you." Mercer got up on his knees and began making small, passionate circles on Thomas's chest as he kissed his neck. "And the best part," Mercer whispered between kisses, "is that we'll be together. I'll have you always by my side."

It was Thomas's turn to want to vomit, but he knew better than to let his tense muscles betray him. And he was keenly aware of Parry's over-flowing mouth. Wishing to keep the stream flowing, Thomas started to run his hand up and down Parry's chest, working at fastenings as he went.

"No," Parry said suddenly as he pushed back from Thomas. "Not now. Put on some music."

Thomas picked something soothing, but Mercer overrode him. "Faster! Something with more energy!"

Thomas complied, then sat again to watch Mercer dance around the room wildly, almost like a dervish in some somnambulant trance. On and on he went, circling madly, till at last he collapsed on the sofa, slipped off, and knocked his head on the coffee table on his way down, putting himself to sleep.

Thomas stood over him. *It would be so easy to finish him now. Just a twist of his already-twisted head, and it would be over. But...I'll undress him, put him to bed, and get word to Loni. When he wakes, I'll tell him how wonderful he was, and minister kindly to his hangover. But, Mister Prime Minister Mercer Parry, I wouldn't be a bit surprised if Loni didn't decide your time is up. And if she does, I'll take you to bed one more time, feed you great quantities of roed, and then I'll gut you like the pig you are. And I promise you no one will ever disgrace me again.*

Mikal was pacing up and down outside Tabber's door trying to decide what to do. The corridor was hot. But he couldn't feel the heat, except for what he himself generated. He was too angry, and his blood was boiling. Worse than that, he was disordered, undecided, and uncalm. How could that mere human have such an effect on a Nidean?

And Ki! Whatever was in his head? *How could he?* Mikal wondered. *How could he retire without consulting the pride? Without consulting me? How could he? Why, his tour of duty is over in a matter of weeks!*

But Mikal knew. Mikal knew that Aubin Tabber, that tiny, shriveled human, was at the bottom of this. He had to be. For some reason, Ki called this human "friend."

Mikal finally rang the buzzer at Tabber's door. He waited what he considered a polite length of time, but not a nanosecond more, and rang again. And when he still got no answer, he rang and rang and rang until the sound filled both the apartment, and the corridor.

Aubin threw his robe over his naked self and padded from his bedroom to the door in bare and cold feet, trying to scratch the sleep out of his eyes and avoid the furniture. It must have gotten substantially warmer during the night, but his living room rug felt like it was made out of polar bear, especially where the ventilator blew cold air over it. He'd tried to ignore the buzzer. After all, it was the middle of the night, but the one doing the ringing was too persistent to ignore. Finally, he'd gotten out of bed.

When the door at last opened, Mikal's eyes widened in surprise. *How puny he is!* he thought as he stared at Aubin's exposed, sunken chest, the belly under it running to fat. *I could snap him in half with my bare hands!*

Aubin stared out at Mikal in disbelief. "Do you know what time it is?" he asked through a stifled yawn.

"I know," Mikal said as he put one thick-nailed hand on Aubin's chest and pushed him back into his apartment, allowing the nails to make an impression on Tabber's white skin.

Aubin was now fully awake. "Wouldn't you like to come in?" he asked sarcastically. "Make yourself at home." He turned his back on his uninvited visitor and walked to the wall where his *Caryatid* resided. There was only one chair along that wall, and its back snuggled safely against the plastiboard. *If this guy is going to wake me and push me around, he can damn well stand,* Aubin thought caustically. He shifted in the chair until he was comfortable, then asked, "Is there something I can do for you, Lieutenant?"

I hate this human, ran through Mikal's mind

over and over. *The commander is obviously insane.* "Why did you talk Commander Ki into retiring?"

"What?" Aubin asked, genuinely confused. This was the first he'd heard of such a thing, and he was fairly certain Ki would at least have mentioned such an important move to him.

"The colonel has tendered his resignation as soon as his current tour is up. He's going back to Nide to take up the pride occupation," Mikal said angrily, as if Aubin knew all of this. "And you can't convince me you had no hand in it."

Aubin stood quickly. "If I can't convince you, there's no point in your staying. I'll see you out."

Tabber walked past Mikal and started toward the door, then froze midstride at the hissing sound of steel being drawn registered on his ears.

"Do not move, human."

Aubin was careful he did not, though a red mist of anger rose behind his eyes. "If you just did what I think you did, you've made a grave error," he told the lieutenant.

Mikal sneered. "I think not."

Aubin dared to turn his head back over his shoulder. "You've drawn your hoj on an unarmed man who bears you no malice. If you're not going to put it into its scabbard unblooded, you're going to have to put it in my back. How are you going to explain your dishonorable, incompetent behavior to Ki?" He hesitated long enough to let that sink in. "Our discussion is finished, young man. I think it's time you left."

But Aubin was not fool enough to move. He knew Mikal still had to decide what he was going to do. There was a distinct pause, as if the parties involved had frozen for a moment of peace, then Mikal raised the sword to strike. But as he raised his arms, the thought of Ki's reaction to his killing this human stopped him at the last possible second, and he resheathed the sword. Feeling the shame of having made such a cowardly decision, Mikal hurried past Aubin and out the door.

Aubin swayed slightly as he felt the rush of air passing him in Mikal's wake, as he had readied himself to feel the bite of steel. When the door finally shut tightly, Aubin poured himself a glass of bourbon, sat down quietly, and had a bad case of the shakes.

"I'm too old for this," he said quietly to his *Caryatid*.

Mikal stood outside the door breathing hard. His fury clouded his every thought, leaving everything in a muddle, and he spoke to himself as he tried to sort things out.

"This human knows the proper name for the sword, down to the proper inflections. How could Ki have taught this human so much? I would guess he's seen the pride's honor blade. And to know that a blade has to be blooded..."

The blood in Mikal's veins froze and his heart stopped pumping. He had resheathed his sword without the proper respects. And that human had forced him to it! Now he'd have to hold a Bashtrii ceremony to reconsecrate and reblood his blade. That meant cutting off his sidelocks! Everyone, even Ki, would know! He rocked back and forth unconsciously in an effort to console himself.

All I can do is pray to Mmumna that no one will be impolite enough to ask what happened. And that Tabber will not embroider the story, he told himself wretchedly. *Look how easily Tabber man-*

ipulated me! he screamed internally. *No wonder he's gotten to Ki. If the colonel retires, human, I swear to Mmumna so will you!*

Workmen scurried around Loni as she stood at a southeast-facing window staring out at the constant storm boiling over the oceanic low-pressure weather-control zone. Her arms were folded, and she was totally closed in on herself. She had no real feeling for all the remodeling activity buzzing around her. Though her new office was almost complete, she was busy thinking about "the word," and Thomas's report. She shook her head, and her free-flowing curls swirled gracefully to the delight of one of the workmen who had taken to looking at her intently. But she did not see him any more than she saw the sleek new furniture being brought in piece by piece.

She was mad as hell at herself. How could she have been so stupid as to not see the Avoyans were interested in killing the empress in hopes they could swing power to themselves. Certainly the emperor would be easily enough swayed. He twisted in the wind even with Elena's guidance and discreet manipulation. Loni groaned to herself. An Avoyan empire! Ye Gods! That would be a sight worse than the one they had!

Her reply to Thomas's communiqué had been that it was time to get out of the palace and back to her place. She'd hide him. She shook her head again, and sighed. Thomas was a fanatic, but fanatics could be useful. It really was too bad, though, that he'd become a fanatic. He used to be such a sweet and naive young man before he'd encountered Parry. But, she supposed, Parry was enough to turn the hardest old trooper into a fanatic, let alone a sweet young boy.

She rested her forehead against the transparency and felt the coolness of it rush against her skin. It was refreshing, and she turned so that her cheek just touched it, too. Young boys. The entire rebel force seemed to be made up of young boys! Even Colwin, her special favorite, was hardly more than a baby. But at least Colwin was now here in her building with her, along with several others. She could watch over them, and if anything went seriously wrong, she could get them all into her office. Then, if the emperor came looking for them, all she had to do was say the word Caligula. It was that simple. One small word, and this entire floor would be destroyed. She was fairly certain, as well, no one else would be injured. She had seen to the structural reinforcements when she'd begun this remodeling. And they would have a clean death. None of her boys—nor herself, for that matter —would fall into the hands of the vicious Lionmen. Well, to be fair, not the Lionmen *per se*. They had a kind of honor Loni could relate to. But heaven keep her from the emperor's tender mercies!

Chapter Ten

———◆———

PARRY COULD NOT believe his good fortune! He hummed happily and tunelessly to himself as he strode down the corridor. Courtiers he passed no longer ignored him. As prime minister he was deserving of their notice, and he enjoyed their recognition of his new importance. His new quarters were in the nicest part of the palace. The only thing wrong with them was their proximity to Ozenscebo's own apartments. Parry was slightly nervous about Ozie finding out he was keeping Thomas. It wasn't a secret, exactly. Parry was simply not very eager to share.

He reached his new and ornately decorated door, and tapped the palm lock happily, still humming. And his grin grew even wider when he stepped inside. Incense hung heavy in the air. Low, throbbing music wafted through the smoke like a ghost, there, but just out of sight. Parry knew Thomas had something special planned. All the drapes were drawn closed, and the lighting was turned very low. The late afternoon sun and all the empire were forbidden entrance just now.

But Thomas was not in immediate evidence. Parry looked for him in the adjoining sitting room, but, when he was not there, decided to allow the boy his grand entrance instead of intruding on him before he was ready. Parry walked to the roed, which was thoroughly iced and frosty, and poured himself a full goblet. He quaffed it quickly, and refilled it, determined to be ready for whatever his lover had in mind, and sat himself comfortably in an extra-large chair facing the bedroom door.

On his empty stomach the roed took effect quickly. Parry could smell the various scents making up the floral incense, and the music played on his skin in exquisite little fingers of vibration. He was getting impatient. Where was Thomas? He poured himself another goblet.

The bedroom door opened slowly, and Thomas stepped into the reception room, stopped, and placed his fists on his hips. The boy smiled happily at Parry's indrawn breath. Thomas was magnificent. He wore a small white leather thong with narrow straps that came up over his chest and shoulders, and nothing more, except for a thin film of oil that allowed each and every muscle to glisten like a gem when it moved. The white leather gleamed against his dark, golden skin as Thomas moved and stretched, allowing Parry a good look at his perfect shape.

Without looking away from the boy, Parry fumbled for the roed and poured yet another glass. His smile spread from ear to ear, so wide it threatened to let the thick red drug dribble out of his mouth when he downed it. Yes, he was definitely going to take Thomas back to the Avoyan world with him. This boy was too good to let go. *Oooh*, Parry said to himself, I'll have others, of course. *One is never enough. But this one is going to be my favorite. And I'll take good care of him. I'll teach him what high living is all about.*

At last Thomas left the doorway, and started slowly, slowly, to walk toward Parry. Thomas's chin was down on his chest, so that he looked up at the envoy with his big brown eyes peeping through his heavy black lashes. He lingered over his approach, allowing Parry plenty of time to run his roed-enhanced eyes over and over Thomas's body. Then, when he reached Parry, Thomas put out his wide, finely shaped hand, and pulled Parry to his feet.

"What..." Mercer began, but Thomas stopped his mouth with a tiny, gentle kiss, then pulled back and shook his head, indicating he wanted no speech. Then he stepped in close to Mercer, so close that a breath would have had to sigh to get between them, but not so close that they were touching.

The very nearness of the boy was driving Mercer mad. He could smell the perfumed oil Thomas had used, rich and full of sandalwood. His roed-sensitive skin could feel the heat radiating off the boy's almost-naked body, but that was not enough. He wanted more. He wanted the touch of that flesh, the feel of the oil sliding warmly between his fingertips and Thomas's tan skin. But whenever he moved out to touch, Thomas stepped back just far enough to avoid contact, teasing, thwarting, maintaining the control.

Then Thomas gave in. He slipped his hand up to the top frog of Parry's elaborate robe via the envoy's thigh, tracing a little highway of oil from his fingers all along the route, and Parry quivered at his touch. Thomas kissed him as the fastening opened, and kissed him again for the next, and the next. Then the kisses followed his hands lower and lower down Mercer's trembling torso, as one by one the fastenings fell open, till Thomas stood up straight and with the flat of his palms softly pushed the fabric away from Mercer's shoulders. His body rippling so badly with desire that he could hardly hold the emperor's heavy goblet, Mercer made a move to set it down before he dropped it.

Thomas forestalled him by putting a finger under the edge of the stem. "Finish it," he whispered huskily to Parry. "Everything I do will be better."

With weakened grip, Parry obliged, then realized he was almost going crazy, drowning in sensation. He could see the various colors making up the candlelight, feel the low, throbbing music as it raced over his skin in pulsed vibrations, smell Thomas, the oil, the roed, the incense, the flowers, the dust, the sunlight behind the curtains. It was almost too much to bear and remain sane.

But Thomas had been watching carefully, and now that Parry was rising to the occasion, the boy knelt and pulled on his keeper's hand gently but insistently so that Parry knelt also. As they faced each other on their knees, they swayed, Parry in response to roed and passion, Thomas in response to Parry.

"I've thought of something new," Thomas whispered in Mercer's ear as he brought his mouth and tongue into play on the prime minister's earlobe.

"What?" Mercer breathed heavily.

"It'll be good. I promise," the boy responded, and moved so that his oiled chest pressed against Mercer's, angering Mercer with the fact that the white leather straps prevented total contact. Then Thomas moved, swaying from side to side, sliding on oiled skin, pulling with oiled leather. Mercer groaned.

Thomas looked aside from Mercer's fever-twisted face, and watched his hand seeking under the cushions of the chair the pair knelt in front of. At last his fingers found what they sought, and he smiled. He leaned his head forward once more and kissed Mercer fully and heavily on the lips, and as he did so, he slipped the blade of a four-inch stiletto into Mercer's gut, and pulled up.

Innards and hot blood flooded over the reception-room carpet and Thomas. Parry's eyes opened long enough to see what had happened. He lived just long enough to comprehend. Then he fell face forward, burying the dagger even deeper into his body.

Thomas leaned aside to let the body crash, then stood on wobbly but victorious knees. He looked down at the bastard who had defiled him so often. "Was it good for you?" he asked the corpse.

Then he stumbled away, turning his back on the mess on the carpet. He was going to shower, then dress in his finest clothes. He was going to die, but he was not going to die as Mercer Parry's plaything.

Clean, his dark curls still wet from the shower, Thomas stood in front of the mirror as he zipped the skinsuit all the way up to his chin. He knew what he was about to do was going to upset Loni terribly, but that couldn't be helped. There was no life for him anymore, not even underground. He smiled at himself in the mirror, then went to sit on the bed. He picked up a knife that had been resting peacefully on the pillow, and just touched the point up under his chin.

Then he jammed it home with all his might, driving it straight up into his brain.

It was dark in Loni's office, but not nearly dark enough to suit her. Though all the interior lights had been shut down, there was still a smudge of daylight in the sky that allowed some few photons to sneak through the transparency into Loni's domain. All the leaders of the rebellion were present, except Colwin, but contrary to normal there were no near fisticuffs, no shouting matches. The place was like a tomb.

"How appropriate," Loni mumbled to herself as she stood behind her sleek new ebony bar pouring herself a very large brandy. "How utterly appropriate."

Colwin came in tensely quiet, and Loni felt a sense of relief. They were all present now. If it was necessary, she could say the word. "Caligula" could take them all to their just rewards.

"Loni," Colwin said with barely repressed anger as he approached her, "something's happened you should know about. The shuttle flight from Shawati arrived about twenty minutes ago. On board were 179 adult passengers, 19 kids, and 24 crew." He stopped, gulped down a lump, and grabbed the edge of the bar so hard that Loni pictured his fingers penetrating into the black heart of the wood. "When they began to disembark, Lionmen herded them into a large lounge, and killed them all with energy weapons. Ozenscebo had declared them traitors because of Parry's being killed by someone from Shawati." Small beads of sweat were standing on Colwin's brow.

Loni saw the violence in him. It was riding just below the surface. She put her hand softly on top of his, and gently tried to loosen the locked fingers. When she finally succeeded, Colwin grabbed at her hand with the intensity only someone desperately in need of human touch can generate.

"I know," she told him. "I know."

Colwin looked at her oddly. He'd just come from hearing the report. How could she possibly know. Then he looked around at the others scattered around the room. Each of them was struggling with something fierce and personal. It was obvious the room had known before he brought the news. He looked back at Loni. She looked terrible. She looked worse, in fact, than he had ever seen her. Her eye makeup was smudged where she had obviously wiped away some tears. There was no color in her cheeks, and her hair, which had been in a complicated twist earlier in the day, now hung in loose tendrils and tight kinks. She had pulled out the twist without even bothering to comb out her hair, an unforgivable sin she would have fired one of her girls for.

"Loni, we've got to attack the palace. Now. We can't let things like this continue."

"You and everyone with you would be dead in five minutes. If you lasted that long."

Colwin subsided, and Loni returned to her earlier morbid train of thought. *They're all here. Maybe I should say "Caligula." They'd never even know what happened.*

But then she thought better of it. There had been enough death today. Far too much death today. And instead of adding to it, she would contact Shawati. Perhaps Thomas's people would be willing to help. She had told Thomas to kill Parry. And because of that, 222 totally innocent people died. She tried to console herself by wondering how many more would have died if Parry hadn't been eliminated, but there was no comfort at all in the thought.

Colwin squeezed her hand. "Are you all right?"

She shook her head. "No."

"What is it?" he asked gently.

"I hate my job," she told him.

But with Colwin's questions had come a new sense of reality. She was in charge here, and it was her place to see that as few people as possible followed those innocents into Death's arms.

"Listen," she said, raising her voice so that all in the room could hear. "There's not to be any more trouble of any kind until I say so. You're all on vacation."

Aubin had requested Ki's presence on his first free day, so Ki arrived at Aubin's door. It was late in the afternoon, but Ki had, as usual, spent almost all of his free day catching up on paperwork. He rang Aubin's buzzer.

Aubin smiled when he saw Ki, and motioned him into his apartment. "We're going out," he told his leonine friend. "You've been moping."

Ignoring the last part of Aubin's statement, Ki asked, "Where?"

"Outside the palace."

"Why would we want to do that?" Ki asked quizzically.

Aubin exhaled heavily in sheer exasperation.

"Because you're depressed and you need some cheering up."

Ki raised an eyebrow. "What makes you think that?"

Aubin felt the muscles in his jaws tighten with the beginnings of anger. "Because I'm the all-seeing, all-knowing god of the universe."

Ki shifted his comfortable stance to one Aubin knew was suggestive of stubbornness, and rested his hand on the hilt of his sword. "I have work to do."

But this ploy Aubin had been prepared for. "It's your day off. See! I told you I was all-knowing."

Suddenly very uncomfortable, Ki said, "Aubin, I don't want to go outside the palace."

"Do it anyway. Humor this stupid human."

Ki's shoulders dropped. "You're not stupid, and I don't have to humor you."

Aubin could smell victory. "In that case, will you go with me as a friend? I want to talk to you someplace where I can be certain of uninterrupted privacy."

Ki's gut tied itself into a gordian knot. There was no escaping it. He knew what it was Aubin wanted to talk about. And Opal was the last thing in the multiverse Ki wished to discuss. He was about to refuse, but Aubin had requested this as a friend. "All right," he answered quietly.

"I knew you'd agree," Aubin said cheerfully, and pulled some things off the back of a chair. A hooded robe and some leather thongs for the purpose of tying Ki's hair back were proffered.

Ki was not happy. "I don't like pretending I'm something I'm not," he told Aubin, eyeing the garments warily.

"Lionmen are not real popular in town right now," Aubin told him.

"Then, why are we going into town?" Ki asked in frustration.

"Because it's safer there than here."

That had done it. Ki's curiosity was aroused. He took the thongs and tied his hair into a long tail that fell free from the back of his neck. Then he took the robe and slipped it over his hair and his uniform.

Aubin watched the transformation with a critical eye. "I'd be happier if you'd leave those here..." he said as he pointed to Ki's swords.

Ki looked at him.

"But I know that isn't possible," he sighed, "so could you at least shift them so they're not quite so obvious?"

Ki complied. "Happy?"

"No," Aubin answered truthfully.

"Happier?"

"Yes."

The two left Aubin's rooms and started out of habit down the corridor that would take them most quickly to the front gate. But suddenly Ki stopped and tugged at Aubin's sleeve.

"Not this way," he said. "Not this time." And he led them to a service entrance that was a small door guarded by a single Lionman.

Mikal had been following Ki's scent all day. He was trying to figure out just what in Mmumna's hell was going on. He saw it as his duty as a member of the Lawwnum pride. He wasn't about to let Ki disgrace himself or the pride. And he'd caught a glimpse of how Ki was dressed when he'd left Tabber's. That had to be Tabber's fault. A sudden and very strong urge came over him, an urge to run out and kill Tabber where he stood. But with great effort he restrained himself.

He watched as the two friends slipped out the back way, and realized he'd lost them to the outside. He'd not dressed for the outside world, and by the time he changed they'd be out of sight. There would be no way to track them if they took transport. But his spirits suddenly lifted. There was one thing he could do. He could find out just exactly what Aubin Tabber kept in those apartments of his. Maybe, just maybe, there would be something interesting.

Although Ki had been aware of the existence of Loni's Place, it was probably the last place in the universe he ever expected to find himself. Yet here he was, ensconced in a private booth cut off from the rest of the room by a set of thick, heavy curtains and walls at the backs of either seat. The other side of the table was faced with a transparency that allowed the occupants to see the entertainers and the general crowd scene down below them. One could choose whether or not to hear what was happening by pressing buttons. The wall could also be darkened for total privacy, but Aubin did not do that. He adjusted the booth's lighting so its occupants would be invisible to the revelers below, and sat back to watch the frenetic activity while he sipped at his drink.

"Well," Ki said as he played with a glass of fruit juice, "you brought me here for a purpose."

Aubin smiled. "I brought you here to enjoy yourself."

Ki frowned. "I am enjoying myself. Can't you tell?"

Aubin groaned. "Of course," he said sarcastically. "You're just beaming with pleasure."

Ki was beginning to be very annoyed with this human. His patience was wearing thin. He raised his left hand, and rested his elbow on the thick tabletop. Little flashes of colored lights were reflected in his hand's polished metal from the control console embedded in the tabletop. Ki watched the lights dance and move as he slowly rotated and canted the hand. It was a restful occupation.

Aubin, too, was caught up in watching the hand. The soft pink-orange and pale blue reflections swam across the bumps and ridges, forming exotic patterns of color and shadow, and Ki's slow, gentle motion made the effect almost hypnotic.

A sharp *crack* startled Aubin, and he looked down to his wrist where a new sensation was being born. He saw Ki's hand clamped down tightly over his forearm, and noticed the nails were buried halfway into the wood. Aubin wanted to shiver, but didn't dare. Though there was no enhanced strength built into the hand, this was a not-so-subtle reminder that the envoy was not dealing with a human. Aubin carefully told himself to watch his p's and q's.

With difficulty, he drew his eyes away from the engrossing sight of his imprisoned wrist, and matched Ki's gaze. He made an effort to keep his voice level, and came at last to the reason for his conference. "I had a charming visit from your young lieutenant. May I have my hand back? I'm rather fond of it. I'd hate to break up the set."

Ki never moved.

"Why are you leaving?" Aubin asked, sitting

forward over his captured hand to indicate his intensity.

Ki lifted one shoulder casually. "Why are you staying?"

"The emperor is a bastard." Aubin winced as the steel bands around his wrist constricted.

"The emperor is the emperor," Ki said evenly.

"Yes. He is," Aubin agreed. "I'm an old-fashioned man. I believe that a representative government can work. Unfortunately, when those representatives are corrupt, the concept is destroyed."

Ki snorted his derision. "In the thirty-eight years I've known you, I've only heard you speak up three times in council."

Aubin nodded sadly. "True. I'm only one man. But as long as I hold that seat, no corrupt man can take it. If I keep my mouth shut, the emperor forgets I'm around, and I don't have an accident."

There was a pause while Ki considered. "I see," he rumbled at last, and pulled his nails one by one out of the wood.

Aubin sat back, rubbing gingerly at his wrist. "You still haven't answered my question. Why are you leaving?"

"I'm tired."

"Then, take a nap."

Ki sighed. "Aubin, you started this conversation, not me. I'm not in the mood for jokes."

Aubin's head dropped slightly with regret. "I'm sorry. Reflex action."

Aubin's apology released Ki's tension, and he relaxed slightly. Aubin saw it, and listened eagerly for what Ki would say next.

"I'm tired of rebels, responsibility, Mikal's hero-worship, politics, and disgusting courtiers," he said humanly, with no trace of Nidean rumble, and he looked around carefully. Almost in a whisper, he added, "And I'm tired of Ozenscebo's excesses."

Aubin sat back heavily. He was shocked. He had learned to expect almost anything from his Nidean friend over the years, but never, never had there been a word about the emperor.

Both men fell into their own thoughts, and conversation died.

Loni switched off the monitor that rested at a slight angle in the new desktop, and it dropped out of sight as a matching wooden panel slid forward to cover it.

"That was interesting," she said to the empty air of her office. "If we wait until the colonel is gone, we've actually got a chance of success." She stood, and walked around her desk to stare out the window at the lighted city below her. "And if Ki doesn't like Ozie's excesses, what do the rest of the Nideans think?" Suddenly she smiled. "If we could get them on our side, no one could stop us."

Chapter Eleven

————◆————

ELENA STOPPED IN the corridor outside Magnus's schoolroom and put her hand to her forehead. She was feeling light-headed and disoriented, and the necklace around her neck felt like a ten-ton weight. How she longed to rip the thing off and throw it over the palace walls! But she could not. Her husband had decreed she wear it every day. And so she complied, for Natanha's sake, though she felt the obscene jewel was drawing away all her strength. She had been shocked, in fact, when she had looked in her mirror this morning. She had had huge violet circles under her eyes, and her normally pale skin had taken on an unhealthy yellowish cast that reminded her of runny cheese. New lines had sprung up in a few days, and she seemed unable to smooth the worried creases out of her brow.

And Magnus was no help. He was running rampant. She had been called in by a frantic teacher who still had part of a pencil protruding from the back of a bleeding hand.

Elena tried to pull herself together as she stepped into the schoolroom. She would not be able to calm Magnus if she was not calm herself. But what she saw shocked her into believing what the teacher had told her: her child was crazed. The schoolroom bore all resemblance to the throne room after the bomb had destroyed it, even down to the blood spattered across the floor. Every single tape had been pulled from the shelves and thrown, some coming to rest across the room, some in among the biology equipment, one in the fish tank. The shelves themselves had shattered when they'd been toppled, leaving splinters and boards all across the floor. Small hissing and popping sounds emerged from the shorted-out computer terminal, along with a thin stream of yellow fluid that left no doubt as to its method of demise: the young prince had used it for a bedpan. The

Earth globe had been opened like a peeled orange, and a complete map of the empire had been slashed, and hung down from the wall mount like party streamers.

And in the midst of all this carnage lay Magnus, asleep. Elena stepped over the debris till she neared her son, and stood looking down at him. In his sleep he was wonderfully innocent. There was only the round and soft face of a child, and Elena found herself thinking there was hope for him yet.

Then he opened his eyes. He looked up at his mother with the hard, cruel, calculating eyes of a rapist. The innocence was lost to a maniacal grin. But when he recognized Elena as his mother instead of his teacher, Magnus pulled the serpent's fangs and replaced the reptilian grin with the mask of innocence.

Elena's hand went to her throat. She was shocked, and not really sure she had seen what she had seen. Was it possible for such a change to occur in one so young?

But she had to try. In response to the innocence she began, "Yes, Magnus, Mama loves you, but we have to talk." She stooped so that she was more on the level of the prone child. "You must stop doing these things."

He sat up. "I don't want to go to school anymore. It's no fun."

"You don't have to go any more today," Elena said, thinking there was no longer any school for him to attend. "But when we repair all this, you have to go back to studying so you can be a good and wise emperor when your time comes."

Magnus jumped up so quickly it startled Elena, and she almost fell over backward.

Magnus stood over her, and again the eyes of the rapist looked out over the world.

"I'll just tear it all apart again, Mama," he said as he walked away from her. And then he turned back with a feral grin. "And I'll stick anybody you send."

Elena stood, and straightened her back resolutely. "You must not go about impaling your teachers! They're here to help you. In fact, you should apologize to Mr. Daito."

Magnus grinned widely. "Daddy's right. You are a bitch."

Shock and hurt washed thickly over Elena, and she could not have told which offended more. "Magnus, you should not call people names. That's not nice."

Magnus began a casual stroll across the trash-strewn room, kicking wreckage out of his way as he went. Then, in a flash, he grabbed at a sharply pointed piece of a chair, raised it in a clenched fist like a weapon, and turned on his mother. "You think you're so smart," he hissed at her, "but you don't know anything. Get out of here, you stupid cow." He began waving the jagged stake in front of him like a knife fighter. Then he screamed with all the volume and force a seven-year-old child can muster, and charged at her.

Elena stood her ground. "No," she said. She grabbed his arm when he came near, and removed the wood from his grasp with a practiced twist. Then she spun him around and spanked his bottom with all the might she could muster. She had expected tears, but Magnus swung away from her and turned on her a glare of hatred that hit her like a physical blow.

"You're going to pay for this, bitch," he spat

through clenched teeth. "I'm going to tell Father." He wrenched his arm free.

Elena was so surprised at him that she let him go. A kind of shock had settled over her. How could she have given birth to such a monster? She backed slowly out of the schoolroom when a servant entered, and she stood in the corridor breathing hard, so wobbly she had to put her shoulder to the wall in order to remain upright.

Then she heard Magnus's scream of rage, and a returning scream of pain from the injured servant, and Elena reeled as her horror washed over her anew.

Mikal found himself once more standing in front of Aubin Tabber's door. But this time he was bound and determined to be polite. He rang the buzzer. Once. And waited patiently for it to be answered.

Aubin could not cancel the look of surprise that passed over his face. He had not been expecting to see Mikal, but even less had he been expecting to see Mikal with his sidelocks shorn. Though his massive mane was swept back from his face in the traditional Lionman style, there was nothing framing his face. He had taken them down to the size of sideburns. Aubin was stunned. He had never seen any Lionman in uniform, including the women, without sidelocks. In fact, the only Nidean he had ever seen without them was Learaa Maaeve, and she was so odd she didn't count. Without the locks, Aubin thought, Mikal looked positively childlike, with a soft, round face.

"I would speak with you," Mikal said gravely to Tabber. "May I come in?"

Aubin, wondering how the boy had managed to learn some manners, stepped out of the doorway and motioned Mikal inside. "Will you have a seat?" Aubin asked politely. He did not want Mikal to be the only one with manners.

Mikal shook his head and turned to face Tabber squarely. "As you know, Aubin Tabber, Colonel Ki Lawwnum and I are members of the same pride. Having a colonel in our pride is a source of great honor. Having the Commander of the Guard in our pride is a source of even greater honor. Commander Ki's pride is a very important one, being the keepers of legend, and quite frankly, I would do anything to keep Ki from losing the pride's honor."

He paused, and that gave Aubin time to reflect that this was probably the longest speech he had ever heard from the boy, and certainly the most polite. He wondered what had prompted such a change in attitude. Perhaps it had something to do with the loss of his sidelocks. He would ask Ki about it the next time he saw the commander.

Mikal cleared his throat and continued. "I admit I do not understand Colonel Ki's affection for you, but I accept it. I also admit I do not like it, but, again, I accept."

It was obvious to Aubin there was something more the boy wanted to say, and he was having a great deal of difficulty dealing with it. Aubin felt a flash of pity for the lieutenant.

"You seem to have some influence with my pridesman. I'm here to ask you to convince him not to retire."

Aubin was stunned. He was speechless. But he had gotten very good over the years at not showing such things to babes who were still wet behind the ears.

Mikal, who had been watching carefully for Tabber's reaction, began, quite uncharacteristically, to fidget. This was not going at all as planned. "You will, of course," he added into the lengthening silence, "be well paid for this. I assume fifty thousand credits would be sufficient?" Mikal had hoped he wouldn't have to buy this human. After all, Ki saw something in him. But it was obvious by his lack of reaction that he was like all the others, totally without honor and driven to action only by greed or lust.

There was another long pause, and Aubin let it drag out while he suffocated the fire of absolute rage that threatened to flash over him. When he was in control he answered, "No."

Mikal was surprised. He thought his offer had been generous. "That isn't enough? I'm sure I can raise some more."

The tic of an overly tight muscle started at the corner of Aubin's mouth. "I must admit you've got balls," he told the Nidean. "Your offer was most generous. But you've just insulted me by assuming I would take advantage of my friendship with Ki, and you've insulted the commander by assuming he could be so easily controlled. I think you've thoroughly disgraced yourself."

At the mention of disgrace, Mikal's hand went automatically to his naked face. He felt absolutely bare without his sidelocks.

How does this human always manage to infuriate me to the point of homicide? he wondered to himself.

Aubin continued. "As you are, as you have

pointed out, Ki's pridesman, I will not tell him of this incident."

That surprised Mikal more than anything else that had happened between the two. How was it this human was capable of acting with honor when everyone knew humans had no honor? He did not understand.

"Good day," Aubin said, and he did not try to keep the acid out of his voice.

Mikal knew he was being dismissed. It was a thing he had heard often enough before. And he left, feeling equal parts of confusion and anger.

Commander Ki should die in battle, Mikal told himself. *But it has fallen to me to protect the honor of our pride. Ki has become...Mmumna!* He hated to think it! *Ki has become human and mortal. If he goes back to Nide, he'll be only a puppeteer again, just like all the others.*

He continued down the hall, and, in his confusion and ashamed state, knew everyone in the palace was looking at him and laughing.

Magnus, a screaming, whirling tornado, swept into the seraglio fountain room. He was in total disarray, his hair a mess, his clothing torn and stained with what appeared to be blood, and without shoes.

The Lionmen on guard were stymied: they knew he did not belong in the seraglio, but as heir they could not very well keep him out, either.

The screaming continued unabated. And it was getting stronger, as the Guardsmen refused to leave their posts to attend to the prince. But the screaming did bring a partially clad Mamasan, who burst into the fountain room boiling mad. The emperor was in residence! Who had the audacity to make such a commotion! She would see to their immediate punishment!

She stopped in her tracks. She had seen the young prince only a handful of times. Their paths did not ordinarily cross, as he was still far too young to be in need of her services.

"May I be of service, my prince?" she questioned as she hurried toward the boy. She had to find some way to quiet him before he disturbed his father.

"Her ring cut me when she hit me," he shrieked. "She hit me, she hit me!"

Mama-san, now that she was closer, did see a gash on the boy's cheek. She leaned over him, and petted and soothed him just as she would have done any other man. *How like his father he is*, she said to herself. *Most men are just little boys*. And gradually he quieted somewhat.

But now she was caught. The prince was insisting he be taken to his father. But dare she interrupt the emperor? Dare she refuse the prince? She hesitated, but then at last decided it would be safer to disturb the emperor than to ignore his son.

As Mama-san disappeared down a corridor, Magnus's copious tears dried up miraculously. He sat down at the edge of the fountain, giggling at how easy it had been. He had decided as soon as his mother left that she was not going to get away with spanking him. So he'd figured out how to get even. It hadn't even been very hard, really. Oh, he'd had to cut his cheek. But that had only hurt for a moment. And anything was worth seeing Mama in trouble with Father. He laughed openly, and splashed vigorously at the fountain's basin.

Ozenscebo exploded out of the corridor Mama-san had disappeared down a few moments ago, and Magnus was instantly crying as hard as he had ever been. He stood up and ran to his father, screaming.

"She hit me! Look what Mama did to me!"

It took a moment for Magnus's condition to really sink in on Ozenscebo. But when he realized the child was telling him that Elena had struck him, the emperor exploded.

"You!" he shouted, pointing to each of the four Lionmen resident in the fountain room. "Go now and arrest the empress for treason! Bring her at once to the throne room!" He wrapped his arms around his son and pulled him tightly into an embrace. "I don't give a damn about any treaties, Magnus," he said as he quieted his son. "She's an unfit mother, unfit to rule with me. If it means war, so be it. I'll stomp them as easily as I stomp her."

Magnus buried his face in the full skirts of his father's hastily donned robe, and smiled broadly.

Then Ozenscebo pushed the boy back enough to get a good look at his face. "Can't you do something about this blood?" he yelled at Mama-san. Then he whirled the boy into her arms and strode off angrily for the throne room.

It was Mama-san who called his Guard. For the first time ever, they had to catch up with a hurrying emperor.

Ozenscebo had summoned all the people resident in the palace. All over, courtiers dressed hurriedly, set down reports unfinished, and scurried to the throne room to discover what had happened.

The emperor paced the width of the throne room waiting impatiently for a large enough audience to gather. He wanted as many witnesses as possible to what he was about to do.

When Natanha entered the room, Ozenscebo looked at her as if she were a particularly noisome spider that had decided to drop into his soup. "Sit there!" he told her forcefully, and pointed at the throne.

Natanha recognized the tone of voice, and knew it was not to be argued with. She sat on the throne, most uncomfortable at being seated there, and twitched the delicate silky blue skirts into as attractive an arrangement as possible while sitting on an impossibly large chair with feet dangling above the floor. *I did not expect to be summoned today,* she thought ruefully. *If I had known I would be in public, I would have done something more grown-up with my hair.*

When Magnus entered, he sauntered directly to Elena's customary seat and sprawled there as if he owned it. He threw one leg over an arm, and stuck his head on the seat, and then hung it backward over the edge and under the arm.

Natanha watched her brother. There was something new there, a surety that had been absent as short a time ago as yesterday. And his eyes... His eyes were strange, seeing things Natanha could not comprehend. They looked for all the empire like her father's. A spasm of disgust washed over her. Magnus was too young to have those eyes.

The very large room filled more quickly than it had ever done before. This kind of summons was most unusual, and everyone was curious.

When the emperor judged he had enough of an audience, he began, even though people were still filing in at the back of the room.

"This is the reason I summoned you all," he said with a grand gesture, and Elena was brought in from a side entrance walking calmly between two pairs of Lionman Guards, each of them with drawn swords. There was a single intake of breath from the entire room. "This woman, this creature, has defied me on more occasions than I can count, but because of my generosity and great patience, and certain treaties, I have overlooked this. But now she has dared to try to kill the imperial heir, my son." He was warming to his subject, and he was getting redder as he was becoming angry all over again. "I am a generous and kind man, but I cannot overlook treason in my own household. The punishment for treason is death. I will make no exception, not even for one supposed to be my loving wife. She will be taken to the dungeons, where her life will be terminated."

Even with thousands of people in the room, there was a moment of absolute silence. They were stunned, each and every one of them. Except Magnus. He had known from the moment he'd burst into the seraglio that he would get even with the bitch.

Natanha blanched, and had a sudden desire to become part of the woodwork. But her mind revolted. The only coherent thought that occurred to her kept running circles in her consciousness: what was it Mama had said about finding transport?

Sufficiently pleased at his audience's reaction, the emperor bellowed, "Take her away!"

But Elena, even in such dire straits, managed

to steal his show. Although she looked frightened, she did not faint, or cry out. She instead dropped the emperor a most correct and proper little curtsy that managed to be only the tiniest bit unsteady.

It unhinged the rest of Ozenscebo's anger, and he turned positively purple. He knew where the hearts of his people would be now. They'd be with the bitch! "Get her out of here!" he screeched, wanting her gone from his sight and theirs before she could win more of their sympathy.

Her guard started her away, and a path opened naturally for them down the center of the room. It was as if a great gash had opened in the heart of the empire. Some of the braver ones even murmured words of encouragement to the empress as she passed them. She acknowledged them with a regal inclination of her head.

The empress and her guard had progressed approximately halfway down the long room when the lady's soft blue eyes met the tattooed, slitted eyes of her closest friend. She looked at Ki sadly, knowingly, and she chilled the blood in his veins.

He stepped into the gash and raised his hand. There was not another in the empire who could have stopped this progress, but Ki Lawwnum could, and he did.

He had been watching from the heart of the crowd, having arrived too late to take his normal place near the end of the room. And he had feared what he had seen on the emperor's face even before they had brought in Elena. He knew there was no hope for her now. None. But he also knew what had occurred in those dungeons she was being taken to. He knew what had hap-

pened to Opal and the two conspirators Templa
and Paschasia, and others. Mmumna herself
probably could not fathom what gruesome
things Ozenscebo would dream up for an of-
fending empress. Ki had found himself quaking
with fear for his delicate human friend, afraid
she would disgrace herself. That this regal
woman should disgrace herself was unthink-
able. She would not be able to stand up well
under such "pleasures" as Ozenscebo would de-
vise.

He had to still his quaking. *I am Ki Lawwnum,
one of many,* he told himself sternly, *and I am a
legend-keeper of Nide. I have manipulated the
puppets since the day I could walk. Today I will be
nothing more than another puppet. No one here
will know I tremble like a frightened child. No one
here will suspect I intend to subvert the emperor's
plans. I will propel myself as a legend-keeper, and I
will not be found out.*

"My Lord!" Ki shouted to the front of the hall,
his voice pitched correctly to travel the length of
the room.

The emperor glared. Not even Lawwnum
should have dared to interrupt this time.

But Ki continued. "I most humbly beg, Highness, as Commander of your Guard, that I be
allowed to serve you by removing this treacher-
ous woman."

A heartfelt "Thank you" reached Ki's ears
from Elena's lips, though the voice was unre-
cognizable. She understood how much suffering
he was trying to save her from. The thanks had
been meant for him alone, and he was certain
only the two Guardsmen who flanked her were
aware she had spoken.

Ozenscebo's face did one of its speedy, insane

changes. He looked happy now, happy that his commander understood the necessity of removing the bitch and was so eager to act. But there were other considerations.

"No, Lawwnum, no. Your way is too quick." He tittered like a schoolgirl. "We don't want her to leave us too soon. No. With proper caution she will have weeks in which to repent."

Elena arrived at her holding cell still surrounded by her four Guardsmen. They opened the door, and allowed her to enter first. She looked around grimly. There was a small table, a single chair, and a narrow hard cot. The lighting ran in a strip down the middle of the ceiling behind gratings that threw regular, square shadows all over the floor and walls, which had once been white, but were now a dirty and graffitied gray.

The most senior of the Guardsmen spoke. "Will you have a seat, Your Highness? I do not know how long the emperor will be."

Elena laughed as she sat. "I'm in no hurry to see my dear husband, Guardsman. I can tell you that." But she was grateful to these Nideans. They still addressed her as Empress, and, so far at least, had allowed her to retain her dignity.

It interested her enormously that she was not frightened for herself. As she examined the thought, she supposed she had lived with the possibility of Ozenscebo's ending her life for so long it no longer fazed her. But she was enormously frightened for Natanha. There was nothing more she could do for her daughter. Elena prayed Natanha had learned enough to survive.

She looked up and addressed the Lionman

who had spoken to her. "Please. If you can find it in your heart, I would very much like paper and a pen and a few minutes alone."

As soon as she had spoken, one of the Guardsmen slipped out the door and returned with writing implements. He placed them on the table before her.

"A few minutes alone?" she asked plaintively.

"Madam," the Guardsman answered, "we were told not to leave you unattended."

Elena nodded, then stood. She went quite close to the superior.

"Please. I most certainly am not going anywhere, and you can attend me as well on the other side of the door as on this. There are some things I would like to say to my daughter." She leaned in close to his ear so that only he could hear. "I am really very upset, and I am afraid I might disgrace myself in front of you and the others."

The Guardsman considered. She was really quite a lady. It was too bad she had not been born Nidean. She would have been a credit. And it was true they could attend her on the other side of the door. "I will give you ten minutes, madam. But I cannot give you more."

Elena was very happy for their small kindnesses. "Thank you," she said as she pulled the rings off her fingers and gave one to each of her Guardsmen. "Thank you all very much."

Elena sat quickly at the table, unwilling to waste even a moment of her allotted time. She wrote to Natanha, hoping one of the Guardsmen would have heart enough to get it to her. Then she removed the hateful pendant from around her neck. She still loathed the thing, and all the corruption and sickness it represented. But at this moment, it was also her salvation. From the back of the pendant she pulled a tiny off-white tablet she had wedged into an open space in the pendant's golden setting. Then she threw the hated piece of Opal aside, and focused all her attention on the tablet. The pendant had been the perfect place to hide her friend, as Ozenscebo had decreed she wear it every moment she was about the palace. And what a friend this tablet would be. It was a poison of the nicest kind. It bound itself to the hemoglobin in the blood, thereby rendering it incapable of carrying oxygen. There would be no pain. She would go to sleep, and she would quietly suffocate. In this situation one could not ask for a better friend, though she would take with her into the next life the fact that Ki had tried.

She swallowed it, then went to the cot and lay face up. She arranged her skirts for the last time, and placed her hands together delicately. Then she closed her eyes, and conjured up an image of her daughter laughing and playing in golden sunshine that just matched the color of her hair. In moments she was asleep.

Learaa Maaeve sat at her desk and frowned at the paper resting there. She had to finish this report. Her superiors on Nide would need to know as soon as possible what had happened here. But try as she might, she found she had the hardest time setting it all down.

"That's because it makes no sense," she told herself, and once more picked up her pen to begin.

This time, at last, she managed to get some sort of coherency into her report, though she kept having to stop herself from adding her own opinions.

"No," she told herself strictly. "You're here to report, not editorialize."

She managed quite well until it came time to explain why Ki Lawwnum had offered to kill the empress. *It was quite obvious to all that he wished to save her pain,* she wrote, but then she threw down the pen in frustration.

Had it really been obvious to all? Or only just to her? Certainly the emperor had been happy enough at Ki's proposal.

She tapped her heavy nails on the desk in irritation. It was not often she had trouble making up her mind. Yet here she was debating over the wording of a simple sentence.

"Yet so much depends on how these words are read at home," she murmured. "There must be no disgrace for the commander in them."

Then, at last, she made up her mind and allowed the words to stand as she had written them. Those at home could question others if they doubted her word. She folded and sealed the letter with her official seal, rang for her secretary, and sat back once more to ponder. She did not think she would ever understand the feelings that existed between Ki Lawwnum and the humans, but this time, at least, it had done him credit.

Chapter Twelve

———◆———

AUBIN HAD WATCHED for Ki for five days. Now he'd given up on watching, and was headed toward Ki's apartments with a tray of food.

"If I know Ki," Aubin said to himself under his breath, "he hasn't eaten since I saw him last."

He reached the door, and hit the palm lock. Nothing happened. "Shit!" Aubin exclaimed angrily. "The privacy's engaged! He's locked me out!" Angrily, he buzzed.

Inside, in a darkened room, Ki sat very still. *If I'm quiet*, he told himself, *whoever it is will go away*.

There was another buzz, and Aubin's voice came through the door sounding muffled and far away. "Ki, let me in!"

Now I know I want whoever it is to go away, Ki thought as he recognized Aubin's voice.

But Aubin could be as stubborn as any Nidean. "I know you're in there, Ki Lawwnum!" he called. "And if you don't let me in, I'm going to stand out here and yell through the door until I embarrass you right out of your fundoshi!"

He would, too, Ki thought as he creaked to a standing position. *The man is totally shameless. Mmumna, my joints hurt*, he thought, then realized he was massaging his mechanical left hand with his right. *Even my hand hurts*, he groaned inwardly.

When he opened the door, the smell of Aubin and the food assaulted Ki's overly sensitive nose, and his stomach roiled in spasmodic reaction.

But this time Ki was not alone in reacting to a smell. Aubin's stomach lurched and rolled over at the dense, musky smell of Ki and the closed, unventilated room. He was appalled at Ki's appearance, but he was also glad, somewhere in a tiny corner of his heart, that Ki was no longer quite so perfect. But even over that, it was obvious Ki was in extreme pain.

The two stood and looked at each other without speaking. Aubin was overwhelmed. Ki's quarters, which were always perfect, were in total disarray. Everything was toppled, or dirty, or shoved aside. Everything except the puppets. They still hung on the wall and had apparently not been molested. Ki himself was a wild and disheveled creature from another world, not Commander Ki the Perfect. Aubin thought he looked like the old holos of the wild Nideans he had seen in a history of the war for the planet, but he had never connected such wildness with Ki the Immaculate.

At last, Aubin broke the silence. "My god! When did you sleep last?" he asked as he stepped forward.

Ki assumed, quite correctly, that Aubin was about to barge in, so he stepped aside. It was easier to let the envoy in than to keep him out. Stopping him would be too much work, so he walked past Aubin and back to his chair, and flopped down in a flurry of dust motes.

Aubin turned on the lights. "Have a little pity on those of us who aren't mushrooms," he told Ki, then went to place the food in the kitchen. He was both cheered and angered by what he saw. In comparison to the sitting room, the kitchen was clean. That was cheering. But it also meant Ki had eaten nothing. That was stupid.

"You haven't eaten," he said accusingly as he left the kitchen.

But the reek of the place hit him again as he went back into the sitting room, and he held his breath and headed for the French doors. He pulled open the drapes and flung the doors open to a fresh, if slightly chilly, September morning. Then he went to stand in front of Ki.

"You smell like a dead imlowwn—whatever the hell they are," he told the commander.

Ki moved his right hand enough to pull some of his mane off his face.

Aubin looked back out the doors at the fresh, dewy morning longingly. It had to smell better out there than it did in here. "You're getting weeds in your garden," he said.

When he still got no reaction, Aubin shrugged, then walked to the ventilator to start it working. He put on a recording, the first thing he grabbed, for some pleasant noise. Then he started picking up things, clearing a path so he could move enough to clean up the rest. All the while he chattered at Ki like a toy robot stuck in gear.

Finally reaching the point of annoyance, Ki looked up. "What do you want from me?"

Aubin dropped the things he had been picking up in a heap at his feet and placed a fist on each hip. "I want you to stop acting like a pathetic jackass."

"There are no jackasses on Nide," Ki answered with barely any inflection.

"Of course not!" Aubin exclaimed as he threw his hands up into the air. "They all come here and become commanders!"

Ki closed his eyes for a long moment, then

opened them again. "I know what you're trying to do, Aubin. You're trying to get me to lose my temper. But I'm too tired. Why don't you just leave me alone?"

"Leave you alone?" Aubin said angrily. "I haven't heard from you in five days! I've missed your sterling wit and effervescent charm! Surely you don't expect me to leave!" He paused long enough to draw an angry breath. "Besides, haven't you heard?" he asked as he bent down to pick up the pile of oddments he had dropped. "I've been demoted. I'm not an envoy anymore. I'm a hausfrau."

"Aubin," Ki said tiredly, "I'm not in the mood for this. All I have to do is call downstairs and have some Guardsmen escort you out."

"Go ahead!" Aubin yelled. "They'd be delighted! It'd be the first time they've seen their commander in a week! He certainly hasn't been at practice, as I heard *at length* from Mikal two days ago. He thinks I'm responsible for that, too." He turned away, paused, then turned back. "The rumors are interesting, you know. You'll like this one. This one's good. From your actions it's assumed that you and the empress were close, if you know what I mean. Engaged in a few close-order drills."

"Don't!" Ki growled.

Aubin was delighted. He had Ki's attention. "Straightened out the kinks in your sword, did she? Didn't know Nideans went in for exotic types, though she was pretty. Just out of curiosity, is Natanha half Nidean? You were there when she was born, I'm told. Were you there before?"

Ki stood rockily. "That's enough!" he rumbled

as his hand searched for swords he was not wearing.

Aubin was grateful the swords were not in evidence. If they had been, his head would have been rolling about the floor like a soccer ball. "Do I finally have your attention?" he asked Ki bitingly.

The heavy wash of emotion did Ki no good at all. He rocked back and forth like a scarecrow blown in a high wind, obviously on the verge of passing out. Aubin grabbed his shoulders to steady him, and began to gently prod Ki into the kitchen where it was clean and light so that he could eat. Aubin helped the commander sit at the table.

"You really are a bastard," Ki told Aubin from behind a wild mane that had once more fallen across his face.

"Yep. Eat this," Aubin said as he uncovered trays and pushed them at Ki.

Ki turned away, nauseated. "I'm really not hungry, Aubin."

"I don't care. Eat it anyway," the envoy said. "I got a good look at you a moment ago. I could punch you out right now. At this moment in time I'm bigger and tougher than you are, so eat!" He pointed sternly at the dishes. "And after you do, I'm going to leave so you can clean yourself up."

Ki picked up his chopsticks and played with his food. "You know, you really pushed your luck with that comment about Natanha."

Aubin agreed. "I had good reason. I needed your attention."

"How is she taking her mother's death?" he asked quietly. "I suppose I should look in on her."

Aubin shook his head. "Good trick. Ozie has a full cadre of your Lionmen out looking for her. She hasn't been seen since she left the throne room that day."

At first it had been easy to hide in the servants' quarters. All Natanha had to do was change rooms periodically whenever someone was expected off shift. And, of course, pinch some clothes that were not quite as grand as the court gown she'd had on when she left the throne room. She'd pulled her long soft hair up into a sort of sloppy twist, and for several days she sailed among the various retainers without being recognized, listening to their gossip, keeping up with what was happening around her.

But it had to happen. Someone who had served the royal family directly got a good look at her in the sunlight when she was getting something to eat from the servants' kitchen. She'd had to flee when she saw the recognition beginning to form in the retainer's face.

So, she'd moved down into the bowels of the palace. This was a warren of small tunnels, their purposes long forgotten, unused rooms, accessways, and, glory be! long-forgotten storerooms that held treasure troves of antique furniture and clothes, paintings, wines, and even, occasionally, foodstuffs. It was a particular blessing to find the storerooms. Going through them gave Natanha something to do to divert her mind from the horrors surrounding her.

She had surmised from overheard conversations that her father had started a search for her once he realized she hadn't been seen. The fact that it took four days for him to miss her did not distress her. In fact, it was pleasing to know she had been so quiet she had escaped his notice. But because she was now being actively looked for, she'd had to leave the rather comfortable servants' quarters.

Too soon to suit her, she'd have to leave the basements, as well. She'd been having a good time digging through an old chest of clothes. In it she'd found an old lady's dress, the fabric nearly rotten, but covered with what appeared to be natural pearls. She began removing the pearls by biting at the threads. It probably wouldn't be too difficult to grab money, probably not too much more difficult than grabbing food, but there was no sense in wasting an opportunity. And if she was going to get to Midron as her mama had told her, she was going to need enough money to bribe someone. The pearls were perfect. Totally untraceable. But while she was working, she heard something. She put the pearls she had already removed automatically into her pocket, and moved to the door of the storeroom she'd been working in. She just caught a flash of a Lionman's uniform as he passed at a junction in the tunnels. They'd started to search down here! At first she panicked. There was nowhere left to run! But then she admonished herself to think! Not to give in to emotion! She replayed one of Ki's favorite lectures on the subject in her head, and amazingly it cleared her thoughts.

It was hard to admit, but for once in her life Mama had been wrong. Tragically wrong. It had been easy for Elena to tell Natanha to get to Midron. But it was not nearly so easy to get out of the palace undetected. And if she had gotten out, she would have to find someone to take her to Midron who was willing to operate outside the law. Maybe, just maybe, if she had walked out of the throne room and right to the docks, she would have managed to get out—if the Lionmen would have let her go unescorted. But that was a very large and unlikely "if." And now it was impossible. Her father had put out a "reward for information" on her.

Her search for another place to hide did not take as long as she feared. While backing out of the storeroom, both eyes searching for Lionmen, she stumbled into a section of the basements used for engineering purposes, and there spied an open duct. As she was small of stature and not quite grown, she fit into it quite easily, while a Lionman, even the most feminine of them, would never make it. She took a flashlight from the tools hanging on the wall, and crawled in. It was a tight fit at first, but very soon, as it joined other ducts, it was almost a highway. She was able to crawl freely. As soon as she was somewhat comfortable, she put her head down on her arms, relaxed as much as she was able after her scare, and listened. She heard no active pursuit. In fact, it didn't even sound as if the Lionmen had entered the engineering station. She breathed deeply in relief, and regretted it. The dust on the bottom of shaft made her want to sneeze. In fear of being heard, she pressed her hand hard just below her nose to suppress the sneeze, then moved deeper into the ductwork.

It was a surprising place. At various points where several pieces of work joined, there were spaces as big as the playhouse Natanha had had as a small girl. At some points the air moved with the force of a hurricane, and at others hardly a breath stirred and dust settled heavily.

She caught the scent of cooking food, and that set off a tremendous rumble in her belly. She'd been eating cold storeroom stuff for days. Hot fresh food was something not to be passed up—if she could only figure out how to get to it.

She followed her nose through several twists and turns, and at last found herself looking through a grating near the top of the huge kitchen used to prepare banquets, nearly two stories above the floor. It was abustle. Ozenscebo must have some sort of major affair in the works. Dozens and dozens of meat pies cooled on racks. Enormous haunches of meat roasted on spits over fiery-red elements. A wonderful sight. But Natanha's watering mouth was too far above it all to be of any good, and her nose was torturing her unhappy belly. She had to find a way down to a level where she could purloin some of the goodies. And from such a simple need grew Natanha's organized exploration of the interior workings of her father's palace.

For some time after Aubin left, Ki sat considering. It would not be a good thing if someone else found Natanha. Despite the fact all efforts to find her had failed, Ki felt she still had to be inside the palace. Someone would have seen her leave if she were not.

He moved, and his muscles wailed. They were more stiff than they had ever been. He shifted his weight preparatory to trying to stand, and discovered his legs were shaky and his back weak. He groaned, and fell back against the cushions of the chair. He felt like a newborn cub. The only feeling that compared readily to this had occurred when he'd lost his hand. He'd been pretty rocky that time, too. But then all he'd had to do was sit around and be pampered. Now he had to find Natanha before someone else did.

Relying heavily on the force of his hands against the arms of his seat, he thrust himself up out of the chair and to his feet. Cramps started in the long muscles at the back of his legs that had tightened and shortened during his hibernation. He ignored them, and walked unsteadily to the shower. He ran the water over himself, alternating very hot and very cold, for some time, stretching, bending, moving slowly under the needle-fine spray of the shower.

He felt better as he dressed. Some of the drunkenness had left his walk, though his muscles still screamed at him for abandoning them. But it was only Natanha who pulled him up from his chair, he realized as he tied his sash. There was no zest in this, no lust for the hunt. If he did not feel he owed the child all the help he could find for her, he would not have moved. Such feelings were confirmed when he caught a glimpse of himself in his mirror, and he looked away quickly so he would not see more. He was not immaculate. His mane hung down, wet and uncombed. His sashes were twisted, and he did not care. The kimono he'd thrown on was one that had been worn previously. Its wrinkles mirrored the worry lines on Ki's tired face.

And as he thrust his shar and his katana through his sash, leaving the hoj resting peacefully on its stand, he knew he didn't care anymore about what happened to him. He had taken service with a monster, and that monster could destroy an empire. All that mattered was that the spark of unsullied life that was Natanha be safe.

Stopping the first Guardsman he came across, Ki ascertained where Natanha had last been seen. He ignored the shocked and horrified reaction the Guardsman had to his commander's deteriorated appearance, and went directly to the servants' quarters, hoping to catch a whiff of her scent, or find something that would tell him where she was. He knew her better than anyone else alive, now. It was possible something would speak to him when it remained silent for one less familiar.

But he found nothing. Everything had been overturned, ruffled, gone through, by too many hands. If anything remained of Natanha's scent, it had mingled with so many others and faded so deeply it was indistinguishable.

He stopped in a doorframe, and rested his shaking legs by leaning against the jamb. He steadied himself with his metallic left hand, too heavy to shake like the right. And he considered. The child had hidden well. She had remained anonymous here until she'd been spotted accidentally. But where would she go next?

As far as she could get from the hunter, Ki felt, so he was now in the deepest part of the palace, dark, cold, wet, and musty from long disuse. Perfect. The all-pervasive mustiness would mask Natanha's scent very well unless she was very close. So Ki began a systematic search. He visited every nook and sniffed at dusty corners until his eyes watered and his nose ran in fierce reaction to dust and mold. But he did not stop.

And as he searched, he wondered about the fix he found himself in. He had sworn service to the empire. But the empire was governed by a monster. Over and over again he looked at the question of following the orders issued from such a monster. There could be no honor in obeying such orders. But there was dishoner in disobeying. Ozenscebo bore no resemblance to the legendary first emperor, elected by his people to restore some sort of order after the chaos of the Destruction, nor even to the soldier-emperor who had made the pact with Nide. And yet Ki served the empire.

Then something came to him through the dust. Fresh and warm, it had to be Natanha even though he could not be certain yet. He followed the scent, and gradually he snorted through his quandary. He owed his allegiance to the empire, not to the scum Ozenscebo. And if he chose to disobey orders ... He paused to consider. Did he have the right to do this to his pride? They would hold themselves accountable, even if Ozenscebo did not. He continued. There was always a chance no one would find out. He was leaving this world soon, at any rate.

He found her. She was just beyond an old and rusty grating held together only by habit. *Res is a good man*, he told himself. *He is capable of taking over for me. I know I cannot serve this beast Ozenscebo any longer*. He cocked his head to one side. *Perhaps I can take Natanha to Nide with me. She is young. She could learn. The pride would accept her, take her in, for her own sake if not for mine*. He made an effort to picture Natanha on her marriage day with a pride's tattoos decorating her face, and remembered instead Elena's face with the mauve circles under her weary, heartbroken eyes. He shuddered. *It would be terrible for the child*.

Try as he might, he could think of no place else to take her should he somehow manage to get her out of the palace undetected. A Lionman on any world but Nide would stick out like a sore thumb. Especially one with a human child in tow. And there was no one else Ki could trust to guard his princess his way. Perhaps she was safest right where she was, at least for the time being.

He stepped to the grating, aware the girl had managed to stay perfectly still, making no sound, and that she had managed to mingle her scent with that of others by wearing someone else's clothing. *She has learned well*, he told himself as he spoke directly at the grating in a quiet, tired, and scratchy voice.

"Don't speak. You've hidden well. You have increased your chances by keeping yourself very clean and wearing another's clothes. Do not stay in one place. I am not the only one with a nose. Do not go to the port yet. Your father has men there, seeking you. Wait as long as possible, then try to get off this planet. Your father is a butcher. He will kill you without a thought. I'm sorry I won't be around to help you. I'm going home. I can no longer abide what sits on the throne." He paused, resisting an urge to put out a hand to the dimly sensed shape that shook now with sobs just beyond the light. "I didn't hear you, I didn't smell you, I didn't see you. I'm leaving now." He turned, took a few heavy steps, realizing sadly he had just given the child all the help he was capable of giving in spite of all his promises to Elena, then went back to speak once more with the grating. "Be careful," he told the steel bars. "You owe it to your mother."

He walked away feeling impotent, but there

was nothing more he could do. He'd kept his promise to Elena as well as he was able. And if Natanha did as she was told, exactly and with great care, with a dose of extremely good luck she just might make it offworld.

Ki looked up finally, and realized his steps had taken him to the higher basements of the palace. The ground level was only a short flight of stairs above him. He climbed them, and found he was near the exit he and Aubin had used the night they'd gone to Loni's Place. He stopped, his left hand clacking softly, and remembered the smell of the outside air. It had tasted bad, but not nearly so bad as the air in this corrupt palace tasted to him now. He started up again, and knew he was going to walk out that same door, and he was not coming back. His credit voucher was on the dresser, and his hoj rested serenely on its stand, but he was not going back. He would not stay in a place where he was expected to hunt children to extinction. The Guardsman challenged him, but Ki barely paused. "I'm looking for the princess," he said offhandedly, and the Guardsman accepted without further question, in spite of the commander's appearance.

He began to walk to the city under gray skies that produced the autumn's misty drizzle, half of him aware that he might be able to find transportation there, in spite of the fact that he had no ready credits. Perhaps there would be a Nidean ship in port, or perhaps he could sell his sword, either literally or figuratively. The rest of him reveled in the sheer joy of walking, of using the muscles he had so long neglected. He was still stiff and weak, as weak as a cub, but as he stretched with every step, he felt more free, and the rain, as it soaked his mane, left him feeling clean of the palace's pollution.

It was a long walk into the city's center, a distance of some twenty miles. And it was an interesting tour. First he encountered the slums, the thrown-together shanties circling the city illegally. There he saw no one. People who lived in the area had long ago learned not to be seen, especially by someone in imperial uniform. Then he came to the legal suburbs, the areas inhabited by minor officials and well-to-do, if not wealthy, businessmen and their families. Children peeked at the bedraggled Guardsman from behind opened drapes before their mothers pulled them deeper into snug little houses. Then he hit the outer ring of the city itself. In some ways it was worse than the illegal squatters' quarter. At least there one had been able to see the sky. Here it was obliterated by tall buildings and awnings that hung in tatters. There one had been able to draw a fairly clean breath. Here the concrete held the stink of garbage.

Gradually Ki became aware that here people were not scattering at the sight of him. They turned to look, and one or two even followed. He ignored them. They were totally inconsequential. All that mattered was that he find some sort of rest for his beleaguered mind and a way off this world.

Another man joined the followers, and Ki turned down a side street in hopes of discouraging further pursuit. But the followers, too, turned, and alarm bells in the back of Ki's mind he had been totally ignoring suddenly demanded his attention. He was being shadowed. He continued to walk, and began to listen. There were four of them at varied distances. They were not a threat, at least not yet. None of them had shifted out of nonchalance. He turned again, and found himself in an alleyway. It was narrow, with small doors opening directly onto the pavement, and it was dark. If there had been lights here at one time, they no longer functioned. The broken concrete was slick with a combination of reeking, greasy slime that oozed out of the back of a butcher shop, and cold drizzle.

Ki looked down the alley toward its end, trying to determine in the bad light if there was a way out at the back. He blew out heavily, trying unsuccessfully to clear his nose of the stink of garbage. And as he raised his head, a figure stepped out of a slightly recessed doorway and into the rain.

Asses! Ki thought as he realized there would be no way of merely walking away from this trouble. *But they're only muggers. Maybe I'll leave the swords sheathed. I've had enough of killing.* Then several more stepped out of various nooks, and Ki took a reassessment. *The one at the head of the alley. He's the leader,* he told himself. *And as with all bullies, if you take out the leader, the rest will run.*

Another sound caught his ear from behind. Five back there now. A total of nine. *Difficult, but not impossible,* he thought. *As long as they don't have energy weapons. But I will need my swords. A pity.*

The man Ki had determined was the leader brushed his soft golden brown hair out of his eyes and made a small signal with his hand, and the group began to close in, moving closer and closer to Ki one ragged step at a time. Ki remained perfectly still.

He smiled when he heard the rattle of the chains. There would be no energy weapons among this group, and the clank of a piece of pipe confirmed it. That meant this would be a fair fight, though he would resort to his swords.

He considered the men he could see in front of him. One of them was determined, grim, the leader. One to his left looked like a thug, the type who would beat on anyone for the sheer joy of hearing them scream. The two more he could see looked scared, but were unwilling to show it, in spite of their position about ten feet behind their leader. A gust of wind shot coldly down the alley into Ki's face, and it brought with it the scent of their fear. That evened the odds, and Ki growled, deep and heavily in his throat, using the wild sounds that shook Aubin to help their fear blossom.

His hand found the hilt of his sheathed katana, and he shifted until the grip sat well in his palm. *I wish I had the hoj,* he mourned inwardly. *This little toy is too short and too light.* Even with all the practice he had taken with the katana, he was not totally comfortable with it. His hoj was part of his arm.

He pulled his hanging wet hair back off his face with his free hand, and shifted his shoulder to loosen them from the clinging wet silk. He filled his lungs, and with a bloodcurdling yell rushed forward, charging those in front of him. As he hoped, the ones behind him, figuring they were safe for the moment, also came forward. Ki turned swiftly on them and downed the center three before they could react. They died surprised.

The thug took the opportunity to come at Ki's neck with a knife. The blow would have landed, but Ki had expected an attack from the rear and continued his sweep of the katana into a full circle. It took the thug across the belly, and he went down, yowling, trying to hold in his guts.

It was too much for one of the cravens. He pulled an energy weapon from inside his jacket, and fired. That burst was answered by one from somewhere behind Ki. No one, not even the attackers, had expected those bright bursts of light, and there was a split second devoid of motion. But Ki, with long-practiced battle sense, recovered quickly. He used his shar to end the thug's agony, leaving the short sword in the corpse in order to free his hand, and then rushed at the leader. Golden slitted eyes met pale blue, and Ki was stunned by the hatred he read in the human's round eyes. This was not, then, a mugging.

Ki, with his nanosecond advantage, managed to grab the leader by the throat with his cold left hand, and shoved him hard into the wall. He spared a glance for the two cowards who had been backing this fighter, and realized one had been spattered with gore from the thug's stomach wound, and was in a state of complete shock. When his gaze brushed over the other, the man was in the process of hitting the dirt and covering his head with his hands, and weeping, totally freaked by the addition of energy weapons to this battle. The sight disgusted Ki, but he could not spare the time to think about it.

"If you're fond of your throat, tell them to throw away their weapons."

"Drop 'em," emerged bitterly from the captured throat.

No one moved, and Ki did not hear weapons hitting the concrete.

The steel fingers tightened unmercifully.

Strangled sounds emerged from the leader's mouth, then, "I said 'Drop 'em'!"

Reluctantly, weapons clattered to the ground. Another wind gust blew down the alley, and a fresh scent made Ki look up. At the same instant, a voice called down from above.

"Colwin, look out!"

Above Ki, the man on the roof let fly with a steel ball from a slingshot. It caught Ki at the temple, and the Lionman realized that had it not been for his hair he would have been dead. As it was, he felt himself crumbling. *Should have killed the bastard when I had the chance*, he thought as he folded.

Chapter Thirteen

———◆———

AM I ALIVE? danced repeatedly and drunkenly through Ki's mind. *Mmumna, I hurt! My head is throbbing, my ribs hurt more. I must be alive. I hurt too much to be dead.*

Ki tried to shift to ease the ache in his side, and couldn't. Then he vaguely remembered being hit in the side of the head. His inability to move suddenly scared him. What if the blow on the head and his immobility were connected? He clamped his eyes shut more tightly, and

fought the thought down. One thing at a time.
Was he suffering from a concussion? He tried to
remember what Aubin's apartments looked like,
and succeeded, down to the twisted maiden that
was Aubin's special favorite. Ki's last conversation with Mikal also replayed itself for him
without a blank spot. He was satisfied. His
memory was intact.

He tried to open his eyes, and could not, so he
relaxed some of his efforts to fully waken. As he
relaxed, some things came gradually to his attention. He could hear and smell a ventilation
system working close at hand, and felt the wash
of it across his aching shoulders. Then he recognized a scent, female, and realized he was not
alone. Now he would not move even if he could.
Voices and words came to him as the fog in his
brain gradually cleared. He recognized the scent
of the one whose throat he should have ripped
out. He regretted his generosity anew. If he had
killed the boy, he would not be in whatever fix
he was in now. He sniffed purposefully. The female's hair lacquer and perfume came to him
strongly. She must be nearby. And there was another male, this one some distance away.
Flowers from various worlds were somewhere
in this spacious room. And over all of this there
was a curious electrical ozone scent Ki could
not identify. His eyes were beginning to func-
tion, and he caught some reddish sunlight
through his eyelids. He began to find the ends of
his body, and he realized he was in a chair with
his hands tied together behind its back. Unfortunately, the chair felt as if it was metal, and
heavy. So much for simply breaking the chair.
His bare feet rested on carpeting, thick and very
soft. There was no noise outside of that created

by the occupants. Either this place was very remote or very well insulated.

"Wake him up, question him, then kill him! It's the only way to handle the pussy!"

Now Ki was making sense of the conversation floating around him, and he was not terribly pleased by what he heard the boy saying. But he was not surprised. He'd seen the hate in the boy's eyes when they'd met in the alley.

Things began to fall into place. The quiet, the thickness of the carpet and the absence of odors. It all added up to a private house or office. And the actions the boy was advocating made it fairly certain Ki was in rebel hands. No smells, thick carpet, privacy. That added up to money and power. So these were not just common soldiery.

"Yes, Colwin," the female answered. "I want to question him, too. But first I just want to talk to him. Wake him up."

Without moving, his hair hanging dirty and limp in his face, his head hanging forward, Ki said, "That won't be necessary," though his voice sounded very strange in his ears because of the dryness of his mouth and throat, and the grittiness around his lips. He raised his head, sat as straight as his bonds would permit, then tossed his head to clear his mane from his line of sight. His gaze fell immediately on the boy, Colwin, and instinctively Ki's eyes narrowed and his teeth bared. Colwin cringed, and Ki turned his head to the female who rested casually at the front edge of the desk. She looked anything but helpless, in spite of her tiny stature.

Up to this point Ki was not really angry. He was hurt and in trouble, yes, but anger was not part of what was happening. This was the way the game was played. Then he saw, behind the female, a human playing with his naked swords, running his greasy, acidic fingers along his revered blades. It was unforgivable! And Ki was furious.

The growl grew from deep in his chest, and rumbled coarsely along his throat. "Put that down!" Ki ordered reverberatingly in a low and threatening tone.

The startled human went snow white and dropped the sword on the desktop.

Colwin stiffened. "You're in no position to give orders, pussy!" he snapped viciously.

From somewhere behind Ki stepped the tallest, thinnest human male Ki had ever seen. He was dressed in a black skinsuit which, on his emaciated frame, hung in baggy folds, making him look skeletal. He walked to the desk, and as he passed close to Ki's chair, Ki was fascinated to discover that the ozone scent emanated from this human. The thin one bent from the waist over the desk, and with a look of rapture began an exacting study of the swords. He did not, however, touch them.

Through all of this, the female had remained unruffled. In fact, she looked almost bored. Ki found himself beginning to respect her, though he knew she was someone to be careful of. She moved from the front of her desk to behind it, shooing the frightened male out of her way so that she might sit comfortably. Then her eyes narrowed as she noticed a freshly cut notch in her desktop where the sword had fallen.

"You'll pay to have this repaired," she told the man coldly. Then she thought for a moment before she continued. "Colwin, take them out of here. I want to talk to my guest privately."

Colwin spun away from Ki and faced Loni savagely. "Are you crazy?" he screamed.

"Probably," she answered, totally unruffled, "but do it anyway."

Everything froze into a tableau, and remained there, balancing precariously, while it was decided who was in charge, Colwin or the female. Then she made a small waving motion with her hand, shooing them out, and the tableau broke. The female held sway.

But Colwin still hesitated. "We'll be right outside. Just scream if he tries anything. We'll hear."

She waved them out once more, thinking, *The hell you'll hear. This place is so well soundproofed you wouldn't even hear the explosion that would take this pussy's life until the walls came down. If he tries anything, I'll just say "Caligula." Couldn't be simpler. We'll all get to hell together.*

The skinny male had taken up a position just behind the female's chair. He remained behind when the others began to file out, his eyes moving almost rhythmically between Ki and the woman.

Loni escorted her cohorts out the door and closed it tightly behind them. Then she pulled up a side chair and sat down right next to Ki. He looked her over, taking note of the very expensive suede skinsuit she was wearing. The jewelry was as real as the rest of her.

"Is this the common treatment for all your 'guests'?" Ki asked sarcastically.

"No. But it is not often I have a pus— Lionman come to visit. Some of the young men tend to get just a little overzealous."

Something in the woman's speech pattern reminded Ki of Aubin, and he found it alarmed him slightly. Perhaps she was just a touch too self-assured. Her accent was nothing like Aubin's Lunar drawl, however, and Ki found he really couldn't place it with any certainty.

"You know you're taking an awful chance being alone with me," Ki said before he realized even he had begun to forget about the skinny one's presence.

"I really don't think so," she answered pleasantly. "You're tied with polycarbonate rope. You're strong, but you're not that strong." She paused a moment, and smiled. "If you'd like, I'll get you the p.s.i. for polycarbonate. It might be interesting."

Ki smiled back at her. "No, thank you. That won't be necessary." But she had told him exactly what he wanted to know. The tensile strength of polycarbonate was such that he would never break it no matter how long he pulled at it. But it would cut. He began rubbing the bindings against the spot where his left hand joined his wrist. There was a rough spot there that had bothered him for years, but he'd never taken the time to have it fixed. Now he was glad he hadn't. *And if I'm very careful*, he told himself, *I may live long enough to get out of here.*

"You're very thorough, whoever you are," Ki said to the lady.

She smiled again. "I've been very remiss. Forgive me. My name is Sara Korlon. My friends call me Loni. You are in my office. Welcome to Loni's Place. I usually treat my guests a little more ... casually, but you're very special."

It dawned on Ki that this Sara Korlon must

have a small empire. And that meant the rebels had more money and power than anyone suspected. No wonder the emperor had never been able to find them and root them out. And if this office was any kind of measure, it must be quite a far-reaching little empire. There were several sculptures, and each of them came from a different world. The paintings on the walls would have done honor to the Imperial Museum. The two walls of windows showed Ki he was at the very least ninety stories above the street, possibly more, and if he could judge from what he could see from his seated position, he was in the very best part of Capitol Center. And the lady had taste. The sofa and drapes were done in a soft, neutral beige that had just a touch of pink in it, and the pink was picked up by the dusty rose of the carpet. It was perfect for her, and yet Ki could understand how the many men who revolved around this lady could be comfortable here, too. None of the furnishings were small or fussy, and everything looked as if it could and should be used.

Loni broke in on his thoughts. "And the reason you're still alive and I'm here alone with you ..."

Ki cocked his head to one side. Alone? The skinny one didn't exist for her either?

"...is that I have a proposition for you."

Ki met her gaze and raised his eyebrows in questioning curiosity.

But Loni did not proceed immediately. She stood, moved to a small bar that was nestled into a nook in a bookcase, and poured herself a drink. Then she brought the very fine crystal wineglass back to his side and seated herself once more.

"You have my undivided attention," he said as a prompt.

She took a sip of her drink, and enjoyed the taste of it. "It's quite good," she told Ki. "A combination of white wine and cognac. Would you like to try some?"

But Ki was becoming annoyed, and he was afraid his sawing motions would be noticed if she became too relaxed. "Get on with it," he said brusquely.

She set her drink aside and leaned close to Ki's face, as if she were imparting a secret. "As you have already figured out, you are in the hands of the illustrious rebels. Also as you know, we don't like the emperor. One way or another, he's on the way out. If we don't get him, other groups will. There are those who would like to eliminate the empire entirely, but most of us, myself included, don't subscribe to that philosophy. We believe Ozenscebo has betrayed a trust put on him by his fathers and has raped the empire. We are forced to remove him for the sake of the empire. We had hoped we could eliminate Ozenscebo, leaving Elena in charge. She was certainly more qualified for the post than Ozie. Unfortunately, Ozie has precluded that option. This leaves us with Magnus, who is even less acceptable than his sire. If permitted to live, the abomination will put his father to shame." She paused, and put a finger to her lips while considering. Then she nodded to herself and continued. "Your personal dislike for the emperor is known to me."

Ki was astonished, but he dared not let that show. "Is it really?" he asked coolly.

Loni waved her hand in a circular motion at the skinny male, who still stood behind the desk. His eyes dropped half closed, and he drew one deep breath and exhaled slowly. It appeared to Ki that he had fallen into a trance, but it should not be possible to do so so quickly. Skinny began to recite in a singsong monotone.

"Lawwnum: 'I'm tired.'"

"Tabber: 'Then, take a nap.'"

"Lawwnum: 'Aubin, you started this conversation, not me. I'm not in the mood for jokes.'"

"Tabber: 'I'm sorry. Reflex action.'"

"Lawwnum: 'I'm tired of rebels, responsibility, Mikal's hero-worship, politics, and disgusting courtiers. And I'm tired of Ozenscebo's excesses.'"

"Stop!" Loni called, and the man's eyes fluttered open. All traces of any trancelike state vanished.

Ki was both astounded and furious. "That was a private conversation! You can take your proposition and go to hell. If you untie me, I'll be happy to see you on your way."

Loni was shocked, and it showed in her face. That was not the response she had expected. She did not believe Lawwnum could be so angry simply because one little conversation had been "overheard." And besides, if he was so tired of the emperor's excesses, why wasn't he delighted with the chance to join the rebels?

Ki noted her shock, and was pleased. How naive she had been!

The male had not moved from his place behind the desk, but his face had changed again. This time he drew his brows together and seemed to be listening intently, although Ki, if he had seen the change, could not have said listening to what, as all conversation in the room had died. Then he nodded once, and walked to

Loni's side. He bent over, put his mouth next to her ear, and whispered, "Natanha." It was done so softly that only a Nidean would have been able to overhear.

Loni's face lit up as she understood, and she turned eagerly back to Ki while the male returned to his place behind the desk.

"I've outlined three possibilities. There is a fourth. The princess favors her mother, and to date has escaped her father's kind attentions. I'm told she's smart. If she continues to avoid discovery, I'm sure she would make an acceptable empress." Loni grinned broadly. "I see I have your attention again."

"You have."

"This is where you come in. Although our ranks are growing daily, and we have extensive information on the palace, we have almost no information on Nidean battle strategy. That makes it impossible for us to enter the palace. We need you to teach us Nidean battle techniques. With your assistance we may be able to spare hundreds of lives which would otherwise be thrown away while we learn, and thus insure that the princess is placed quickly on the throne."

Ki flashed his somewhat long and moderately pointed teeth at Loni in a broad smile. "What makes you think I won't agree, then call in a cadre of Lionmen and level your little building around your ears?"

Loni leaned forward with a very sober expression on her face. "You're a Lionman," she told him eagerly. "More importantly, you are *the* Lionman. You would rather slit your belly open than break your word. Your word will suffice for me. If you'll join us and work with us, I'll untie you here and now. You'll be given quarters here and treated as an honored leader."

Ki looked intently at her face, and considered. She was right. The emperor was not fit to hold the throne. But Ki had promised to uphold the empire. Ki had learned very painfully that the emperor and the empire were not the same thing. The question remained: Could he kill the emperor and still serve the empire? Yes, if Ozenscebo died with dignity. Ki could not let him die at the unclean hands of the rabble. Ki had to kill the bastard emperor himself.

"You have my word," he told Loni as he pulled his hands from behind his back with bits of rope dangling loosely from his raw wrists.

Ki felt clean and, although very sore, whole once more as he made his way down the warren of back hallways in Loni's Place to the appointed room where he was supposed to be debriefed. It was an interesting tour past kitchens, linen closets, janitorial closets, and all the other behind-the-scenes necessities that made a place like Loni's work. He had showered and taken some time to meditate. And surprisingly, but true to Loni's word, except for the young man who had come to take his uniform to be cleaned and then returned it a few minutes later, he had seen no one. As far as he could determine, he had not been followed or spied upon.

It was oddly uncomfortable to be dressed in his uniform, however, and he tugged repeatedly at the corners of his tunic as if it needed straightening. Loni had promised him some new kimono and hakama. He couldn't very well continue to wear his uniform—he'd stand out like a sore thumb. But they probably wouldn't arrive until tomorrow. At least she didn't expect him to wear either the flowing robes Ozenscebo had made popular or the skinsuits Aubin was donning lately. He'd have been mortified to be seen in either.

At precisely the appointed hour, Ki knocked on the door of the debriefing room. Loni answered it, and Ki stepped in.

"You're punctual. I should have expected that, Commander," she said with just a hint of a smile. "You live up to your reputation."

He raised his eyebrow at her skeptically. "Which reputation is that?" he asked.

She laughed, and asked him to sit down. He did, and took the opportunity to look carefully around the room. The center of the room was brightly lit, and in the circle of light stood a functional but not fashionable desk. Its metal top reflected none of the lavishness of the furnishings upstairs in Loni's office. The chair he took was comfortable, but, like the desk, not fashionable. There were two more chairs, and aside from the clutter on the desktop, no other furnishings.

In the shadowy corner behind the desk there was a figure. At first even Ki's excellent eyes had trouble making it out, but as he studied it the odor of ozone came to him, and Ki recognized the skinny one who had been in Loni's office earlier. There was another large man in the farthest corner, but Ki dismissed him as a bodyguard only, having no real purpose as far as this meeting was concerned other than to see that Ki did not harm Sarah Korlon. The skinny one, however, was present at Loni's invitation. There was a purpose there that Ki did not understand, and Ki did not care for puzzles.

He did not have to wonder long, though, because Loni spoke while she was taking her seat behind the desk.

"This, Commander," she said as she gestured behind her toward the shadowy figure, "is an Interface. He would like to know everything."

Curiosity stimulated, Ki asked, "What's an Interface?"

Loni smiled smugly. It pleased her that the Commander of the Imperial Guard did not know of their existence. "This is half of a team. They are members of a religious sect who moved to a colony on a small moon of Changwo so they could practice in freedom. They had been persecuted and chased out of just about every other place they'd tried to settle. Their purpose is to know everything—and that is not an overstatement."

"Half of a team? Where's the other half?"

"In the basement in a suspensor field. This one"—and she gestured behind her again—"has no thoughts of its own. It merely gathers information for the Cognoscitive, leaving the Cognoscitive free to process and collate the information fed into her."

"I see," Ki said, dismissing the problem of bizarre religious sects for the moment. "But what is it you want to know?"

The Interface stepped forward into the light, and leaned across the desk eagerly, resting his weight on his hands on the desktop. "Everything. All that you know."

"Specify," Ki answered coldly.

The Interface appeared to cock his head

slightly as if to listen, then said, "Information on your homeworld is scarce."

"We have a red sun—" Ki began in a textbook fashion.

The Interface cut him off. "We know the physical properties of your planet. We wish to know the cultural things your closed-door policy keeps hidden from us."

Ki snorted. "Our doors are closed because we prefer them that way."

The Interface straightened, and looked to Loni. "Please ask the commander to cooperate. Anything said here will be kept in strict confidence."

Loni stood, and walked around the desk until she stood very near Ki, and she looked down at him with mink-brown eyes. "Commander," she said sweetly, "please?"

Ki looked up at her and sighed heavily. His position was a decidedly uncomfortable one. But he had promised to help. He reluctantly nodded.

Ki was alone in his new quarters trying to make sense out of everything that had happened to him during this overly long and dangerous day. As he rested on his heels with his back to the wall, his eyes traveled around his new room. The walls were thick. No outside noise came through at all. But they were plain and painted a light cream color. There were no windows. He shifted uncomfortably on the hard concrete floor that even the light brown wall-to-wall carpeting could not hide from his knees. He had looked carefully when he'd come back, however, and the room appeared to be all his. There did not seem to be any listening devices anywhere.

He was mightily uncomfortable with all the talking he'd done. It was usually he who asked the questions. Still, he hadn't told them everything. If Natanha was to get to the throne, he had to be there. And if he was going to be there when Natanha made it, he had to be in control of the situation here and now. That meant some things were to remain his alone.

He had found it disturbing that the Interface kept returning to Nide and things Nidean. Over and over again Ki had had to dodge. But it had been amusing to see the Interface's face when he had flatly said "No!"

Ki shifted again. *I'm willing to betray the empire*, he thought, but then he screamed inwardly at himself. *No! That's wrong! I'm willing to betray the emperor, not the empire! And I am not willing to betray Nide!*

He calmed himself once more, and turned his thoughts. *Loni seemed very intelligent. Elena probably would have made good use of her if the empress had known the entrepreneur existed. But Loni does have a serious flaw. She relies too heavily on her alleged oracle, the Interface-and-Cognoscitive team. That reliance will be her downfall.*

That triggered something, and Ki paused to consider it, turning it over in his mind and looking at it from all sides. *Yes*, he told himself finally, nodding his head. *If things don't go my way, the Interface will begin to get false information.*

Chapter Fourteen

———◆———

AUBIN WAS MUTTERING to himself as he walked determinedly down the hall toward Ki's apartments.

"This time I'm going to nail his ass to the wall! I thought I'd gotten him to move! I thought he'd go back to work! But no! No one's seen him!" he fumed to himself. "It isn't like him to mope, especially since I talked to him. I'll get him this time! I'll pick up a spoon and offer to feed him. And when he looks at me like 'What are you doing, human?' I'll offer to burp him and change his diapers! That'll get him. He'll react to that! Then, when he says, 'What now?' I'll tell him if he doesn't want to be treated like a baby, he shouldn't act like one. That'll get his attention!"

But when he stopped in front of Ki's door, Aubin suddenly discovered he was afraid. He stopped.

"One of these days, Aubin Tabber, you're going to push Ki too hard," he told himself. "Ki isn't human, and you saw what he did to that servant in the throne room. When you finally do push too hard, your head is going to roll around like a soccer ball, too." He sighed. "At least it'll be quick." Then he smiled wryly. "And, of course, there is some pleasure in knowing that *after* he cut my head off, boy! would he feel guilty!"

He stared at the palm lock for a moment, then inhaled deeply and let it out slowly. "My pension isn't that good anyway," he mumbled, and opened the door.

Except for a small amount of light coming from a closet in the bedroom, the apartment was dark. The drapes were still drawn, and the place had that unused smell Aubin associated with coming home after a long vacation. He knew Ki wasn't there.

A burst of fear exploded in Aubin. He began talking to himself again.

"He's not here. But no one's seen him. People remember when they see him. So where is he?"

He started turning on lights and looking around the place to see if he could find something that would help him determine where Ki had gone. But he didn't really find much that was of help. The living room was still a mess, though Ki's traditional puppets still hung neatly on the wall. They were only just beginning to get dusty. The bedroom was fairly orderly, though the closet door was open, as was a drawer in the chest. On the chest the hoj rested in its stand like a baby in its cradle. The bathroom was more disorganized. What had been wet towels had been dropped on the floor, and now the room smelled musty and old in spite of the ventilation system.

Aubin walked back into the living room. "Nothing," he said aloud.

He walked over to the wall where the puppets hung, and stood looking up at the almost-life-sized figures where they dangled from their thongs as if waiting for one of the puppeteers to insert his hands and feet and begin a tale of Nidean history. "It would take a strong man to manipulate these," Aubin muttered as he fingered the rare fur that formed a breechclout on a wild

Nidean female. "A strong man. A Lionman." He looked into the female's face. "How many stories have you told, pretty lady?" he asked the puppet. "How many times have you told your people their history? I wish you could tell me one more tale. I wish you could tell me where Ki Lawwnum has gone."

Aubin forced himself to take heart from the fact nothing disastrous had happened here. And Ki had his swords, because the stands for the katana and the shar were empty. With those swords Ki could take care of himself in almost any situation.

In reaction to his fear, Aubin began to get angry. "If I know that bastard, he's sitting on his heels somewhere in the palace watching the grass grow while all the rest of us worry about him!"

He pounded his fist into his open palm with a smack. "Grass! I haven't checked the garden!"

But any hope that thought might have brought was dashed as soon as Aubin opened the doors. He was shocked at its state. Weeds were everywhere, bending over the path, hanging into the stream. The grass was shaggy and uneven, spotty brown in places where the weeds had taken over.

"No one's been here for some time," he said as he stepped out the door onto the path. "It looks wilder."

A breeze blew across from the water, and brought with it a chill Aubin was not used to. Being from Luna, he spent almost all of his time indoors. The out-of-doors seemed unnatural and ferociously dangerous to him. But instead of retreating, he pulled his arms across his chest and walked out a little farther. After the closed-in feel of the apartment, the breeze was almost welcome. It was at least fresh. He walked to the area of grass where Ki usually did his meditating. It had grown high, and much of it was heavy with seed. The patch of flowers across the way was blowing madly in the wind, weeds mixed in with the remnants of colorful blooms that were also heavy with seed and ready to die.

Aubin stared at it, and his imagination created out of the little patch of flowers a world where all were wild and fierce. He had a vision of Ki, far more leonine than he actually was, with a wild, flowing mane that tumbled totally free, and the pointy face of a meat-eating beast. And this Ki did not speak, but only rumbled and growled.

Now Aubin knew he was really frightened for his friend, and it took considerable effort to shake off the image. It was an illogical fear, Aubin knew, but it remained with him all the same.

"Something's wrong. I feel it," he whispered to the wind. Then he snickered at himself. "Listen to me. I'm starting to sound just like Ki. Nothing's wrong. I'm going to go in and sit down and wait for him. He's got to come back eventually."

He shivered as he closed the doors gladly behind him, but he took one more look at the sky. "It will be winter soon," he said sadly.

Then he shook himself, trying to throw off the morose mood he'd fallen into. He went into the kitchen and poured himself a stiff dose of stawwshwa, even though he loathed the stuff. It was the only alcoholic beverage Ki kept. He went to the large, comfortable chair where he had last seen Ki sitting, and made himself at home. Then he closed his eyes and downed a big gulp of the stawwshwa as if he were taking a particularly foul-tasting medicine.

"Foul-tasting it may be, but it helps my aches and pains," he sighed, and shifted until he was comfortable. Then, as he relaxed, he realized he was very tired. His emotions had drained him. And soon he began to drift, and then to doze.

Something was digging painfully into Aubin's shoulders, and his feet dangled above the floor. He was being shaken like a rag in the grip of a playful puppy, only as he opened his eyes, Aubin could find nothing playful about the situation. A furious Mikal was on the verge of breaking his collarbones.

"What are you doing in here?!" screamed the livid lieutenant. "What have you done with the commander?"

Aubin was only just beginning to wake up. He realized gradually there were three other Guardsmen in the room, including— *What's his name?... Res.*

All this time I've been worried about what Ki was going to do to me, and now this kitten is going to break my neck! he thought. Then the anger caught up with him again. *The hell he is! I've got to look as angry as I can. That shouldn't be hard. I'm furious.*

Masterfully, Aubin put all of the fury into his face. Then he slowly turned his head so that he was looking down at the hands on his shoulders. Then he looked at Mikal squarely.

"Take your hands off of me," he said slowly, enunciating each word precisely.

Shocked that a mere human could generate such anger, Mikal released Aubin.

"Excuse me," the envoy said as he shoved his

way past Mikal in order to address Res. "Captain, as you are the senior officer here, I demand to know why one of your subordinates has attacked me!" Aubin could feel Mikal's hot and angry breath blowing down his neck, but he ignored it.

Res was completely calm. "We have not seen the commander in over a week. We were worried about his health and safety. We've come here to see if the colonel was in need of assistance. When we arrived, the rooms were empty except for you. You will kindly explain the colonel's absence and your presence."

Aubin put a tight rein on his anger and faced the captain in a more subdued manner. But as he was about to answer, Mikal spoke from behind him.

"You'd better tell us the truth, human," Mikal growled. "We'd know the difference."

Res looked up, annoyed. "Enough!" he spat at the lieutenant in Nidean. Then he looked at Aubin. "Well?"

"The last time I saw the colonel, several days ago, he was not feeling very well. I came back because I haven't seen him since. I found the apartment empty." He paused significantly. "My palm print *does* give me access. I did not break in. When I didn't find him, and I saw the state of his quarters, I thought there might be trouble and decided to wait for him. But instead of a colonel I found a lieutenant. Rather a letdown, wouldn't you say?"

Res looked down into the human's face, assessing the truth of what he'd heard. The piercing stare was a hard one to bear, and Aubin was tempted to turn away from it. But he didn't dare. He had learned as much from Ki.

Res broke the scene. "I see. I'm going to initiate an organized search for the commander, both inside and outside the palace." He turned and began to leave the room, followed by his men, but not by Aubin. Res turned back to the envoy. "Are you coming?"

Aubin shook his head. "No. I'll wait here. He's bound to pop in eventually. I find it more sensible to stay here than to run around."

As the Guardsmen began again to leave, a wicked gleam came into Aubin's eye. With as much of a Nidean rumble as he could muster, he called, "Aallaard Lawwnum, I like your haircut."

Mikal's red face read "I'm going to kill you, human," and he turned back, his hand reaching for his sword.

Res's deep bass voice whipped hard against Mikal's back. "That's very ill-advised, Lieutenant."

Mikal stopped, breathing heavily, his control almost gone. But he finally turned toward the door, stepped out, and shut it behind him.

"Gotcha!" Aubin tossed after him.

The subbasement was a completely cheerless place, cold and damp and smelling of disuse. The feeling of being closed in, surrounded by spongy earth, was heavy, as if the whole structure could collapse any moment. Pillars of unfinished concrete held up an overhead structure of steel beams and more concrete. Bare light fixtures cast a cold blue wash over everything, making the area even chillier. The concrete floor was covered with thick, padded practice mats, but they were dusty and smelled of mold, in

spite of looking as if they'd hardly been used.
The far wall was covered with scorch marks, obviously from repeated energy-weapons practice.

Ki looked through the light haze of spider
webs and grunted. It was obvious the rebels put
more store in their contraband energy weapons
than they did in hand-to-hand.

"I've got a lot to teach them," he said quietly,
shaking his head.

The twin doors to the private, key-operated elevator opened behind Ki and he turned to watch
the first of his group of trainees. They were a
conglomerate of men and women, apparently
from every kind of background imaginable. The
men started at about age seventeen, mere
toddlers in Ki's view, and ranged up to about
forty-eight. Ki thought several of them were
probably too old for this, but he'd give them all
a chance to find that out for themselves. The
women, too, started at about seventeen, but
they ranged only up to about twenty-seven. An
interesting dichotomy.

Ki took a purposely casual stance, leaning up
against one of the concrete pillars with his arms
crossed, and watched the groups as they left the
elevator. Most of them, men and women alike,
were carrying knives, supposedly concealed, but
only a scattered few looked as if they knew what
to do with them.

He recognized two from the brawl in the alley,
and allowed that they were probably pretty
good street fighters. They'd be no match for the
Lionman Guard, however. And the rest were as
soft as putty.

Gradually, his students formed a crescent
around him, waiting for him to begin. *Some students*, he thought. *Most of them want to kill me.*

But not as much as that one they call Colwin. It's a good thing he's not here.

He straightened. "My name is..." He checked himself. He'd been about to use the correct Nidean pronunciation. He softened it to something human. "...Lawwnum." He was not ready yet to spook them, and Aubin never could stand to hear him speak his native tongue. *Mmumna, I wish I could have a long talk with Aubin.*

"As you no doubt know," he continued, "I was until recently commander of the Lionman Guard. I have developed, however, a difference of opinion with our emperor. I have recently made the acquaintance of your Loni, and she has requested I instruct you in the art of hand-to-hand combat."

He paused to look around, checking on reactions. A few looked eager, almost too eager, for the chance to fight a Lionman. A few openly snickered at him, as if there were nothing he could teach them. They were less dangerous than the ones who were quiet.

He answered the snickers. "I can see a few of you question the need for hand-to-hand when you have your energy weapons. Some of you are quite secure in your skills, and some of you are very eager to try me. I assure you energy weapons are effective even against Lionmen." He held up his left hand and turned it slowly in the cold blue light. "Effective, that is, until you get close." He smiled, showing his predator's teeth, and laughed a good Nidean rumble that started deep in his chest and vibrated wildly out of his throat. "If you should be unfortunate enough to be within fifty yards of a Lionman, he can move fast enough to dodge your blasts. He'll get you. My— or rather, the emperor's, men and women are to date the best-trained fighting force in the empire.

"Lionmen, however, have one weakness that will serve us. They have an overall contempt for the training and experience of the average human. With my help, you may be able to surprise them and walk away with your hides intact."

A rudely sneering human interrupted. "I would remind the colonel," he said sarcastically, "that we mere humans brought you down."

Ki felt he should answer, as he recognized the one who had caught him with the sling. "True. But it took nine of you to do it, and even then you only managed it because you were already in hiding above me. If you'd been down on the street, you'd all be dead." He paused, grinning, allowing his teeth to show once more. "Of course, if you wish to prove me wrong, we have mats over here. I'll even let you use the three knives in your tunic and the two weapons in your boots, while I shall be, as you can see, unarmed."

The slingsman hesitated. There had to be a catch. But his confreres were laughing and urging him on. Finally he shrugged. There was no easy way out.

With a clipped, choppy walk he took the mat and bent without ever turning his golden-skinned face from Ki to pull his pants legs up. He pulled a pair of sai out of his boots, and placed them reverently in front of him in an X before tucking the trousers firmly into the boot tops. Then he turned more gracefully than his walk should have allowed, and whipped the sai in quick and very menacing circles.

"You picked the wrong person to fuck with

today, pussy," he said through clenched teeth, black eyes flashing, angry he had been forced into this by his peers. He tucked one sai into his belt, and grabbed a dagger. In the same motion he threw it at Ki and rushed forward.

Ki stepped aside, unruffled, though bothered slightly by the billowing of his unfamiliar hakama. He should have taken the time to tie them up, but it was not important now. This boy, for all his machismo, would be easily bested, as long as Ki paid attention. Ki was certain the boy could be sly, and this was one fight Ki could not afford to lose. He heard the knife clatter against the wall. It sounded as if it shattered, but he did not turn to confirm his ear, as the human was bearing down on him.

The charge was handled easily, and Ki had the sai in his hand now as he threw the human aside to allow him to try again. The man stood, red-faced and angry at his loss, and threw another knife at Ki, who laughed as he grabbed it out of the air with his left hand. The action made a loud *chunk* sound, and several of the onlookers shivered involuntarily.

Once more the human attacked, having drawn the other sai, but Ki struck down firmly on the man's arm, and the sai flew like a small silver eaglet just trying its new flight vanes. Spectators scattered, and it finally clattered to the floor.

But Ki was tiring of the ease of this. There was no challenge here. So he dumped the man to the mat, planted his knee firmly in the scrawny human chest, and, with the sai he still held in his right hand, nicked the man's cheek deeply enough to draw blood.

Ki met the man's furious black eyes. "It could

have been your throat. Did I make my point?"
The Lionman stood fluidly, allowing the other
his freedom, and turned to face the student
group, calculating the one on the floor would
have to make one more face-saving move.

The man on the mat reached for the last dagger in his tunic.

Without turning, Ki said heavily, "Don't."

Then he continued walking toward the group.
"Next?" he asked cheerfully.

Chapter Fifteen

THE WORKOUT HAD been a good one, and Ki had
enjoyed it. It was hard to believe, though, that
he had been here for only two weeks. This place
would never be home, but the unfamiliarity was
wearing off. And there were some good feelings
growing. After a few difficulties in the beginning, he had established himself as the master,
and now had the respect of those in his charge.
He didn't dare work them too hard yet, though.
He was afraid they wouldn't come back, and
they needed to know what he could teach them.

He stepped into the private elevator, still
sweating. He had a right to be sweating. He had
taken on five opponents today, some of them
fairly good. He'd only asked one match apiece of
his pupils. At least the basement didn't smell
too rancid. It must be because they hadn't used

it previously for much of anything other than weapons practice.

He felt the elevator begin to lift, and leaned back against the wall while he toweled off his face. *I need a shower.* He sighed. *The hot water is going to feel good,* he told himself, and draped the towel around his neck.

The elevator stopped, and he walked down the corridor to his room, already working at undoing a stubborn knot in his sash. There were a few people in the corridor, but he'd become enough used to the place that he felt he could safely ignore them, and he did so.

But one woman called out to him. "Colonel Lawwnum?"

"Yes?" He turned to face her.

She walked up close to him, and looked up at him with the air of a shy seductress. "Colonel Lawwnum, I've seen you forever on the newscasts, and I just wanted you to know I'm so happy you've decided to join us. With you on our side we really have a chance." She batted her dark lashes at him, and smiled. "I really just wanted to meet you," she whispered confidentially.

Ki looked down at her, amazed at how tiny she seemed after dealing with his fighters. Were all noncombatant human females so small? But there was something different about this one. The black lace dress she wore made it obvious she was not one of the fighters. And her features were what Ki had heard described as Mediterranean, a rounded face with olive skin, a real rarity, black eyes, also round, and wonderfully thick dark hair.

"Who are you?" he asked.

She extended her hand to him while she introduced herself, and heavy bangles jingled at her wrist. "My name is Teresa. I'm one of Loni's girls," she said sweetly as she moved closer to him so that she had to look up sharply at him, accenting her obvious womanly charms in her low-cut dress and draping her heavy lashes over her eyes.

When he did not take her extended hand, she reached out a little farther and touched his bare chest where his kimono had parted. "You're so warm," she said languidly. "Were you going to take a shower?"

Quite taken aback, Ki answered truthfully. "Yes."

Teresa stepped even closer, so that Ki could feel her warmth against his chest. "Would you like some company?"

Ki stepped back quickly, and tucked his kimono closed.

She giggled sweetly. "Don't tell me you're shy!"

Mmumna help me, Ki whispered internally, aware of where this was going and not liking it. Humans were, after all, not so very far removed from the beasts. "Not shy at all," he said honestly. "And you're a very attractive young woman." He allowed his voice to rumble heartily. "I thank you for your offer. It's tempting. But I'm afraid I might be too alien for you," he lied chivalrously, being really horrified by the thought of loving a non-Nidean.

She laughed gaily. "I've taken care of all kinds."

Ki started backing toward his door, which seemed a very long distance down the hallway. "But I can guarantee you've never taken care of a Nidean." He continued to back, his steps becoming ever more hasty.

She followed him, closing the distance between them. "There's a first time for everything."

Colwin stepped out of the elevator, and just caught a glimpse of Teresa out of the corner of his eye. Deciding his current errand would wait a few moments, he turned in her direction, hoping to find her available. He stopped short as he saw her facing down Lawwnum, and ducked aside to watch from concealment.

At last Ki reached the door, and opened it without glancing back. This female was one adversary he did not dare turn his back on. "Perhaps," he told her as he stepped over the threshold. "But today is not a day for first times." The door slid shut, and Ki collapsed against it. "Mmumna be praised!" he murmured shakily. "I got out of that one. Barely."

On the other side of the door Teresa was stamping her foot in frustration. "He turned me down!" she said angrily. "I can't remember the last time someone turned me down!" She turned and walked back in the direction of the bank of elevators, speaking quietly to herself. "When Loni sics me on someone I always come back with the goods! I will win! I will! After all, he is male. But it may take a little longer than I thought." She sighed, not wanting to face what came next. "I suppose I'd better go tell Loni I didn't get what she wanted yet, but I will."

Colwin stepped out of hiding as the elevator doors slid shut behind Teresa, and smacked an angry fist loudly into an open palm.

* * *

Mikal's hands trembled slightly as he took the pride's honor blade off its stand. He was feeling a stronger remorse than he would have thought possible for Ki's passing, and a violent anger directed at the rebels who must have gotten him. The search Res organized for Ki had determined Ki had left the palace, but he'd completely vanished from sight after that. The assumption was that he had found something pointing to Natanha's leaving the palace, and when he'd followed the lead he'd been downed by rebels. Mikal gave vent to a low growl. It must have taken twenty or thirty of them to bring down Ki Lawwnum.

Mikal was also feeling a repressed sort of glee. Finally and at long last, the sword was his! It was no wonder his hands were shaking!

"But I dare not make any more mistakes like I did with that looney, Aubin Tabber," he told himself sternly as he ran his hands lovingly over the sheathed blade.

There was something unsettling going on inside Mikal, however, and he felt it strongly, though he did not understand it. "I deserve this. I worked hard for this. So why do I feel like it's not mine?"

Then his pride overcame his senses, and he laughed at his womanish whimsies. "Of course it's mine!" he told himself sternly. He stuck it into his sash, and moved so he could see himself full-length in Ki's mirror. It was wonderful, perfect! And it belonged exactly where it was. Mikal adjusted the angle slightly, and straightened his mantle, smiled at himself in satisfaction, assured he was a handsome figure in spite of his missing sidelocks, and then moved into the living room.

He stood and surveyed the room, letting a whistling vibration out of his throat. "I have my work cut out for me! All this stuff has to go back to Nide." He turned slightly, and looked at the puppets in their place of honor. "Those should go back to Ki's father." Mikal shook his head as he remembered Ki had actually wanted to go back to Nide to be a historian once more.

His mind sheered away from that thought, and turned instead to the ceremony that was to be held the next evening. How touching it would be! Mikal would be there in the place of honor, looking bereaved but dignified. Of course he would be wearing the sword. It wasn't usual for a mourner to wear a weapon at a memorial service, but everyone would understand.

Mikal picked things up and looked at them without really seeing them, and put them down again. All the while his mind sped from one thought to another.

Now that the commander was gone, someone would have to take his place. It would probably be Res. He was the one Ki trusted the most, and he was very senior. There would probably be a promotion for Mikal, too. Then, if this business with the rebels got messy, and Mikal was beginning to sincerely hope it would, if anything happened to Res they just might promote one Mikal Lawwnum to the commander's post. He smiled. That would make him an even younger commander than Ki had been.

He grinned. "Of course I deserve the sword."

Ki stepped into Loni's private office, somewhat surprised at the summons to this particular room. Previously, if Loni wished to speak to him, she met him in one of the lesser offices. That way he did not have to traverse as many corridors, and there was less risk of his being seen by someone outside the rebel organization. He was curious.

Loni stood as soon as he entered, and gestured at a fine, old telescope. It was brass, ornately worked and highly polished, and stood on its own stand. It was pointed northwest in the general direction of the palace.

"I think there's something you should see," she said in a tone he had not heard from her before. "Look at the palace courtyard."

Quizzically, he bent to follow her instructions. He saw a courtyard filled with figures in white, and it hit him in the heart. He stood and faced Loni, his anger barely in control.

"I've seen this ceremony too many times before. Why did you call me to see this one? Did you want to remind me that my kinsmen are dying at your hands?"

His voice was cold and his eyes were blazing, but Loni did not blanch or shy. She met his gaze steadily. "That is not a ceremony for the dead."

"Yes, it is. I've presided over enough of them to know," he said coldly.

Loni repeated herself forcefully. "That is not a ceremony for the dead!"

Impatient with her, Ki made a cutting gesture with his hand and loomed angrily over her. "Human, do not tell me about Nidean customs!" he rumbled wrathfully.

Loni took a step back in surprise, then took a deep breath to steady herself and started again. "You have very sharp eyes. I suggest you take another look. You may see enough to recognize the next of kin."

Still angry and impatient, Ki bent once more to the telescope, but he could not make out anything more. He stood, and shoved the thing angrily aside. "I can't make out anything but white shapes."

Loni nodded. "It's your funeral," she said as kindly as she could. "I thought you'd want to watch. Not everyone gets to see their own services."

Ki was stunned! Why in the universe would they be holding a ceremony for the dead for him when he was perfectly fine now that his bruises had disappeared? It took just long enough for the thought to pass for him to realize no one inside the palace knew he was well. It had never occurred to him they would assume he was dead. He stumbled awkwardly to the nearest chair and sat down, his eyes very blank.

Loni began to talk, giving him time to recover. "You've been here for two and a half weeks. Colwin tells me you're doing well with the troops. They're learning fast. He still hates your guts, you know. But he's changed his attitude somewhat. Now he doesn't want to kill you until you've stopped being useful. Quite a compliment, coming from Colwin." She paused, looking at Ki's face to see if any of this was registering. "I'd like to compliment you, too. You're looking surprisingly good for a man who's been dead for over a week."

Ki looked up sharply.

"Are you eating properly?" Loni continued. "Are the chefs still overcooking your meat? If they are, I'll have a talk with them. Is there anything you need? Larger quarters? More clothes? A girl?"

Decidedly uncomfortable with all that had happened in the last few moments, Ki cut her off. "Everything's fine. Thank you. But if this is all you called me up here for, I think I'd like to go back to my quarters." He left dazedly.

Loni watched until the door slid shut, then quickly got on the com to Teresa to tell her Ki would be about the corridors and very upset about his demise. It would be a perfect opportunity for her to try again. Then she sat down, and spun her chair around so she could use the telescope. She felt sorry for Ki. She knew what it was like to be thrown into a completely new situation and be cut off from your past. But that was not a reason for her to let an opportunity slip by.

Chapter Sixteen

———◆———

KI WAS AGHAST when he stepped off the elevator into the basement dojo. There were wounded men and women everywhere, and more streaming in. The red of their blood washed over his vision, the thick, copper odor of human blood assaulted him, and he felt his stomach heave. Only his anger cleared his head.

Everything was in wild commotion. Medics running, volunteers moving those most seriously wounded. Some of the less seriously wounded wandered, not understanding what had occurred or where they were. Utter chaos.

It shouldn't have happened. The periodic raids that had been taking place against the palace were meant to be harassment and a setup only. Nothing serious was to take place. The men sent on those raids weren't even supposed to take heavy weapons with them. They were supposed to display no obvious military planning, and they were to be easily and quickly repelled. So how in Mmumna's name had this carnage taken place?

Ki stepped into the chaos and began to tread lightly through it, slipping on the wet blood smearing the slick concrete, and sticking into puddles that were already beginning to dry. He continued, hoping to find answers to his questions. A groan came from his right, and he looked down. There, lying on a blanket on the hard and cold concrete, was a man whose face Ki recognized.

"What in Mmumna's hell was he doing out there?" Ki asked the blood-soaked air.

As he walked, he became angrier and angrier. Face after face he recognized, faces belonging to people who were not ready for any kind of action, people he had not approved to be outside Loni's compound. And they were damaged, some of them severely. Then he knelt at the side of a boy, a cub not more than eighteen, and closed his eyes for the last time. Ki's anger exploded within him.

Colwin walked into view covered with blood, but not a drop of it his own. He wiped ineffectively at his hands with a thick towel.

Rumbling so heavily with anger that his com-

mon was almost indecipherable, Ki called to
Colwin across the sea of misery. "I want to talk
to you. Now. Come with me."

Colwin, immersed in the painful business
around him, barely heard, and shrugged Ki off.
"I'm busy, puss— ah, Colonel." He did not like
being interrupted, especially under such circumstances, and his dislike of Ki showed. He
made the word Colonel sound like the worst of
epithets. He started to move away.

Naturally falling back on his command voice,
the one that carried with it immense power and
fierce determination, and with a rumble that
started over his angry heart, Ki said, "Come
with me!"

Colwin had been trying to clean some of the
gore off his hands. He hadn't succeeded very
well. Now he threw the towel aside angrily, and
followed Ki.

The quietest place Ki could find in the basement commotion was a supplies closet. It
smelled richly of cleaning agents and solvents, a
smell that pierced the lungs and brought tears
to the eyes. But Ki welcomed it. It was clean
after the odor of blood.

As soon as Colwin shut the door behind him,
Ki whirled on him, furious. "These raids are
meant to be harassment," he said, his voice a
barely restrained scream of rage. "There aren't
supposed to be any injuries. Most of the men out
there weren't even supposed to go outside these
walls. They aren't ready. I've told you that." He
took a menacing step closer to the rebel. "So
why were they out there?"

Colwin got his back up. "I don't have to explain my actions to you," he said, and turned to
the door as if to leave.

Ki slammed his hand into the door to keep it shut, and curled his fingers deeply into the wood, trapping Colwin in the steadily narrowing space between Ki and the door. "The hell you don't," Ki hissed.

"The hell I do!" Colwin retorted hotly.

Ki inched closer, and Colwin saw a red mist of anger fall like a sheet of blood over the Lionman's golden eyes.

Colwin relented. "It was their turn. I can't play favorites. They knew the risks before they ever stepped out of here." He paused, and drew a deep breath before he could continue. "No one here expects a bloodless revolution. *Almost*," he said with heavy emphasis, "almost everyone here is fighting for a cause they're willing to die for."

Ki's fingers crunched deeper into the wood. "There is a difference between being willing to die for a cause and committing suicide. These men shouldn't have been on this mission. They weren't ready for it. *And* this was meant to be harassment, not open warfare. They were injured needlessly and their blood wasted. *And I will not* have the lives of my men wasted."

Colwin's head snapped up. "*Your* men? *Your* men did this damage! You're one of the enemy! You have a lot of nerve telling me how to handle *my* men!"

Ki's lips curled back from his teeth. "Let's get this straight right now. I've put up with your garbage for months. I don't care if you like me or not. I'm here for a purpose. I'm here to see this revolution succeeds with as little destruction as possible. You seem hell-bent on killing off your troops before they have a chance of succeeding. You're the kind of leader men will follow gladly, but you have no feeling for the men you lead. Whether you believe it or not, these are my men, too. Every drop of blood that comes out of them is on Loni's hands, my hands, and, whether you like it or not, your hands. Yes, these people know the risks, but they're trusting us to bring them back alive." His cold steel hand grasped Colwin's wrist with a force just shy of that needed to shatter bones, and Ki pulled the man's still-blood-smeared fingers in front of his eyes. "This blood doesn't wash off!"

Wild Nidean drum music filled Mikal's quarters, spilling down off the ceiling and bouncing up off the floor of the single sparsely furnished room that was allotted to him as a lieutenant. He reveled in it; and it reflected perfectly his wildly happy mood. The Guardsmen had repelled the feeble rebel attack with ease, just as they'd repelled all the others. They had become, in fact, almost fun. Why, Guardsmen were vying with each other to see who would draw duty when the next attack was due. It might even be fun to have a lottery for the posts, because fighting with rebels was a lot more interesting than fighting with robots or static dummies. Every once in a while a rebel might actually come up with something new.

This evening's attack had been great fun for Mikal. He'd even managed to nail one rebel himself with his new sword. With any good fortune, Mmumna had sent his puny human soul directly to hell.

He rested himself in his one chair, and threw his feet across the narrow space to his bunk. He raised his arms in the air and stretched mightily. How pathetic and amusing the rebels had become! The attacks were coming at regular intervals, and invariably at the front gate. How could they begin to believe they could get in that way? It was beyond understanding!

He sat up far enough to pull a tray across the top of his desk toward the chair so he could reach it more easily, then settled back again. On the tray was a Nidean gourd-shaped vessel used to contain potable liquids, and a small liquor glass. The vessel was of fired clay sealed with a clear glaze and decorated with a white drip pattern that was ancient beyond memory. Mikal picked up the canteen and twirled it in his hands, watching the pattern change in the dim evening light. He sat that way for some time, holding an internal debate. Finally he picked up the glass, pulled the stopper on the flagon, and poured out a small measure of the sticky red fluid the flask contained.

"Just a sip of roed to celebrate," Mikal told himself. "Just a sip."

He stood, walked the few steps to his bookcase and turned up the percussion music, then went back to settle into the chair to let the drums and the roed caress him.

Natanha was rearranging her furniture, and though she felt like humming, she did not. She worked in total silence, careful not to make the smallest sound when she shifted something, even though she had lived safely in this space for over three months. She found she liked changing things around, as it gave her something to do while she waited. She liked the small roomlike area she'd discovered where five ducts came together, too. It was almost the size of the playhouse she'd had as a small girl, and that memory made it feel a little safer.

She shifted another large floor pillow, and scooted back to take a look. She nodded her satisfaction. Her odd little collection of pillows and blankets and the short stool and table had taken on a decidedly homey look in the small space, especially now with the little personal things she had managed to get.

Her odd assortment of clothes, a collection meant for both male and female and of all sizes, was neatly folded into a plastic packing crate. Another crate turned upside down acted as a dresser, and had several important items on it. There was her mother's hairbrush that she'd had to run a severe risk to obtain, a picture of her mother she had returned to her own room to get (along with a doll she thought she'd long since outgrown), a bottle of her mother's perfume she sniffed when she was particularly blue, and a bottle of Mama-san's perfume. When she'd first begun to hide in these ducts, and was popping out only occasionally, everyone was looking for her, especially the Lionmen. Before she would make one of her raids she would douse herself with Mama-san's perfume. That way the Lionmen paid little if any attention to her scent, dismissing her as the older woman.

A row of small flashlights stood on the floor next to the "dresser." They were of all sizes and shapes, but they all worked. When they didn't, Natanha returned them. On the table was her collection of plates and flatware, enough to serve her needs. If something became too dirty to be serviceable, she simply took another. There was also a little food, though she'd given up the idea of keeping more. If she kept too much, it merely attracted the rats. Food was easy to come by—she simply had to stick her hand out a grating over the kitchen.

She never took anything importantly personal. Mama would not have approved of that.

Her candelabra was ornate and filled with the finest of beeswax tapers, but she rarely lit it. She rarely used any light at all, in spite of her collection of flashlights. It was too likely a light would be seen. But every child needs a nightlight once in a while, and she sometimes used a flashlight under cover of her blankets, and, when she was traversing an area of ducting she was not familiar with and there were no openings, she did need to see.

Her video player and headphones rested on the stool. That was one pleasure she did not deny herself. It allowed her the feeling of being with people, something she needed badly.

Because she could not stand fully erect in her little home, she quickly sat down on the floor pillow. It was uncomfortable to constantly stoop, especially because her mother had always told her to maintain a good posture. She took another look around. There were a number of her own personal items she longed to have with her, but it was too risky to try to rescue them. Soon perhaps. They'd all but stopped looking for her inside the palace.

She hugged herself. Her mama would be mad because Natanha hadn't done as instructed and gotten off Homeworld. But she couldn't have gone. Her father had been looking too hard for her. And, from what she overheard, the ports were still guarded. But, she was sure, her daddy would forget about her soon enough. Then perhaps she would go.

But Mama would have liked how she had evaded them. And now that she'd gotten used to it, hiding was almost fun. It was almost like when she'd been a small child and she'd played hide'n'seek with Ki. It was really very easy, and getting easier as she had more and more practice. She'd only had a few close calls since the time Ki had seen her.

How well she knew the palace now! Why, she'd seen places her mother never saw, places her father probably didn't even know existed. She knew the place better than when she'd played in all the forbidden places.

Soon, though, it would be time to get off Homeworld and out to Midron. Now, that would be fun! It would be an adventure just to get from the palace to the port. After all, a princess is very rarely allowed out alone, and never into a city that hasn't been duded up just for her. Now she'd get to see what it was really like.

She crept over to the corner of her "dresser," and lifted it carefully so the things on top of it didn't spill. Her stash was still there, and she was pretty sure it would be enough to buy her a passage and anything else she'd really need, like some inconspicuous clothes fit for a merchant girl. She opened the blue suede-cloth pouch that had once held a bottle of whiskey, and dumped the contents into her lap. Then, counting them carefully as she replaced them, she dropped into the bag forty-seven natural pearls the size of fully mature peas, ten gold pieces with her father's picture on them, and a small gold ring with a tiny shanshen, Nide's native gemstone, set in it, a gift to her from the Lionman Guard on her last birthday. Though she hated to part with it (she was sure Ki had picked it out), she would if she had to. Satisfied it was all there, she replaced the pouch under the corner of the crate.

She curled up on her bed of blankets and snuggled with her doll. There were some things she missed, of course, like her mother's quiet advice and a good hot bath. But she'd have a bath before long—as soon as she could get off this world.

She sat up again, and giggled silently to herself. She hadn't forgotten how to have fun, even in this weird life she now lived. One day she'd snuck into Magnus's room and stuffed towels into the euphemism until it had backed up. How he'd screamed when he'd stepped into the icy cold water with bare feet!

She froze. She suddenly had the feeling there were eyes on her back, cold and unwelcome. She turned her head back to look over her shoulder toward the one vent that opened into her space, and there he stood, staring directly at her, a Lionman.

The glance into the heating duct had turned Leenoww to stone. He couldn't possibly be seeing what he was seeing, a little playhouse with a princess in it. He blinked, but she did not disappear.

"See anything?" came floating to him from down the corridor where his fellow watch was trying to hunt up the errant sound.

For the space of one breath Leenoww did not answer. There was much to consider here. Everyone knew how fond Commander Lawwnum had been of the princess. In fact, there were some pretty nasty rumors floating around.

But Commander Ki had made one impression on Private Leenoww, and the emperor quite another.

Without taking his eyes off Natanha, he answered, "Nothing. It must have been my imagination, or rats or something." He turned away from the princess and started back down the corridor in the direction of his fellow watch. "These long shifts in the lower levels are starting to get to me."

Natanha listened to the conversation as it grew fainter and fainter as the pair moved away.

"Getting to me, too. But that's what happens when Lieutenant Lawwnum says 'Jump!' and you don't jump high enough."

When she could no longer hear them, she began to pack. It was now necessary to find another place to camp. But try as she might, she could not figure out why the Guardsman hadn't taken her. He was, after all, a Lionman.

Colwin Dene, a Nidean, Loni, and eight human males sat around the large conference table that pulled out of a wall in Loni's office. Ki was holding his peace. Loni was trying to listen to everyone. The rest, except for Colwin, were all talking at once, each fighting for dominance, demanding his view be accepted.

"Lawwnum's done a fine job of training, but leave him out of tactical."

"Just because he ran the Guard he thinks he can run us too. That's just not the way it works."

"He promises us a hit on the palace and he never delivers. We don't think he intends to carry through."

Loni sat back in her chair and let them run

while she poured herself a glass of water from a silver carafe. Now that she knew where they were headed, she didn't pay them much mind. She'd heard it all before in one way or another, most of it repeatedly. But she was paying very strict attention to Ki Lawwnum, late of the Imperial Lionman Guard. He had not heard most of this before, and she wanted to know how he would react to it. After all, the others could be right. Lawwnum's word was supposed to be good, but she had no direct proof of that. And then there was his stubborn, infuriating refusal to tell anyone anything about Nide.

"Caligula" popped into her mind again. This Nidean was capable of much damage, even unarmed as he was now. If he began to look hunted, if he reacted badly to being called to task, she would simply say her doomsday word. It would kill her—and she was not ready to die, not by a long shot—but he'd die too. And a quick death in here would be ever so preferable to being turned in to the emperor.

That question nagged at her, bothered her more than all the rest. *Everyone else says we're ready. Lawwnum says we're not. Is he stalling so he can turn us all in?*

Ki was sitting very quietly. Though he had not heard these things voiced before, he had suspected them. But he knew very well you can't disprove a negative. But for all of that, it was rather unpleasant to have his word questioned. He wasn't used to it. It made him feel a little dishonorable, as if just because they questioned his word it became a little less trustworthy. *General Raashta would have understood. Because the humans decided the Talmac Incident had been dishonorable, though it was not by Nidean stan-*

dards, they decided he was to be relieved of command and demoted. To this day it is against the law for a Nidean to hold a rank above that of colonel. Never mind that Raashta's courageous act won the war for them.

The humans were becoming excessively emotional. Arms were waving madly, two were on their feet. How would he behave if they actually found the nerve to turn on him? Unfortunately, he could not allow them to lay hands on him. It was a thing he could not accept and remain Ki Lawwnum. He would fight back. He really had very little to lose, now. Natanha was probably dead, though he'd heard nothing about her. She was, after all, only thirteen. It still amazed him that after all these years of dealing directly with humans, even liking some of them, that humans and Nidean would never understand each other. The basis for trust was simply not present.

Colwin's two fists cracked down on the tabletop hard enough to make it jump, and the report put an end to the yelling and gesticulating. "That's enough!" he spat into the sudden silence. "I've been listening to you bitch for a long time, and I've come to the conclusion you're all a bunch of shitheads! You question Lawwnum's loyalty without knowing anything about him. You've never taken the time to learn how he thinks. You just assume that because he is the infamous Colonel Ki he can't be trusted. I know! I believed the same thing until recently. Now, I hate it, but I find I trust this man. I don't like him. I don't think I ever will. But I'd lead my men into hell if he said it was necessary. If you want to replace him, you can replace me, too. Because he's the best shot we've got. If we ignore his advice, we might as well commit suicide. And I'm not ready to die. There's a difference between being willing to die for a cause and committing suicide!"

There was a moment of astonished silence, and Colwin sat down. Then some grumbling began.

Loni saw a need for some privacy. "Colonel Ki, would you be good enough to leave us for a few moments?" she asked as politely as she could. There had been enough improprieties today.

He nodded and stood, and went to stand at the window in the reception room. He looked across the city toward the palace, wishing he knew exactly what was going on inside it, and whether or not his princess was still there.

When he was asked to rejoin the group, Loni told him it had been decided they would keep him on. "But there is one thing we must know, Colonel Ki. How soon can we attack?"

"One month."

Loni nodded. "Thank you, Colonel. Gentlemen, I think that's enough for today. Will you excuse me?" Loni asked as she stood.

Ki left quickly, followed by the others, but, as Colwin was about to walk out the door, Loni grabbed his arm.

"Except for what you said in here today, you've been very quiet," she said as she drew him toward a sofa. "Is something wrong?"

"No," he said as he sat down.

Loni crossed her legs delicately, not believing a word of it. "Colwin, this is Loni. What happened between you and Colonel Ki?"

Colwin's blue eyes flashed anger for a moment, but the spark was quickly killed. "Nothing important," he answered flatly. *But*, he told himself, *I trust Ki Lawwnum more than I trust you right now. You sicced one of your girls on me!*

Loni, sharp as ever, caught the change. She put a hand gently on his knee. "Colwin, is there anything you want to talk about?"

"No."

Chapter Seventeen

———◆———

KI STOOD IN front of the narrow mirror that made up part of his closet door and watched his hands tie back his white hair. He used a piece of sash, and gathered the heavy mane in at the base of his neck. He wrapped the cord around the hair several times, and tied a strong knot.

Then he looked at himself as he reached for a kimono. He was not in as good condition as he used to be. He was training at a human level now, after all. But he would do.

The kimono was black utilitarian cloth. The hakama he tied on over it were the old ones from his uniform. Over all he flung a cloak of heavy black silk. It was too short because he'd "borrowed" it from one of the girls, but it, too, would do.

Carefully he opened his door and looked out. The corridor was empty, and he made quickly for the elevator. This time, however, instead of going down to the basement levels, Ki went up.

The date for the attack on the palace had been

set. Weather Control had said it would be cold and snowing, which Ki considered optimum conditions. The snow would be a help in muffling some sounds, and Lionmen instinctively disliked cold. Of course, there had been arguments. Most of the humans wanted to wait for clear weather. Ki had repeatedly and patiently explained that they had established a pattern of attacking at regular intervals and only in clear weather, and that they were now about to break the pattern.

But before the attack took place, there were some things he wanted to do. He wanted his hoj. He still felt unhappy with the katana. It was a lovely thing, a marvel, but it was too short and too light to fight with. And he needed to see Aubin.

The elevator reached the top floor, and Ki stepped out. He was headed toward the port, and he intended to "borrow" one of Loni's jumpers. If all went well, it would be back in its parking space before first light.

All Colwin had really seen as Ki stepped off the elevator was a flash of white from his hair. But something about the color made Colwin curious, and he walked in that general direction. He actually had to have a full view of Ki before he recognized him with his hair pulled back and wearing a short cloak. Then he was really curious. Where was the colonel going dressed like that?

Allowing plenty of room between them—Colwin was all too aware of the sensitivity of Ki's nose—he followed the Lionman. It really wasn't too difficult. It was around midnight. There was very little traffic at this time of night. It was too late to arrive at Loni's for the evening, and too early to go home. And now it wasn't too difficult to figure out what Ki was up to. There wasn't much else in this direction except the port.

But when Ki opened the door to the outside and a gust of wind flung back the cloak, Colwin had a surprise. Tucked neatly into Ki's sash were the two swords they'd taken from him when he'd arrived. He wasn't aware they'd been returned. Ki started across the open area toward the jumpers parked on the edge of the roofline.

When Colwin reached the door, he called out after Ki, "Going somewhere?"

Ki stopped and turned back toward the door. Even though he could not see the face because the light was coming from behind through the open door, Ki recognized the voice. This could be trouble.

"Yes. I have business."

Colwin approached across the plascadam. "Like letting the palace know we're coming?"

Ki snorted, turned his back on Colwin, and proceeded toward the jumpers once more. He selected one, and started to get in.

Colwin stood in the cloud created by his own breath in the cold, and watched. He was fearful of letting Ki go. Too much was riding on this one Nidean. He crossed his arms over his chest, feeling the thin material of his skinsuit rasp over his hands when he tucked them under his arms. This certainly was not the proper dress for this kind of weather.

Ki stopped, and put his head out the jumper door before he closed it. "Trust me, Colwin," he said, then slammed it tight. He looked back, and the human was still staring. He waited. But when Colwin did not move, Ki took off.

Colwin watched the jumper's lights as it moved into the sky, then looked up at the real stars. "My head is screaming at me to turn the bastard in. 'We're all going to die in the most horrible way possible. Don't trust that pussy!' But my gut says I saw his eyes and he's not lying." He exhaled heavily, watching the plume of his breath. "I trust that man more than I've trusted anyone in my life. If I'm wrong, hundreds of men are going to die, and it will be on my head. They're my responsibility. Isn't that what he told me?"

He turned and walked back toward the door. "I'm not wrong."

Ki followed the prescribed path for personal pleasure vehicles into the palace, and used Mama-san's code for entry. He landed the jumper in his garden. It was close enough to the seraglio that unless someone really checked, the discrepancy would not be noted. Of course, he took the chance that Mama-san had landed only a few minutes before he had, but it was a necessary risk. As no one came bursting through the garden doors, he assumed his ruse worked.

He opened the door and stepped out into the cold night air. He regretted the fact that he had to smash his garden, but the regret only lasted until he saw the state of it. Then he was angry. Although everything was dead, brown and dry for the winter, he could see the grass was far too long and the flowers choked with weeds. He shook his head. No one had bothered to care for the little bit of green.

Though there was a skin of ice over his little stream, he stretched his legs and stepped over it. He could hear the water running under the ice, and he did not really want to spend the evening in wet footgear.

He walked to the French doors that opened into his apartment, and was forced to stop. He had bumped headlong into his old life, a life he could never again take part in, and the blow had left him breathless. This was something he had not been prepared for, the aching emptiness.

But he would find time to mourn later. Right now there were things to be done. On a whim he tried the palm lock, not really expecting the door to budge, but it popped open. Evidently they had not bothered to change the prints. After all, he was dead. And who would want such austere chambers when there were others, much more elegant, standing vacant? He smiled toothily. Their mistake gave him the one thing he needed tonight—easy access to the palace.

The skinsuit that had fit Aubin like a glove six months ago now hung on him baggily, and he caught a fold of material as he entered his apartments. He angrily tugged it free, then entered without turning on any lights. The spotlight over the *Caryatid* was on, and there was a small light in the kitchen. It was enough.

He was tired. Tired of sitting in a council where nothing happened. Tired of listening to men who made no sense. Tired of being useless. Tired of being. He, quite frankly, didn't care about anything anymore. And when his term was up in a couple of months, he was going home to Luna. He was going to buy an apartment in the most remote portion of the caverns, take his music and his *Caryatid*, and tell the rest of the universe to stick it in their alternating current outlet.

He found his way to his controls, and turned on Pachelbel's Canon in D Major. He found a bottle of bourbon sitting on the bar, and poured himself a stiff one, straight up.

He shook the nearly empty bottle. "Have to remember to get another," he mumbled, and took a long sip. "Aaaaah. That's better."

He liked his bourbon, and he'd stick to that, thank you. He'd tried roed again about a month ago, and found he still choked on the stuff. It was too sticky-sweet.

"I definitely need a quiet place," he said to himself as he sat down facing his sculpture. "Maybe I'll get a dog. No. Too much trouble. A cat?" He shivered. "I've had enough of felines to last my whole life. A bird. That's the ticket."

He hadn't eaten all day, and he was already beginning to feel the booze as it slid smoothly into his system. "When you've got my friend Mr. Bourbon, who needs food?" He took another long pull at his glass.

Now that he was certain Aubin was alone, Ki stepped out of the shadows and into the *Caryatid*'s spotlight. It hit him full in the face, and the strong light framed and reflected off Ki's white skin. But he hadn't quite counted on the effect that would have. Because he was dressed completely in black, standing in front of a deeply shadowed recess, his face appeared to be floating, unattached, just behind the sculpture.

Aubin's mouth dropped open. He was seeing a ghost. The glass he was holding shook, then tipped, then spilled all over his legs before Aubin dropped it.

Ki smiled warmly at his old friend.

Aubin could not help but stare. Then he shook his head and tried to turn away. "Mr. Bourbon is not being good to me tonight," he said pathetically. Then he straightened his shoulders. "I am an intelligent man. Intelligent men do not see ghosts," he told himself firmly.

He was answered by Ki's rumbling laughter, and, as always, Aubin's hackles rose.

He stood up, but very unsteadily. "I've been drinking too much. I'm seeing things."

Ki stepped forward and turned on the room lights. It was only then that Aubin registered the black kimono and hakama. But he was still uncertain. He poked Ki in the chest several times just to make sure he was solid. Having satisfied himself on that point, he turned back to his bar.

"I need a drink," he groaned. He picked up an empty bottle, and threw it aside, careless of where it landed. He found a half bottle of gin and a reasonably clean glass and poured—and poured. "I'd offer you a drink, but I don't believe you're real anyway, so I'll save it all for me."

Ki smiled again. "What? No stawwshwa?"

"My god! You are real!" Aubin exclaimed, believing at last. "But you're dead. I went to the ceremony. Don't you think I'm handling this well? The emperor even had a day of mourning. Great pomp and circumstance. If you were there, you'd have loved it. Don't you think I'm handling this well? By the way, Mikal's laid claim to your sword. He's sent some of your things back to your family. And I am not going to handle this well at all." He'd said it all, in a rush, in one long breath.

Ki watched Aubin's hand shake as he took another drink. He thought it couldn't be easy to have your friends come back from the dead.

But now that he was getting over some of the shock, Aubin was feeling more like himself. "Where the hell have you been?" he carped. "Do you know what you've put me through? Why the hell didn't you let me know you were alive? Have you told Mikal yet? He'll be *thrilled* to have to return the sword," he told Ki with great sarcasm.

Ki was relieved. He'd begun to think that Aubin's load was one brick shy. "That's better. Now you sound like yourself. So do me a favor and *shut up!*"

Aubin opened his mouth to protest, then snapped it shut so hard there was an audible click. It probably wasn't wise to argue with someone who could come back from the dead.

"I have to make this fast," Ki told him. "I have a lot to do tonight. I took your advice and looked for Natanha. I found her, but there was nothing I could do for her. I then left the palace with the intention of going home. On the way to the port, I met some delightful gentlemen who kindly invited me to join the rebellion. For the past six months I've been training them, and next week I'm leading them in an attack on the palace. And I need your help."

Aubin's reaction was immediate and extreme. He shook his head and waved his arms. "Oh no. No. I am not crazy. You obviously have gone crazy, but I am not crazy. I've already made arrangements for my retirement. I'm going back to Luna and live in peaceful solitude. I'm not going to get mixed up in anything like this. You've got a lot of nerve, you know," he scolded. "You think you can just die and then come back and ask anything you want. I make it a policy not to grant favors to dead men. No way. Count me out."

"Aubin," Ki pleaded, "I need your help. Someone has got to stop Ozenscebo. His merest touch shrivels whatever it lands on." He stopped, cocking his head to one side, and looked Aubin over critically. "Look at yourself! Look at what's happened to you in six months! The same thing is happening to the entire empire! I'm going to lead the attack next Wednesday, with or without your help. Without your help a lot of men are going to die. All I need you to do is open the bakery door and let me in. The main battle will be going on at the other end of the palace." He paused, trying to gauge Aubin's reaction. Then he continued quietly. "You once told me you believed in the old democracy where one man made a difference. So, dammit! Make a difference! I need you, Aubin!"

It was all but completely black inside Mikal's quarters. But Ki was totally familiar with them. He'd lived inside one exactly like this long enough. There was a desk, a set of bookshelves, and a bed containing a lump that would be Mikal. The scent was his.

Ki stopped to listen. Mikal's breathing was easy and shallow, even and regular. He was asleep. Ki registered the strength of his scent to use as a marker. If his pulse rate went up, if he began to wake, it would get stronger.

But while he was doing that, something else came to him. Something that should have been familiar, but that he could not place. It was sweet and thick, and the odor was not unpleasant though Ki reacted very badly to it. He cursed himself inwardly. This thing was bad, and he should know what it was!

But he had a reason for being here, and regardless of the unidentified scent, he had to take care of the sword first. He began to move, but slowly, slowly, blending into the darkness like the ghost Aubin had thought him.

Aubin. Aubin would help. Ki was certain of it. He said he wouldn't, but Ki knew better. If Mmumna pleased.

And no matter what happened, the sword really would be Mikal's soon. But not now. Not yet. He didn't deserve it yet.

He moved with the aching slowness he had learned as a tiny cub from his masterful father. Inch by gradual inch, he made his way toward the bookcase, the logical place to begin his search for the sword.

He checked on Mikal once more. He was still asleep. So, slowly, listening for Mikal's breathing, smelling for his pulse rate to increase Mikal's scent, he searched.

Nothing.

He made his patient way to the desk. If the sword was not in the bookcase, it had to be there. He put out his hand, gently, patiently, and knew the blacker shadow in the shadows he'd touched was his sword. A rush of feeling swam over him, relief at having the rest of his arm back. And more. Things it would take him years to sort out fully. But most of all there was a gladness at being whole again.

But as he leaned forward to take the sword, the sweet scent grew stronger. He couldn't place it no matter how hard he tried, but something inside him told him it was important.

He slipped the sword into his sash with the

most natural of motions, then began to search the dark for the source of the sweetness. Unfortunately, he extended his left hand, and it brushed against a glass with a slight *clink*.

Mikal's breathing changed, and his scent became instantly stronger. He was beginning to come awake, aware at least subliminally that something in his space was not as usual. He started to lift his head groggily, then Ki heard him sniff and sit bolt upright. Puzzlement, then fear, came rolling off the younger Nidean, and Ki knew he had been recognized.

He had to put Mikal out, and quickly. He raised his arm and swung his left hand down directly into Mikal's temple. He was extremely careful about the blow: it was meant to stun, not kill. He would have felt much better about it if he had been able to see Mikal. Then he could have been sure he wouldn't kill him, but ...

Ki turned on the light now. Mikal had fallen half out of the bed, his head resting oddly on the floor while his feet stayed under the blankets. Ki grabbed him under the arms and swung him back onto the bed. He was alive. He had a slight cut, and he was going to have a terrible headache in the morning, but thankfully Ki had been correct in both direction and force of the blow.

But what was it that had caused all this? What was that odor? He turned back to the desk and saw the Nidean pottery flask and the single glass which now resided tipsily on its side. Ki picked up the flask, unstoppered it, and sniffed.

His stomach heaved. Roed! Anger settled coldly around the remains of his dinner. Everything Ozie touched was corrupted, even Mikal.

In pure anger, he threw the flask at the wall over Mikal's head, shattering it, strewing shards and ugly red spatters over everything in the room, including himself. He wiped unconsciously at the gobbets on his clothes as he watched the sticky red fluid ooze down the wall and into Mikal's blankets and hair.

The anger found its way out Ki's mouth. "I hope you have a *real* headache tomorrow, cub!" he breathed almost inaudibly.

Chapter Eighteen

SNOW WAS FALLING heavily in big, heavy flakes the size of microdisks, though there was very little wind. It settled thickly over the rocks and evergreens in front of the palace, and over Loni as well as she hid among them.

She was cold, colder than she could remember being since she was a kid. She tucked her full-length blue-fox coat closer about her, and pulled the cape collar up to shield her neck and face. "I knew this damn fur would come in handy for something," she mumbled into her cupped hands while she blew on them, trying to warm them.

She was wearing no jewelry except her watch, and she felt positively undressed without it. But Ki had specifically told her he wanted her neither to shine nor to clank. So she'd left it all home. But that didn't change the fact that she felt like she had just stepped naked out of her bathtub into the midst of a formal dinner party.

She looked at her watch for the hundredth time. It was still only 2:30 A.M. The attack wouldn't begin until 2:37. Somehow that seemed an eternity. How many seconds were in seven minutes, anyway? Quick calculations gave her 420. Too many.

She looked around her for the others concealed as she was. Some she could see from her vantage point, most she could not. She hoped they were still where they were supposed to be. This was the real thing.

This attack was not going to be the game the others had been. This time there were explosives and energy weapons. Lawwnum wanted a very loud and continuous diversion from them, and Loni intended to see that he got it, even if she had to make all the noise herself.

She looked at her watch again. *They can't be in position yet. They'd better be in position.* But it wasn't time yet, and she forced herself to settle down and wait.

She waited, watching the seconds run past ever so slowly. And finally, inevitably, it was getting close to 2:37. Now she wanted to wait. *They couldn't be ready yet, could they? I should wait just a little longer. But Lawwnum said 2:37.*

At 2:37 precisely, she closed the connection on a very large explosive.

Mikal stood on the wall with all the others from this watch. This attack was much better organized and much more fierce. The rebels were not merely throwing themselves away.

They were picking their targets carefully, and even managing to do some minor damage.

Mikal grimaced as he faced into the snow. He pulled in a long, searching breath, looking for the scent of the one he expected to find. But Ki wasn't there, at least not in a place Mikal could reach from this high on the wall. But there was no doubt about it. Maybe Ki's scent didn't reach this far, but Mikal could smell him all the same.

The young Guardsman sneered. How foolish could Ki have become in his old age? Did he really think he could come back into the palace and steal his sword and then not have everyone on the watch for him. Did he really think he could waltz in the front gate like an invited guest? There was no way past the front gate short of atomic weapons. There was no way that feeble rebel force could possibly win with a straightforward frontal assault. Ki should know that...

He groaned. Ki did know that.

"Mmumna, I've been an ass! This is a diversion!" he said angrily as he turned on his heel and started back across the gardens for the living quarters. "He's coming in the kitchens or the bakery. He's either by himself or with only a few picked men." He ran at his considerable top speed. "Mmumna, I hope I'm not too late. I've got to stop him! I will stop him!"

Leenoww's head came up sharply when Mikal sped past him at an open run. "Lieutenant," he called acidly, "the battle's back here!" He never did think much of the blowhard. Didn't understand how the commander ever put up with him.

Mikal never broke his stride. "Come with me!" he yelled back over his shoulder at the private.

Leenoww shrugged, and obeyed.

"I've got to get my sword back before he dishonors it!" Mikal hissed into the falling snow he was rushing through. "I've got to get my sword back!"

Aubin paced the length of the huge stainless steel table that served the bakery for kneading and mixing. His gait was uneven and he stumbled slightly as he walked, tripping heavily over the hems of his emperor-style robes. Because he had lost so much weight, they were too long. And because he had not cared in some time how he looked, he had not had them altered.

He stopped his pacing, and hoisted himself unsteadily onto the table. His hand slipped out from under him, and he lurched to one side, almost falling off his perch, but at the last moment he righted himself. He sat, his feet dangling like a child's, wishing himself somewhere else. He looked down at his distorted reflection in the scrupulously clean but use-scratched table, and sighed at the sight of himself. His skin was paper thin and the veins showed through over his nose and cheekbones. His mongrel Lunar genetics, strong over the long haul, seemed to have deserted him, and his face looked tired and worn-out, blurry in the scratched steel. He let his shoulders sag and dropped his head.

Suddenly he jumped off the table and walked directly up to the door. He struck it with his fist with all the strength he could muster.

"Damn!" he yowled. The pain in his hand startled him back to where he was and what he was contemplating, and the ringing of the door

from his strike was exceptionally loud and unsettling in the bakery's deserted stillness. He
thrust his hip against the door to silence it.

"Ummph," he grunted as he shoved his injured fist into his mouth, a gesture meant to
soothe himself, but one that was necessary, he
found, to keep him from crying out further.

When the thrumming in the hand at last
began to recede, he pulled his fingers out of his
mouth and addressed the door, talking to it as if
it were his oldest friend—or newest enemy.

"He really is a son of a bitch, ya know that?
He's got one hell of a lot of nerve. Who does he
think he is... Dying, putting me through the
hell of that, then coming back and expecting me
to turn traitor! Who does he think he is?"

He started to pace again, swishing his robes
out of the way of his disorganized feet, then
turned back to the door.

"What did I do to deserve this?" he asked the
portal. "I'm not a bad guy. I mind my own business. I haven't tortured any puppies or anything. What did I do?"

His pacing resumed, and it became more
frenetic as he let some of his anger and fear
surface.

"I know what I did!" he said as he made a
grandiose speaker's gesture with his injured
hand. "I started talking to that goddamned
pussy!" He paused, the hand coming to his chin
in thought. "I should've known he was trouble,"
Aubin said as he turned to speak to the jamb. "I
should've seen it. Too foreign. Too exotic. Ego-
centric and hidebound!" He found his feet walking again. "He's not even human!"

Aubin stopped, legs apart, feet firmly planted,

arms akimbo. "And I am not going to open this door!" he said with determination.

He jumped up onto the table once more, and began to muse. "If that pussy should somehow manage to kill Ozie, I'm in deep shit. And if he doesn't kill Ozie, I'm in deeper shit yet." He shook his head. "Well, I'm not gonna do it! I'm going back upstairs, get drunk, and not think about it. Ki's already dead. I've been to his funeral. And he can damned well stay that way. So all of this makes no difference!"

He jumped down from the table and actually managed to take two steps before he slumped back against the stainless steel, remembering.

"Ki said I could make a difference," he said sadly. "But I can't. Look at me. I'm sixty-three years old. I'm out of shape, I drink too much, I've got no family or friends—except for that goddamned son of a bitch who's trying to get me killed. We're talking empire here! I don't make a difference. It doesn't even matter if I'm alive or not . . ."

And suddenly the weight fell off his shoulders. "So what have I got to lose?" he asked gaily.

He looked at the door once more. "I hate you, you son of a bitch," he said happily, uncertain of whether he denigrated the door or the Lionman. He reached out his hand.

A low, rumbling growl crept up Aubin's spine from behind him, freezing him, sending tremors of reactionary fear through his body. Woodenly, carefully, he turned. Mikal filled the doorway, limned in the bright yellow light of the hallway. He looked bigger than any Lionman Aubin had ever seen, puffed up with his self-righteous anger. His lips were drawn back, and his sharp

Nidean teeth glistened wetly, whitely, as he stepped into the bakery's half light.

Aubin felt his insides running wetly down his legs, warm, sticky, disgusting. Beautifully unadulterated terror replaced the blood in his veins. Ki with a sword was nothing compared to this. The one before him was animal. Totally. Purely.

Aubin watched as Mikal took the three exceptionally long strides it took to reach him. He saw the heavily nailed hand reach out, and, amazedly detached, felt the claws pierce the skin beneath his floating ribs, crushing them, coming together with the thumb to collapse his lung. He felt Mikal's other hand grasp his opposite collarbone, and snap it like a paper straw. As his spine crumbled and ribs cracked between Mikal's callused palms, Aubin breathed, "I should have opened the door..."

Mikal dropped the trash and wiped his hands down the front of his kimono, rubbing his long nails deeply into the fabric to clean them. His teeth still bared, a rumble still in his throat, he stepped heavily over the garbage to unlock the door.

Ki, Colwin, and four others crouched in the heavy snow. There was little cover here, and they stayed close to the wall and motionless to draw as little attention to themselves as possible. The door in front of them was solid constanadium, and built so that it slid into the wall and became part of it. There were no hinges, no cracks. The only locks were on the inside. An obvious weakness, it had long ago been reinforced, although when the reinforcements had been designed, no one had considered there might be an organized attack with a little help from the inside.

Ki's mind was running in circles like a rat in a cage. *Aubin said he wouldn't help, but I know Aubin. He'll be here,* he told himself. *He's a good man. He'll be here. He's my friend. He'll be here.*

Finally there was the sound Ki had been waiting for. The attack had begun at the front of the palace. He looked back over his shoulder at the ones with him. Four of them were nervous, even scared. One was not. *And he's an idiot!*

Ki's eyes inadvertently met Colwin's. He had not intended such an intimate touch at a time like this. It was rude, and far, far too personal. But Colwin took it well. His gaze remained steady, and he nodded his head in recognition. Ki nodded back, then turned away, slightly embarrassed.

Aubin would like Colwin, Ki thought. *Colwin has Aubin's rough edge, and if they didn't kill each other they'd be best of friends.*

It was time, and Ki stood, pulling his snow-laden and damp hair back out of his face. He hesitated just long enough to realize he was not really certain the door would open. Then he put out his hand and pushed. The door was heavy, but it opened. *I knew I could count on Aubin!*

It had been dark outside, but it was not quite so dark in the bakery. Light filtered in through open doors from the corridors beyond. And as Ki stepped in, it took a moment for his eyes to adjust. He stepped around the long table where bread was shaped, and discovered a large lump on the floor beyond it. He looked at it dumbly, and discovered he could make no sense of it. It was not something that belonged here. Then the smell of death reached him, and, only after that, the scent of Aubin. Ki moved a few steps closer and looked again. This time he understood. The broken mass of flesh that looked so much like *The Caryatid Who Has Fallen Under Her Load* had been Aubin Tabber. There was no doubt he was dead. Blood trickled from his nose and ears, and people simply did not bend that way.

Ki raised his head at the slightest of sounds from in front of him, and there stood Mikal, and behind him Leenoww. Ki knew instantly that Mikal was crazed. The cub's face was a contortion of rage, and his scent reeked of insanity.

There could be no doubt Mikal had killed Aubin. His physical strength was prodigious. It was far greater than Ki's. The colonel had always been considered rather anemic. Mikal carried fifty pounds of muscle more than his uncle, and was inches taller. And, at the moment, he was quite mad. There was no doubt how Aubin had died. Mikal had folded his bones together as one would crumble a piece of paper.

Ki unsheathed his hoj and motioned Colwin and the others to continue. Leenoww stepped into their paths, and Mikal roared and started for Ki.

Ki defended himself from Mikal's blows, which were heavy and rapid. But Mikal's attacks were not well planned. He was lost in his frenzy. The blows rained down steadily on Ki, and though they were easy to parry, they kept coming and coming. Ki turned to dodge another blow, and swung near the edge of the door. Mikal, not paying attention to the direction of his strike, hit the edge of the door, and his blade snapped. He howled in frustration, and drew his shar. He thrust out quickly at Ki, but Ki disarmed him by pulling the blade out of Mikal's grasp with his left hand. Mikal barely felt the absence of the shar, and continued his stroke before he realized he didn't have a sword. Even more frustration showed in his twisted face.

He stopped, and, breathing deeply, calmed himself enough to speak. "I'll kill you, traitor!" he snarled at Ki, and lunged for his uncle's throat with his claws.

Ki held his hoj in both hands, and swung in a high arc, bringing the blade flashing down toward his nephew. Only at the last nanosecond did he decide to turn the blade so that the flat hit Mikal at a nerve junction, leaving him unconscious.

Puffing heavily from his exertion, Ki answered the cub who was now at his feet in a heap. "I think not. There will be enough killing today, and I see no need to add to it."

He turned his attention to Leenoww. The private was effectively, though far from easily, blocking the progress of the rest of the group. Ki felt a flash of pleasure that the cub had learned so well, but knew he did not have the time to enjoy the feeling.

He walked closer to the wildly shifting group and called off his five men. Colwin was battle-mad, and not ready to stop. Ki saw it, and realized the old habits would die very hard in this one. But habits can be killed, and finally, reluctantly, even Colwin stood aside.

In his best authoritarian voice, Ki addressed the young Nidean. "Private Leenoww, I am going past you. I do not wish to kill you, but I am going past you. Will you stand aside?"

There was a pause, a rather long one, and all was still for that moment except for the ragged breathing of men who had been fighting for their lives. Then Leenoww sheathed his sword, and bowed deeply to Ki.

"You are my commander," he said simply.

Ki smiled, and rested a hand on the cub's shoulder. "When we first met, I said I had need of good men at my side."

Leenoww was surprised Ki would remember such a thing, and wondering, suffering from hero worship, stepped off behind Ki Lawwnum.

The Mighty Emperor Ozenscebo XVII sat in a huge chair that had been put in front of the window wall in his audience chamber. He was watching the battle as it took place far below him. By his hand sat a small table, and on it was a tray with an immense beaker of roed, now more than half empty.

The goblet tipped drunkenly sideways, and a few drops fell into Ozenscebo's lap. He looked down at it and became enmeshed in the color. Red. Luscious. Rich. He looked up. That was what was missing from the battle below him. Red. Blood. Luscious. Rich. He touched the red droplets in his lap, feeling the slight pull of them against his skin when he moved his fingers in the sticky fluid.

He placed his glass tipsily to his lips, and discovered it empty. He waved his hand exaggeratedly over the arm of his chair toward the carafe, and immediately a little girl child came running from across the room to fill it. The emperor turned to look at her. She was dressed in almost nothing—bare-chested, although at her age it hardly mattered—with a diaphanous little skirt made up of petal shapes that the breeze split open when she ran. He enjoyed watching her run, displaying herself for him, so he kept her stationed all the way across the room. She struggled mightily with the pitcher almost as large as herself, and after she poured he smiled at her, patted her curly blond head, turned her about, and pinched her hard on her little bruised buttocks to send her scurrying back across the slippery polished floor. He giggled girlishly. That one would be a beauty when she grew—if he allowed her to grow.

He sat back with a satisfied smile. Life was so much better for him now that Elena was gone. He'd discovered all kinds of new and exciting things, but the things he enjoyed most were his babies. He kept them near him now, always, and Mama-san was under instructions to see to it there was always an ample supply of tender meat.

He dropped his other hand over the arm of the chair, and a small boy presented his bare back to act as an armrest, kneeling on the cold floor and supported by his hands. The emperor began stroking the boy's pale yellow skin, liking the silkiness of it. The child, high on roed, began to arch his back in response to the caresses. Ozenscebo leaned forward just enough to kick one of the boy's hands out from under the child and send him spilling to the floor. The boy rolled, landed on his back, and then, without leaving his back, wiggled like a worm back to the emperor for more caresses. Ozenscebo leaned down and tore away the brief loinwrap the child had, and began to play absently with the child's genitals. It amused the emperor to see a boy so much on the young side of puberty with an erection. The child had an amazing little toy, velvety soft and barely firm, filled with wonderful delicacy. He fondled the boy for a few moments, watching him writhe with pleasure, then crushed the child's organs between his fingers. How sweetly the child sang, and with such projection!

But these things required exertion, and Ozenscebo soon let him go to check on the progress of the battle. There was still not enough blood down below. It was noisy and busy, but hardly anyone was having the good grace to be killed.

"Foolish rebels," he said to the four-year-old, already roed-dependent, who was licking his feet with fervor, causing the choke chain around her neck to rattle rhythmically. "They really thought they could get in here." He laughed. "They'll never get past my Guard. So I can sit here and watch the excitement, even if there isn't enough red to suit me."

He turned to look behind him where, on the far wall of the room, a group of ten or so, all under eight, were occupying themselves, waiting the emperor's pleasure. All were feeling the effects of heavy doses of roed, and it showed in their glazed eyes and craving for stimulation. Some played with themselves, masturbating till they moaned in ecstacy incapable of being fulfilled. Others shared their caresses.

There was the hollow rattle of a substantial chain moving on the marble and poured-gem floor, and the sound brought the emperor's attention back to those near him. There were two chains, actually, one attached to each of the front legs of his chair. At the ends of those chains were a boy and a girl, both with the palest white skins and blondest of hair, both with cornflower eyes and tiny bee-stung mouths, a set of twins. Each was attached to the chain by a large stainless link that pierced the arm between the two bones in the forearm. Short of a surgical procedure, they would always be at the emperor's beck and call. He loved these two particularly. He used them often, the girl especially, because she reminded him of Natanha, and he missed his daughter very much at times.

He yanked on the boy's chain, which drew a small moan from the child, then he pulled the boy into his lap so that he would be handy for what the emperor was going to want in the very near future.

An infrequently used set of side doors with etched-glass panels opened, and several men stepped into the audience chamber. When the emperor heard the heavy tread of adults, he called, "Get out. I didn't send for anyone!"

The doors did not close, and he turned, angry at being interrupted while he was playing. "I didn't send—"

Ki and his group stood just inside the door. Ki looked around, his eyes seeing but his brain refusing to comprehend what was before him. Children, all of them small, dressed in leather thongs and chained to chairs, performing obscene acts. And in the midst of it, orchestrating it, the emperor, now so perverted that Ki was having trouble crediting it.

Ozenscebo stood, throwing the child to the unforgiving floor. "Guards! Guards!" he yelled, panicking.

Ki walked slowly forward, sick and fighting down blinding fury. "The Guards are napping," he said with a wildly reverberating rumble.

The Mighty Emperor Ozenscebo XVII pissed himself, and Ki wrinkled his nose, finding the emperor's terror disgusting. He continued to advance on his lord, and the playthings began to scatter, screaming, as they realized this was not a social visit. The two chained to the chair, however, did not have the option of running. Fruitlessly and awkwardly they attempted to pull the chair away.

Ozenscebo cringed, pushing himself against the window as if he would become a part of it. "You can't do this! I forbid it! I'm the emperor!"

Ki still came forward, step by relentless step.

"I order you to stop!" the emperor screamed hysterically.

And Ki did. He stopped, and he ran his thumb along the blade of his hoj, then sheathed it.

Ozenscebo almost cried with relief. "That's better, Lawwnum. Much better."

Ki drew the katana.

"What do you want?" pleaded the emperor. "Money? No. I know. I'll give you a planet. A whole planet, Ki. Just for you! How about Delena? You liked Opal. Imagine a whole planetful of them, all yours!"

Ki began to move forward again, and Leenoww started to move with him. Colwin dropped a firm, restraining hand on the Lionman's shoulder, however, and when the private looked at him questioningly, Colwin shook his head.

Ozenscebo tried to dart aside, and discovered there was no avenue of escape through his heavy syn-silk drapes. Ki was close now, almost on him. The emperor bolted. He was almost comical as he ran, for physical exertion was not something the emperor was overly fond of.

As smooth as water running coldly over ice, Ki moved in a graceful circle when the emperor ran past, and the royal torso continued to run a step before it fell, and the head tumbled madly and bounced as it began its separate existence. Sticky, red, coppery, human blood fountained across the floor. Here was all the blood the emperor would ever need.

Ki looked down at the katana and at the traitor's hands that held it, spattered with the emperor's blood. He threw the katana across the room as hard and as far as he could. He would not use the human's blade again.

Chapter Nineteen

NATANHA STOOD ON the balcony that overlooked the Guardsmen's courtyard. It was snowing, but she did not feel the damp or the cold, though she wore no cloak, but she squinted at the reflected light behind her veiling. So much had happened so quickly! Why, she hadn't even had time to clean herself properly before this ceremony. She'd merely washed her face and hands and pulled her hair back into a twist that kept all but a few errant strands out of her way. Her dress was clean and white, however, and, thank God! her own.

Magnus stood with her. The boy was also dressed in white, and for the first time Natanha could remember, he'd kept it that way for almost an hour. He was frightened, very badly and thoroughly. He was so scared he barely squirmed.

Natanha was accepting none of his nonsense. She had a firm grasp of his wrist, and every time he moved in a way she considered excessive, she dug her nails into Magnus's flesh. She had also told him before the ceremony that there would be two Lionmen standing directly behind him, and that if he misbehaved she would turn him over to them.

Indeed, there were two Lionmen behind the princess and the prince. One was Leenoww, the other a man Leenoww had told Ki could be trusted. When Natanha had been demanding good behavior from her brother, Leenoww had reinforced the demand with a large, toothy smile and a low rumble.

So far, Magnus's fear had kept him in line. Natanha smiled. It hadn't even occurred to him yet that he was the emperor. It would eventually, of course, but she would take care of that when the time came. For the moment, all she wanted was enough good manners not to disrupt this ceremony.

The courtyard was gradually occupied with Lionmen wearing white kimono. Yet another death ceremony. This one was different, however. Many of the Lionmen were not present. Few had actually died, but many were banged up. Those who had sided with the emperor, and there were several handsful, were locked securely in the depths of the palace. There were many, many Lionmen on duty, however. No one wanted anyone to get any funny ideas right now. Yes, there had been a coup, but if the empire was very lucky, the repercussions could be kept at a very low minimum. After all, the regency rested with Natanha right now, and Ozenscebo's designated heir would soon be crowned emperor. If things stayed calm, those in the outworlds would hardly even know anything had happened.

Rank upon rank of folded white kimono lined the walls of the courtyard as more Lionmen arrived, many carrying more than one garment meant to represent their absent friends. Sadder, there were several who brought personal items to the center of the courtyard to represent friends they would see no more.

The formal ranks of the Guardsmen began to form as they stood shoulder to shoulder, waiting, and Natanha, who stood above them where she could be seen, watched their white breaths in the cold air. So many of them had believed her dead, too. A few even smiled when they saw her.

Then Ki entered, dressed in the traditional mourning, except for one thing. It was not common to wear a sword to a death ceremony. Ki wore two, the shar and the pride's honor blade. He would not be separated from them just now. There was the possibility of trouble, and something more, something very personal.

The small bundle he had under his arm was covered in white silk. It would have been a handful for a human, but Ki barely felt the weight of it. He approached the center of the courtyard and looked down at the memorabilia laid out there. Too many were represented, and he was about to represent one more, this one the most tragic and unnecessary of them all. He set his burden down, and pulled away the silk. The little caryatid gleamed in the frosty sun, and as he stood and tucked the silk into his sash, Ki studied her. He thought that perhaps, now, he understood her a little. She'd tried very hard, against impossible odds, and even now would not give up.

He turned his back on her quickly when he felt the wellspring of his emotion beginning to overflow. There would be time enough for that before tomorrow. Right now there was a duty to be performed.

He stood once more at the head of his troops, and bowed his head in painful reverence.

The cold, watery sun threw a pale yellow cast over the blue-white snow. There were no clouds, and the sky had a greenish tinge in the thin early light. The large white cloth spread on the snow made an island of solidity among the fluffy drifts, and on that island knelt Colonel Ki Lawwnum, Commander of the Imperial Lion-man Guard.

He was dressed only in kimono of a white so hard it refused to take on the yellow cast of the sunlight, and, instead, glistened. His hair was pulled back off his face in a massive tail tied with a thick piece of syn-silk cording, and challenged the snow for sheen. His breathing was regular and shallow, and only the smallest of plumes drifted in front of him like dreamy clouds. His immaculately groomed hands rested on his knees, the natural one looking very blue next to the kimono, the steel losing its gray till it gleamed like polished hematite. Before him, immediately in front of his knees, rested his hoj, clean and peaceful in the early light, and just beyond that was his shar, also resting. His eyes looked straight ahead, but they did not see the activity bustling silently around him. He looked instead into another place.

The audience was beginning to take the chairs that had been set up off to the side of the cloth. The few invited Guardsmen present understood. The humans did not, and their agitation splashed off them like droplets of hot acid dripped onto glowing steel. Colwin and Loni sat in the first row as instructed. Leenoww, sad but resigned, sat next to them. Nide's ambassador, Learaa Maaeve, sat just behind Colwin's left shoulder. Mikal Lawwnum stood at the back of the chairs, waiting, turned aside from the others so that his bruised neck and face were not readily seen.

Colwin's black skinsuit stood out starkly against the snow. Even though it was winter-weight, he was feeling a cold that penetrated beyond his hands all the way to his heart.

"I don't understand why he's doing this," he said plaintively to Loni. "We won."

Loni pulled her black mink close about her and buried her face in the collar so that Colwin would not see the tears already falling. "I don't understand it either," she said as clearly as she could.

Maaeve heard this conversation, and was struck by their sorrow. These humans were here because Lawwnum wished it, but they had no understanding of the release he was about to obtain. She decided she felt sorry for them. She leaned forward to speak to them, her brown Nidean robes looking rocklike where the folds fell in mounds on the ground.

"Forgive me," she began, embarrassed at having overheard their inadequacies. "I could not help but overhear. Colonel Lawwnum is one who cannot live without his honor," she said softly, "and that honor has been put aside in order to rid the empire of Ozenscebo. In order to take it up again, there must be a sacrifice. This is his way out of dishonor."

Loni turned and met the older woman's leaf-green eyes. She did not understand, even now, but she grasped something of the cost to Maaeve to speak of such things to a human. "Thank you, Ambassador," she managed, no longer hiding her tears.

Colwin pulled his head down to his chest. "Yes," he stammered brokenly, avoiding Maaeve's look.

All had settled with an oppressive stillness when the princess entered. She wore one of her mother's dresses, a black lace with enormous full skirts. It did not really fit her properly, and there had not been time to alter it correctly, but her maids had managed to make it look present-able, though they had protested loudly over such a child wearing black. Natanha insisted, saying that after living the way she had, there was little of the child left in her.

Her chin high, little red spots of emotion col-oring each pale cheek, she walked directly to Ki so quickly that her bodyguard had to scramble to keep up.

"I don't want you to go," she said, her voice quaking.

For the first time Ki moved, turning his head slightly and focusing his eyes on his princess. "I must," he said with a voice that was as aged as the earth he knelt upon.

Natanha put out her hand, which still showed the signs of its long neglect, pleadingly. "I can't do this without you!"

Ki sighed lightly, and turned his eyes back to the other place. "You must."

Natanha's chin trembled, and her eyes filled with tears, blocking her sight. Then unthinkingly, she straightened her skirt, and the motion reminded her of her mother. She managed to pull herself erect, though her eyes refused to dry. "You're right. I'm regent now, and, unfortunately, my poor brother is accident-prone."

Ki nodded once, only just deeply enough to let her know he understood, then moved once more, taking from his sleeve the rock she had given him for his garden. He extended it to her, and reluctantly, with trembling fingers, she took it.

She turned from him, because if she did not, she would throw her arms around him and beg him to stay, disgracing both of them. She found her hand compressing the rock seemingly hard enough to liquefy it, and forced herself to relax the grip so she could see the rock. It was not polished yet, but it would have to do.

She swallowed once to clear the lump in her throat, then said aloud, "I, Natanha Accalia, Regent for Emperor Magnus the First, give you back your honor." She extended her hand, and a retainer placed into it a long white silk-wrapped package, which she turned to place in Ki's hand.

His detachment cracked slightly open, enough for him to be startled by this. He had not expected such understanding.

Quietly, painfully, Natanha said, "You have our permission to continue."

As she took her chair, the princess couldn't help but think, over and over again, *I'm not*

*going to make it through this. I don't want to
watch this.*

Mikal moved from his place behind the chairs
and took a position behind Ki. He had assumed
he would act as Ki's second. Ki, however, raised
his hand, stopping him. Mikal stepped away,
feeling what would have been fury in another
circumstance.

Ki turned his head toward the audience, and
focused his far-seeing eyes on Colwin. They
rested there, they clung there, demanding.

Colwin tried to turn his eyes away, but could
not. "Why is he staring at me?"

Gently Maaeve put a hand on Colwin's
shoulder. "He wants you to act as his second.
You will remove his head after he's made his
cut, so that he does not shame himself."

Colwin's eyes bulged and he snapped his head
around in disbelief. "I can't do that!"

Maaeve's grip on his shoulder tightened for a
moment, then fell away. "You would deny him?"
she asked.

Colwin wanted to run like hell, but found it
impossible. As he stood, he found himself mumbling, "I am responsible for my men." His knees
barely supporting him, Colwin walked to Ki's
side. His heart was pounding heavily, as if trying to break out of his chest and run away on its
own, and he was light-headed.

Ki swung his ponytail over his shoulder so
that it rested against his chest, to give Colwin a
clear shot, then he leaned forward enough to
touch his shar. Colwin picked it up, feeling the
ponderous weight of it dragging at his arms and
his spirit, and moved to stand at Ki's exposed
shoulder.

Ki picked up the silk-wrapped package and

exposed the katana, clean and polished now, a blade he had not expected to see again. But as it was the instrument of his destruction, it was fitting that it remain so. He would use this. He set it across his knees, and pulled open his kimono, exposing his blue-white chest and abdomen to the frigid morning. He pulled the square of silk he had used when he cut Natanha's umbilical, one of the happy moments of his life, from his sash and wrapped it around the katana's blade about halfway down its length. He turned the point toward his belly and made a deep and long gash across his gut.

Colwin froze. This was not a thing he could do. And he'd never even held a sword before. Exactly what was it that was expected of him? Then Ki groaned softly from between clenched teeth, and Colwin realized the Nidean was in agony. The longer Colwin waited, the worse the agony would be. With an enormous effort of will, he raised the sword and struck off Ki's head.

It was over, and Colwin, spattered and dazed, was surprised at how easily it was accomplished. He looked down at his hands as if they belonged to another, and dropped the weapon they held.

Natanha wanted to cry, wanted to scream till the very gods heard her. But she restrained herself with the thought that her mother would not have done so. She stood unsteadily, walked to where Ki had knelt, and picked up the Lawwnum pride honor blade. She called Mikal to her.

"If I understand correctly, Mikal Lawwnum, this is yours now," she said, her voice still full of unshed tears.

He reached out to take it, not quite managing,

even with everything that had happened to and around him, to cover his eagerness.

But Natanha held it back, her grip firm. She forced him to meet her eyes. Her tears falling freely now, she said, "You'd better live up to it!"

About the Authors

In a collaborative fervor that will thrill science fiction aficionados, P. J. Beese and Todd Cameron Hamilton have created a masterpiece of alien adventure about a futuristic interstellar empire. Writing, however, isn't their only pleasure. Both have received numerous awards as artists—Beese for space-age jewelry design and Hamilton for graphic artistry. Both are residents of the greater Chicago area.

Reading—
For The
Fun Of It

Ask a teacher to define the most important skill for success and inevitably she will reply, "the ability to read."

But millions of young people never acquire that skill for the simple reason that they've never discovered the pleasures books bring.

That's why there's RIF—Reading is Fundamental. The nation's largest reading motivation program, RIF works with community groups to get youngsters into books and reading. RIF makes it possible for young people to have books that interest them, books they can choose and keep. And RIF involves young people in activities that make them want to read—**for the fun of it.**

The more children read, the more they learn, and the more they **want** to learn.

There are children in your community—maybe in your own home—who need RIF. For more information, write to:

RIF
Dept. BK-3
Box 23444
Washington, D.C.
20026

Founded in 1966, RIF is a national, nonprofit organization with local projects run by volunteers in every state of the union.